DARK ANGELS

A TALE OF THE HUMAN / KNACKER WAR

THE HUMAN-KNACKER WAR SERIES

Slaughterhouse World, by Ardath Mayhar
Knack' Attack, by Robert Reginald
The Battle for Eden, by Mark E. Burgess
Dark Angels, by Mark E. Burgess

ALSO BY MARK E. BURGESS
Dog Daze and Cat Naps

DARK ANGELS
A TALE OF THE HUMAN / KNACKER WAR

MARK E. BURGESS

WILDSIDE PRESS

To my brother Mike, whose sterling example spawned yet another demented purveyor of words and worlds. To stardust you return, but your legacy lives on in each key stroke. You will be missed always, big bro. Fare thee well.

I.

The long-haul destroyer *Goliath* probed the vast emptiness of space, floating in the endless dark like a speck of sand adrift in the ocean. Its armored hull and bristling weapons offered mute testimony to the legacy of violence and conflict which had forged its purpose. This was a special ship, with special capabilities. But out here near the Cluster's rim, where even the stars scarcely dared to venture, the vessel's imposing mass might as well have been a few atoms of frozen hydrogen scattered against the backdrop of infinity.

The warship was currently running in stealth mode, with lighting muted and nonessential systems on standby, to reduce its energy signature to the bare minimum. *Goliath*'s bridge was a twilit landscape, brightened here and there by the multihued glows of work station data screens. The hushed stillness of the room belied the intense work of the officers seated at those stations.

The expansive chamber measured roughly circular. Its vaulted ceiling formed a huge hemispheric dome upon which was projected a panoramic view of the cosmos, fed by input from dozens of sensor arrays on the ship's hull. From here one could look in any direction except down, and even that view could be provided with the push of a button. With lighting minimized, the illusion of floating unprotected in open space was disturbingly realistic.

To the ship's stern spread a vast glowing panorama, the giant globular cluster that humanity had colonized centuries ago, comprised of hundreds of thousands of stars with uncounted habitable worlds, floating just outside the rim of the Milky Way galaxy. Its glory filled the sky behind them. But ahead of the ship there awaited…*nothing*.

Captain Taramay Dent felt the pull of the void as she stood staring out the fore viewscreen. Beyond the ship's bow the stars thinned and vanished, leaving only the scattered embers of distant galaxies. The dimensions of intergalactic space were incomprehensible, tempting one to madness if contemplated too long. She was a woman of strong will and determination, a career space officer, but out here she felt fragile, insignificant, and she knew that her tiny spark of existence could vanish into that abyss and the universe wouldn't blink.

She fought down a pang of anxiety, her secret fear of imperfect technology and her utter dependence on it. Only a few layers of steel separated the ship's crew from the deathly cold of interstellar space. It enveloped them like a tangible entity, inimical, lifeless—except for that one small blip on the scanners. Somewhere not far, hidden among the asteroid field that they were currently exploring, was a tiny island of life. The elusive energy trace of organic beings emanated from there, and the instrument telltales identified the signatures as human. But where were they?

Her mood as black as the void, Taramay turned her gaze to the bridge crew, sighing in exasperation.

"C'mon, people, give me something!" she implored her subordinates. "It's been five days since we cycled out of hyperspace. We should have found our target by now." She looked down from her command dais and to her right, where crouched the main scanner control station. "Talk to me, Mr. Cotton."

The tech officer, a young auburn-haired man in a sky blue Service uniform, glanced up from the screens in front of him. His grimace mirrored his commander's impatience as he replied, "These accursed asteroids are continuing to play havoc with our readouts. I've never seen a star system with so much debris."

The captain scowled. "The unmanned probe that came through this sector picked up life emanations easily. We have far better equipment, lieutenant, so why can't we find that alien ship? It's supposedly a harvest pyramid, full of thousands of human prisoners. The damned things are huge, and the life signs should be off the scale."

The young man shook his head and said, "It's not that easy. Detecting an energy source briefly is one thing. Pinpointing its exact location within an area millions of cubic klicks in size is entirely another." He waved his hand in disgust at his instrument panel. "The nickel-iron composition of the rocks is causing heavy scanner ricochet and echoes. It's nearly impossible to triangulate the origin of the life readings we're chasing. The signals are weak and sporadic, which isn't helping."

Taramay turned back to contemplate the viewscreen, tapping her foot as she said, "I don't like us sitting here naked in normal space, so far from reinforcements. The Cluster's edge is unknown territory. The enemy could be anywhere out here."

She glanced to the first officer's station directly to her left. "Mr. Caine, have you found any additional data on this region?"

"I'll give you what I've got, which isn't much." Her second-in-command tapped his control board, the glow from his screen highlighting his face and blonde hair against the shadows around him. His green eyes darted rapidly across the data readouts. After a pause he replied, "I've been searching the archives since we arrived. We're well beyond the grid usually patrolled by SpaceForce, so the information on this sector is sparse. Star systems are mostly unexplored, but the reconnaissance data on record suggests that the Knackers may have colonized planets out here. Survey drones have picked up energy readings and snippets of alien transmissions in this region. The drones stayed in passive mode at a safe distance to avoid detection, so they weren't able to collect more detailed data."

"Wonderful. We can't pinpoint the location of enemy bases, but there could easily be one in our area."

"Essentially," the first officer said. "Especially when you consider that the loaded harvest pyramid we're searching for was headed this way."

Yes, that would make sense, Taramay mused grimly. Knackers invaded worlds, Knackers captured the inhabitants, and Knackers took people away in giant pyramid ships, never to be seen again. Over the course of the war, humanity had learned that the hulking crustacean-like creatures ferried their captives to distant factory-planets, where their prey were "processed" into convenient food-stuffs for later consumption. The horror of that discovery had emphatically silenced the peacemakers, unifying the human worlds in a desperate fight against their approaching doom.

Not that it would matter in the end, she feared. No species had stopped the Crabs (as humanity had nicknamed them) in their entire nomadic history, which supposedly spanned tens of millennia, maybe longer.

And in the process of resisting this menace, what would humankind become? It took violence to fight violence; this warship she commanded was testament to that. The entire destroyer was death incarnate, a machine designed with one purpose: to take the lives of their enemies. It might even do its job well, for a time, but Taramay felt in her gut that someday the *Goliath* would be defeated by the enemy's superior firepower. When that happened, this ship would bring death to its own crew as well, becoming an icy tomb drifting silently between the stars.

Her morbid train of thought was cut short as the tech officer spoke up again. His voice held an edge of tension.

"Captain, there's something coming into range of our scanners. At first I thought it was another asteroid fragment, but the readings are odd. I'm not sure yet; there's too much interference."

Her sour mood boiled over, and she rounded on the unfortunate junior officer, glaring.

"Do you have any idea how many times I've heard those words over the past few days? And where are we? Still chasing false leads and ghost images with our butt exposed to the enemy, inviting them to come shoot it off. Do me a favor, and wait until you have something concrete before you announce it."

The lieutenant's eyes widened, and he stammered, "My apologies, Captain. I'll keep on it." He lowered his head, making a show of studying his data screens, but he couldn't hide the deep flush creeping across his youthful features.

Taramay regretted the words as soon as they had left her mouth. Glancing around the bridge, she caught expressions of dismay from several senior officers. Dammit, she couldn't lose control like that. She had always believed it was the captain's responsibility to present an image of strength and stability. Well, it was time she lived up to her own standards.

Fuming, the captain took a couple of deep breaths and steadied herself. Hands on her hips, she cleared her throat and said, "The apology should be mine, Mr. Cotton."

The younger man stared up at her, surprised. Taramay met his gaze steadily and continued. "I don't want my staff censoring themselves. You've only been aboard a short time, but I need you to speak up whenever you might have something to contribute. I'm competent enough to filter the information for myself. Okay?"

The tech officer grinned and nodded. "Yes, ma'am."

She smiled back at him, saying, "Keep on your scanners, and let me know the instant the readings are clear."

Her subordinate nodded, rubbing his tired eyes as he turned back to squint at his glowing console. The captain's brow creased slightly, her smile fading as she watched him work. She wasn't the only one riding the edge; the crew members were all showing signs of strain. They had been on constant alert and pulling double shifts since arriving in this sector.

It wasn't so bad when travelling through hyperspace; the voyages were usually quick, and you could see constant motion and know you were heading somewhere. But out here in normal space, without a planet underfoot, there was no visible measure of movement, no signal to the primitive animal brain that they were doing anything more than floating forever in the black. A hundred thousand klicks could pass by, yet the distant background of stars and galaxies looked unchanged to the naked eye. And behind that dreary sameness loomed the constant threat of attack, as they sat here alone and exposed. Monotony and stress made a lethal combination, steadily wearing down a ship's crew. With fatigue came human error, and out here mistakes were potentially as deadly as their enemy.

"Captain." The navigation officer's voice drew her gaze forward to the starboard side of the bridge. Leofric DeBartolo was a seasoned pilot who had been in SpaceForce since before the arrival of the Crabs. His light brown hair was brushed with gray at the temples, and lines around his eyes hinted at decades lived and conflicts endured. He had served with her on the *Goliath* for the past two years. Over time they had built a comfortable interaction borne of long familiarity.

As their eyes met he continued, "When we were outbound, I asked for mission details. You said it was classified, but that you'd reveal our orders once we arrived at our target location. Well, it seems that we're getting pretty damned close. It might be a good time to brief us before the iron is in the fire, yes?"

Taramay nodded with a weary smile. "You're right, Lef. The officers should be brought up to speed." She raised her voice for all to hear. "Attention, everyone."

The handful of bridge crew swiveled their faces toward their commander. Clasping her hands behind her back, Taramay swept the room slowly with her eyes as she began, "It's time to reveal our mission orders. You already know that we're searching for an alien vessel which may be carrying human captives. Officially this is a rescue operation, but we have other directives as well. First, headquarters wants technical data on the Knacker ship, if we find her. We desperately need to learn as much as we can about the enemy.

"Secondly, we're in outland territory. We are instructed to chart and log as much information as possible on the star systems we encounter, especially those any with evidence of alien activity."

"You think HQ wants to attempt a repeat of our Xenopus offensive?" Leofric asked, catching her gaze with his.

Taramay smiled thinly and said, "Very possibly. Hitting the Crabs where they roost may be our best hope for victory."

"What about Xenopus?" the tech officer asked, glancing from the navigator to the captain. "Do you mean the recent battle fought there?"

"Yes," Taramay answered. "What do you know about that campaign, Mr. Cotton?"

"Not much," the lieutenant confessed, shrugging. "I was stationed out in G-sector at the time, and news was sparse. I also didn't have the clearance to be privy to the details when it happened."

"Well, you've come up in the galaxy since then," the captain replied. "Let me fill you in. You know about the factory-planets where the Knackers bring prisoners for processing." It was a statement more than a question, and the smoldering fire in the young man's eyes was answer enough. Taramay continued, "Xenopus III was such a planet. SpaceForce discovered a Knacker stronghold there, via tracking a harvest vessel to its destination. With a fixed target in hand, we were able to turn the tables on our foe, taking the attack to the aliens. The *Goliath* took part in the assault, so I saw it firsthand."

"Wow! What happened?" Bruce asked, his boyish face alight with curiosity. "I never heard more than the basic news hype, you know, SpaceForce winning a glorious victory and so on, but no details. What was it like?"

Meeting his gaze, Taramay had to suppress a grin. Lieutenant Cotton was a sharp officer, and she had been impressed with his service record when he had been assigned to the *Goliath* at their last port of call. Nonetheless this was his first tour on a destroyer-class vessel, and he was still green. Sometimes it really showed.

"What happened is we caught the Knackers completely off guard," the captain told her subordinate. "Their confidence in their own superiority was their downfall. They didn't even have any ship patrols or sensor grids arrayed around the planet to warn them of our approach."

"And we stomped their butts into the ground," Alena Stepanovich added from her com chair.

Taramay chuckled despite herself. "Yes, we did indeed," she agreed. "Our destroyers and dreadnaughts emerged from hyperspace and encircled the Knacker world. From near space we rained down a firestorm of plasma bolts, heavy missiles and even meteorites thrown from mass launchers. The result was devastating. Target areas up to fifty klicks in diameter were vaporized. When the smoke had cleared, the major Knacker ground installations were gone, and the world had ceased to be a military threat in that sector. All that remained was to eventually land and engage the surviving aliens with ground forces."

"Didn't the Crabs fight back?" Bruce asked incredulously.

"Well, yes, they did attempt to launch fighters into space to counter our attack. Most were shot down before leaving the atmosphere. A few larger ships cleared the gravity well and disappeared into hyperspace, with human destroyers close on their heels. A few other Knacker vessels got clean away during the heat of battle. Which leads us to our present mission."

"How's that?" Leofric interjected.

Taramay glanced toward the navigator. "Space Command tells me the human fleet encountered harvest pyramids over Xenopus III. Their size makes them lumbering and slow, so normally they would have little chance of eluding pursuit. However, several loaded pyramids chanced to emerge from hyperspace near the planet while the battle raged. Before the human fleet could close with them, they had vanished once again.

"After the planet was subdued, unmanned probes were launched to track the energy trails left by the alien vessels. One of these eventually beamed back data suggesting that a harvest pyramid, or part of one, had been located."

"The ship we're after," Leofric concluded for her.

"Yes," Taramay confirmed. "We know a loaded harvester can contain thousands of human lives, worthy of a rescue mission. Along with SpaceForce's desire for intel on the enemy, it was enough reason to send us out here. And as you noted, if we happen to find the harvester's intended destination, we may also be able to give SpaceForce another Crab planet to target."

The captain paused, her eyes scanning the bridge crewmembers. "One last thing, and this is strictly classified, for your ears only, people. Our stealth probes picked up bits of alien transmissions that hinted of a new weapon the Crabs were developing, perhaps in response to our recent successes. We have no idea what it might be, but we're tasked with gathering any data possible, and capturing one of the weapons for study if the opportunity presents itself."

She paused and spread her hands, saying, "That's all I've got. Now you know as much as I do. Any questions?"

Silence met her as the crew on deck mulled what they had been told, each person lost in contemplation of the war and their place in it. Taramay let her gaze roam slowly upward once again, wishing the tension inside her could bleed away into the depths of space-time.

Such moments of quiet are a luxury during periods of conflict, and duty inevitably intrudes. It was only a short interval later that the tech officer spoke up again, and this time the urgency in his voice was unmistakable. *I've got something!*

The rest of the bridge crew swiveled their heads to look toward the young man. The captain kept her voice steady as she folded her arms and asked, "What do you see, Mr. Cotton?"

"There's a large mass of metal, *refined* metal, about ten thousand klicks to starboard and slightly behind us. The signals are clear now. It's definitely not an asteroid; scans indicate a pyramidal shape consistent with a Knacker harvest ship. It seems to be dead in space. I'm getting no emissions to suggest an active propulsion system or defensive screens."

"Do you read any power output at all?" she asked, squinting at the viewscreen as if she could make their quarry visible by force of will.

"Just a faint energy pulse, but I suspect that environmental support is still on line," the tech officer replied.

"How can you tell that?" the captain asked.

"Because this object appears to be the source of the life signals we've been chasing," the younger man said.

Taramay stood motionless for a moment, her thoughts racing. Then she swiveled and rapped out orders to her crew. "Ms. Stepanovich, send a tight beam transmission to Space Command. Summarize our activities to date, and inform them that we're moving to investigate a probable Knacker vessel."

"On it, Captain," Alena replied, tapping in commands on her console.

Next Taramay looked to her navigator. As his furrowed gaze met hers, she cocked her head and said, "What do you think, Lef? Can we approach safely, or are the Crabs up to something?"

He grimaced as he glanced at the viewscreen, saying slowly, "I don't like it, but then I feel that way about anything Knacker. I have no concrete reason to suspect a ruse here. If that ship was under power, we'd know it, and it's not like the Crabs to shut down their primary systems just to lure us in. They know that Space-Force tends to shoot first and inspect the remains after. I don't think they'd leave themselves vulnerable on the slim chance that they'd catch someone off guard. Especially not out here in the middle of nowhere."

"Agreed," Taramay replied. "Pyramids have minimal weapons systems in any case, unless this one was specially modified. As you say, a trap seems far-fetched. But something is bothering you."

"Well," Leofric mused, "if the ship is a derelict, what wrecked it? SpaceForce hasn't fought any engagements way out here. And it's odd that a vessel of that size has been stranded this long, without having been rescued. That's a big chunk of hardware to abandon. Not to mention the captive humans supposedly on board; the Crabs would value that commodity highly. So why is it just sitting there?"

"Perhaps the asteroid field has scrambled the Knackers' scanners as well as ours," the captain answered. "Maybe whatever disabled the harvest ship also knocked out their communications. Regardless, we'll need to take a closer look. Turn us about and set in a course to approach the vessel. Mr. Cotton, monitor your readouts closely. I want to know if someone so much as breaks wind on that ship."

Over the next two hours the navigator cautiously brought the *Goliath* in to their target. As they approached, the bridge crew stared at the image growing on the main screen. Straight ahead of them a roughly triangular area of stars was obliterated by the outline of something substantial. The lightless area kept growing until it seemed that they must be right on top of the object, but still they continued to creep forward. There was no sense of perspective in the depths of space, and Taramay was forced to reassess the alien ship's bulk several times as they closed with it. Against her will she found herself in awe at the size of the structure. It was obvious that the pyramid far out-massed any ship SpaceForce had ever built.

Finally the navigator sat back in his chair and said, "That's it. We're at a full stop, approximately a half klick from the vessel."

The captain gazed out the viewscreen, contemplating the dark mass which now filled their forward view. In the years since the Knackers had first appeared, harvest pyramids had become a symbol for all the loathing and horror that the aliens elicited in their human prey. As she faced one up close for the first time, Taramay felt a chill slither down her spine like the touch of a scurrying insect.

Not a single light showed on the flat face of the pyramid; the silent vessel appeared devoid of life. Even at close range the vast structure was barely visible, just a murky jumble of shadows blotting out the starlit sky. Out here in the lonely reaches of the asteroid belt, the solar system's red dwarf sun lay far behind them. At this distance its weak light was so attenuated as to be almost undetectable. The alien ship remained shrouded in mystery.

Taramay kept her gaze fixed on their quarry as she said, "Anything on the scanners, Mr. Cotton?"

"Low level energy output, as before," he replied. "No sign of a response to our presence. Lots of human life emanations inside. This is definitely our target. And I'm picking up...some Crabs as well."

This last statement sounded puzzled, and the captain glanced over at him, asking, "Are you surprised? It *is* a Knacker vessel."

The young officer looked pensive. "Well, I'm only getting a scattering of alien life readings. A ship this large should have thousands, probably tens of thousands. I know they can shield their life signs from scans to some degree, but I'd be able to tell if there were a lot of them. It appears that there are only a few, and that doesn't make sense."

The junior officer might be inexperienced, but he was not stupid. Taramay exchanged glances with the navigator; his unease with the situation was plainly written on his weathered face.

"It seems odd that only a fraction of the alien complement would be on board," she agreed, rubbing her chin. "If they'd been rescued, the entire crew and human captives would have been offloaded as well. We need more information about what happened here. Mr. Debartolo, bring up spotlights on the pyramid. Let's see what she looks like."

The navigator punched his controls, and dazzling beams of white light lanced out from the prow of the human destroyer. The alien ship suddenly flared into stark clarity, every detail of its hull exposed to the observers aboard the *Goliath*. A chorus of gasps swept through the bridge, and Taramay heard Leofric muttering dryly, "I can hazard a guess as to why the ship's marooned."

Alena the com officer simply leaned forward and murmured, "Would you look at that!"

Look, indeed. What had prompted her exclamation wasn't the gigantic perfection of the alien ship. Instead, the crew's gazes were drawn inexorably to the one flaw in that symmetry. The lower right corner of the pyramid had been completely blown away, leaving a raw gaping wound in its place. The crater extended deep into the metallic hull; Taramay could have easily parked her entire destroyer inside the mangled cavity.

Lt. Cotton shook his head, saying, "What could have caused that kind of damage? Did they hit an asteroid?"

The gunnery officer, a hard-jawed blonde named Greta Jónsson, replied from her port-side console, "I don't think so. The metal looks melted and fused. It would take a high speed impact to generate that much heat. If that had happened, the forces would likely have torn the pyramid apart. This appears to be a heavy weapons hit, not a collision with something solid."

"But what sort of weapon?" Lt. Cotton asked. "I've never seen anything in SpaceForce that could maim a pyramid like this."

"I have," Taramay replied, eyes narrowed. The others looked at her quizzically. She nodded and continued, "A railgun round from a Lamprey could do that, and worse."

The young tech officer exclaimed, "A super-dreadnaught? Are those things real? I thought they were still in development!"

"Oh, they're real, all right, though they're new and very few in number. And they're the one spacecraft we have that can strike fear in the Crabs. The whole damned ship is a weapon, a half kilometer long. I've seen a single round from a Lamprey's main gun take out an enemy destroyer, and I mean obliterate it. SpaceForce had super-dreadnaughts deployed at Xenopus III, where this pyramid briefly appeared during the battle. I'll bet that a Lamprey got off a shot before the Crabs fled back into hyperspace. What do you think, Ms. Jónsson?"

The weapons officer nodded. "That makes as much sense as anything." She gestured at the viewscreen and added, "The extent of the damage explains why the ship is stranded. The propulsion system is probably dead, and their communications would obviously be suspect as well."

"How would they have gotten this far if the ship was disabled?" Alena asked, looking confused.

The gunner grunted, and said, "The weapon impact would have generated tremendous heat, especially if it were caused by a railgun. The rounds fired by those weapons contain a depleted uranium core which vaporizes and ignites on impact. The end result is a major fireball. I suspect the ship's hyper drive failed en route, due to ongoing burn damage in sections of the hull which still had an atmosphere."

"Could the weapon hit have killed off the Knacker crew?" Taramay asked, eyeing the pyramid thoughtfully.

"Perhaps," the first officer spoke up. "The intel people think that Crab soldiers occupy the basal portions of the pyramids, to allow for quick deployment when they harvest a planet. Sensor scans of loaded harvesters have suggested that the human captives are moved up into the higher portions of the ships."

"That would make sense," Taramay said, nodding. "It keeps prisoners sequestered and makes escape difficult. They would have to fight past the Knacker soldiers to get to the exits along the base."

"The upper portion of this pyramid appears intact," Lt. Cotton pointed out. "There could be quite a few humans trapped in there."

"Any idea how many?" Taramay asked him.

The tech officer shook his head. "A fair number, but I can't get exact figures. The density of the aliens' hull is interfering with more detailed scans."

"We'll have to board that ship," the captain decided. "Have two shuttles made ready with full troop complements. In the meantime we'll need to find a way in."

"The doorways along the pyramid's base would be the best bet," the first officer suggested. "I'd stay away from the damaged section; it's likely to be a fused mess."

"I agree," Taramay replied. "The challenge will be getting a portal to open, given that the ship is mostly without power."

"The *real* challenge might not be getting in, but rather getting back out again in one piece," the navigator said. No one disagreed.

2.

An hour later a pair of shuttles made their way across the gulf between the two motionless vessels. Lieutenant Atom Granger led the strike team aboard Shuttle One. He was the acting commander of this exercise, and would have authority over the second shuttle's troops as well. A veteran of multiple engagements with the Knackers, he knew the enemy well.

As the hulking mass of the alien ship grew in their viewscreens, Atom briefed his troops on what to expect once inside. "We don't know a lot about the layout in these ships," he told the fifty-odd men and women assembled in the deployment bay. He glanced over his troops as he spoke, nodding to himself in satisfaction. They wore heavy environment suits for work in hard vacuum, and each held a helmet under one arm. Energy rifles were slung across their backs, and grenades dotted their equipment belts. They were going in heavy, and the mood was somber.

All faces were turned toward him as the soldiers listened attentively to Atom's every word. This unit was young, so much so that it pained him to send them into the fire, but they knew that surviving the day could hinge on a small piece of information.

He continued, "There are likely to be a lot of passageways and compartments. We might encounter bulkheads and sealed doors which require blasting. Tomlich, be sure you've got your full ordnance for this one."

The trooper in question grinned and tapped the packs arrayed over his suit; he carried the requisite items for explosives work. Atom continued, "Knackers are waiting for us in there; we don't know exactly how many, but we do know that their numbers are fairly small. We should be able to handle them.

"The enemy will look to assault us from behind protected positions. We've got to proceed carefully. I know it's a huge area to search, but we can't afford to run into an ambush, or to get our line of retreat cut off by Crabs circling around from behind. We'll leapfrog forward by squads, with each group providing cover for the next as it moves up. Any questions?"

"What sort of weapons should we expect to encounter?" a fresh faced young woman spoke up.

"The preferred weapons of the enemy are plasma rifles and grenades, plus a healthy dose of neuro-gas," the lieutenant answered. "The gas shouldn't be a factor, as we'll be suited up for the duration."

"What about our weapons?" another young trooper asked, his face anxious. "Fighting in close quarters will limit our choices, and we've got civilians in there to worry about."

"Good question," Atom answered, nodding. "Our primary weapons will be plasma rifles as well. Once inside, with all that metal, you'll need to watch your aim. Plasma rounds can ricochet, with unpleasant results.

"We'll likely be forced to use some grenades, but judiciously. I don't know how intact the hull is. If we blow out the wrong bulkhead, we may depressurize a compartment that has live people in it. The best advice I have is: fire at clear targets when you have them, and shoot straight."

The shuttles approached the pyramid slowly, alert for any sign of activity. From behind them the human destroyer's spotlights shone like miniature suns, casting black shadow figures of the two transports against the grey metal of the Knacker vessel. The troops on board had fallen silent, lost in private thoughts as they waited out the interminable lull before the action. The shuttle pilots were also hushed, staring ahead at the forbidding structure as it loomed ever closer. Despite their trepidation, the massive alien ship remained inert, floating silent and dark like an artificial mountain suspended before them.

When the shuttles were only meters from impact, they gently turned to creep along the base of the pyramid, searching for a portal. Atom and his troops craned their necks to catch glimpses of the exotic craft through the window of the docking door. Up close the metallic surface was pitted with tiny meteoroid impacts, and crisscrossed with structural complexity not visible from a distance. Knobs and protuberances of unknown purpose bulged from the large metal panels, sliding past in a seemingly endless procession.

Time dragged as the minutes ticked away, yet nothing resembling an entrance came into view. Inside the shuttle bay the tension slowly mounted. Atom could hear feet shifting restlessly in the stillness. His nose caught the sour tang of perspiration in the packed room as stressed bodies in heavy suits began to heat up.

Finally the pilot's voice came over the intercom. "We're approaching what appears to be a doorway. The surrounding surface seems smooth enough to dock. We'll line up and try to achieve a seal."

Atom watched through the docking door, and in a moment a hexagonal hatchway floated into view opposite him. It was wider than tall, at least four meters across, and was inset slightly into the wall of the pyramid. The shuttle's pilot deftly fired the maneuvering thrusters, bringing the smaller ship to a dead stop opposite the doorway. Another couple of nudges from the lateral jets pushed them toward the alien vessel.

"Hold for docking," the pilot said. From the deployment bay they could clearly hear the rumble of the airlock extending. A moment later, a grinding bump told them they had made contact.

Micrograv units instantly adhered the seal to the alien ship, and Air-Tite gel was extruded along the contact points to plug any defects. The thick material conformed to whatever surface it contacted, acting as both filler and glue. Its main strength was that it functioned uniformly well in extremes of cold or heat, vacuum or atmosphere. After a few seconds' wait, the pilot announced, "Air seal confirmed; you're set to go. Good luck out there."

Atom nodded and turned to his troops. "All right, soldiers! We'll be the first to go in; shuttle two will follow. Let's do it by the book. Helmets on, check your seals and suit readouts before we open the hatch! Move it, people!"

The lieutenant then donned his own headgear, insuring that the locking mechanism snapped tight where it met the suit. The glowing heads up display flickered to life inside the helmet, just above the clear visor, and he glanced at the readings as he activated the oxygen flow. He kept his breathing steady, hearing the hollow sigh of his exhales in the confined space. After verifying pressurization, he glanced around the room at the others.

In less than a minute everyone was fully suited, and all hands gave a thumbs-up sign. When he was satisfied that they were set,

Atom raised his arm and said, "Front ranks, weapons at the ready!" He spoke softly, but the suit com broadcast his words clearly to everyone in the unit.

The whine of plasma guns powering up came through his helmet speakers, courtesy of the combat suit's external microphones. The audio sensitivity could be adjusted to give the wearer superhuman hearing, or dampened during combat to insulate soldiers from the percussion of weapons fire. With one last glance at the assembled soldiers, Atom turned and hit the button that opened the inner airlock door.

With a hiss the panel slid aside, and they were staring at the heavy slab of the alien portal a scant few meters away. As one the forward troops leveled their armed weapons at the doorway. The frozen tableau stretched for long seconds as anxious fingers caressed rifle triggers.

Nothing happened, and finally Atom broke the silence, turning and gesturing at a tall soldier carrying two cases of sensory gear. "Corporal Gunnarsson, get a reading on what's behind that door. Life signs and atmosphere." Atom's eyes scanned the suit insignias of the troops near him. In a moment he pointed to a smaller suited figure, saying, "Avery, check out that panel to the right of the portal. See if it's the hatch controls, and test for power supply." The woman nodded and trotted quickly to the wall, pulling a small diagnostic unit from her belt as she went.

Atom and the front troops held position, weapons trained on the hatch, while the two technicians quickly worked. Torvald Gunnarsson held a probe near the door slab for a few moments, watching the readouts on his equipment. He called over his shoulder, "Lieutenant, there's a wide corridor directly behind this hatch, leading straight back into the ship. Side passages branch off to the left and right every twenty meters or so. No signs of explosive charges or other traps on the entrance. No life signs close by. Artificial gravity is on line. The atmosphere is a bit thin, but breathable."

Atom felt a wash of relief at the news. His soldiers could operate equally well in vacuum or air, but moving captives to the shuttle would be a heck of a lot easier if the hull remained pressurized throughout. "Corporal Avery, what's your status?" he called to the other technician.

She turned and answered, "This appears to be the door control board, but the circuits are dead."

"Can you bypass and supply power?" Atom asked.

"Already on it, sir," she replied. Consulting her diagnostic readouts, she pulled wiring from the now-open panel, separating several strands from the tangle. Reaching again to her belt, she grabbed a portable power pack the size of her fist. Quickly she set about adapting it to the alien circuitry.

The corporal knew her trade, and a short interval later she said, "Got it. Ready on your order, sir." Looking over her shoulder, she waited for the lieutenant to give her the go sign. When he signaled, she raised her power source and thumbed a button on its top. As she did, the heavy slab barring their way shuddered. After a moment's hesitation, it ground slowly to the right, and the black maw of the alien ship yawned open.

Atom bit his lip as he sighted down his weapon into the tunnel; there was absolutely no illumination inside the pyramid. A handful of meters from the entrance the passageway disappeared into utter darkness. They might as well have been descending into the depths of a subterranean cavern. Despite the heavy damage to the ship, he had hoped for emergency lighting. As it was, well, he and his team were no strangers to the black.

"Night vision on!" he barked. "Use your scanners; don't rely just on your eyes, or you may end up with a Crab in your face. First squad, move out with me! Hug the walls; stop short of the first intersection. Second squad, behind us up the center of the corridor; advance past unit one after we've checked the side passages. Let's move!"

Atom led the first squad through the portal and into the Knacker ship. "Stay tight," he hissed as the pitch black swallowed them. His helmet display lit up with virtual images of the alien vessel's interior. The suits' visual systems projected energy waves which bounced off surfaces in the environment. The signals were then processed into imagery by the helmet hardware. Unlike some night vision gear which simply amplified existing light, the assault team's equipment allowed for work in total darkness.

The squad advanced down the hexagonal corridor at a slow trot, moving through an artificial gray twilight in which angular metal bulkheads and flooring showed starkly around them. Debris littered the floor, and irregular gaps showed in the corridor ceiling. Although this section of the ship was largely intact, the concussion of the fatal weapons hit had apparently jarred loose some structural panels and other fixtures. Soldiers had to watch their footing as they picked their way around the obstacles.

After a handful of paces, large openings appeared in the walls to the left and right. Atom called for a halt, melting against the left wall just short of its termination. "We're at the first intersection," he spoke quietly through the com link. Who is opposite me on the other wall?"

"Sergeant Harriman, sir" a deep voice responded.

"Sergeant, we'll peek around the corners and check out the side passages on my mark. Ready… *go!*"

The two men whipped around the corners, sighting down their weapons into the side passages. They saw nothing but empty tunnels receding into the far distance. After a tense several seconds wherein nothing moved within their fields of vision, they relaxed and stepped back into the main corridor.

"Second unit, advance past us to the next intersection," Atom commanded. His squad remained against the walls as the rear group came up the center of the corridor and moved ahead.

Captain Dent and her command staff watched the progress of the strike force from the bridge of the destroyer. The port-side wall of the domed viewscreen was overlaid with images transmitted from the alien pyramid. The rectangular projection now showed side-by-side views from the two squad leaders' helmet cams.

Taramay glanced over to her com officer, and said, "Ms. Stepanovich, what's the status of the second shuttle?"

"They're docking with the first boat now, Captain," she replied. "Their squads should be unloading through shuttle one momentarily."

The captain nodded. Both assault teams would board the pyramid via the same entry. The number one shuttle had docked with the alien ship via its starboard docking bay. The second shuttle then could link to the first boat's port-side bay. This allowed the newly arrived troops to cross through Shuttle One's interior and enter the alien ship. "Send a message to the second ship's troops. They are to follow the first team, but leave two soldiers at every second intersection to guard the path of their retreat."

Alena nodded and began speaking quietly into her com link. Taramay turned her attention back to the viewscreen. It appeared that the troops aboard the harvest vessel were approaching a heavy blast door which blocked the corridor. She took a seat in her command chair, and leaned forward to watch with interest.

Atom Granger cautiously approached the metal hexagon obstructing their path. This one was different than the pyramid's outer portal. It appeared decorated, embellished with designs of some sort. He moved closer and realized that what he was seeing was a myriad of bas-relief figures worked into the metal surface. Some appeared to be Knackers, but other life forms were represented as well, including humanoids.

"Scanner readings?" he murmured into his helmet mike.

Corporal Gunnarsson came to the fore once again. His Nordic features were blurred by the mirrored curve of the helmet visor, but his lanky height was evident even within the bulky suit. He quickly ran scans over the portal, and after a few moments he turned to the others. "The atmosphere behind the door is similar to out here: thin but livable. Our rescue targets are on the other side of the barrier, and several levels above us. We've got to get past this door and find a route upward."

"Good enough," Atom replied. Then he spoke a bit louder into his helmet mike, "I need someone up front with xenoarcheology and intel training."

"On my way, sir!" a female voice responded. Moments later a suited figure of medium height pushed its way through the crowd of soldiers. "Sergeant Autumn Desmond reporting, sir," the figure said with a salute.

"Are you trained to collect data on alien species?" Atom asked her.

"Yessir, I have a strong background in archeology and xenobiology," the sergeant replied.

"Good. Take a look at this portal, but make it quick," Atom said. He moved aside, gesturing behind him at the hexagonal slab with its intricate artwork.

"Oh, my..." the sergeant breathed into her mike, her voice fading into silence as she stepped forward. Her helmet scanned back and forth over the portal, craning upward to see the entirety of the vertical face. She reached out one gloved hand to delicately trace the images in front of her. Not a word was spoken, but her breath rasped harshly over her com link, as if she had just run a sprint. Atom let her survey the work undisturbed for a minute. Finally he broke the spell, saying, "Well?"

She turned to him, talking excitedly. "This is incredible! The intricacy and detail in this artwork is totally unexpected. Knackers have never shown much tendency for embellishment in any of their structures. Art for art's sake seems a foreign concept to them. But this! There's a story here, and it may hold clues to the nature of our adversary. I need to see these images more clearly, and capture them for study. Can we light up this portal, please?"

Atom hesitated for a moment before nodding. He gestured to several soldiers standing at the front of the squadron. "Activate your suit beams; aim them at the doorway."

The environment suits had lights installed in the upper torso region. They were not as effective as the night vision gear; any movement by the soldier caused the light beams to gyrate, creating unstable illumination which could confuse the eyes. This could induce a tense combatant to fire at nonexistent foes, sometimes with unfortunate results. A lighted suit also made a clear target for enemy fire. Thus the lights were only used when other options failed, or in special circumstances such as this.

The suit beams flared into life, bringing the bulky doorway into clear definition. The tech specialist moved back and forth, capturing images of the complex figures covering the metallic surface. After a minute she backed away, saying, "That should do it. I'm through here."

Atom nodded, and barked, "Lights out, people! Avery, open this portal." The female tech came running, and immediately set to work on the wall panel adjacent to the doorway. The troops waited in silence, nerves taut as they scanned their surroundings. The walls and ceiling hemmed them in, and the slightest noises reverberated and echoed, making it impossible to pinpoint their origin.

Atom could hear the scuffle and thump of his squad's feet as they shifted restlessly in the packed corridor. The sounds grew, and he suddenly realized that they were originating down the corridor behind them. Something was rapidly approaching their position.

The soldiers whirled, guns raised. In a few moments they could see movement in the distant gray haze of the tunnel. As the gap closed, bipedal figures began to take shape in their weapon sights, and the battle suits' sensors confirmed them as human.

One could hear audible sighs over the com links as the squads lowered their rifles. The second shuttle's troops had caught up with them. When they drew near, the lieutenant at their head announced himself, and the new arrivals fell in behind Atom's men.

Within a couple of minutes Corporal Avery stepped back from the control panel and the doorway slid aside. Behind it another lightless passageway awaited, and they proceeded forward once more.

As they pushed through the portal, Atom spoke into his helmet mike, "Gunnarsson, stay close to the front and scan ahead of us. We need additional sensor capability beyond what our suits provide. Sooner or later we're going to encounter resistance, and I don't want to be surprised. Log this ship's layout within scanner range, and feed the data to our suit computers. If troops get separated, I don't want anyone getting lost. Keep searching for a route to the upper levels."

The main passageway continued on straight ahead, carrying them ever deeper into the silent ship. As they proceeded, Atom could feel the brooding mass of the pyramid bearing down on him. The tunnels were spacious, designed to accommodate ten-limbed creatures with considerably larger profiles than human beings. Nonetheless, as they pushed further into the honeycomb of dark passageways, the feeling of being entombed steadily grew, and with it a mounting sense of isolation and vulnerability. Shadows began to move with half-seen shapes at the corners of his vision. He could tell that his squad was feeling it too. When rows of open doorways began to sprout along the corridor walls, the troopers whirled their plasma rifles to left and right, as their imaginations planted alien hostiles within each darkened portal.

As the tension mounted, so did the chances of someone firing a wild shot which could ricochet back into the massed soldiers. Atom eventually called a halt, and calmly issued instructions. "Gunnarsson, take detailed scanner readings around us. Check for Knackers on this level, and look for a way upstairs. Troops near the front, split off in pairs and see where these doorways lead. Record any useful findings, especially equipment and tech-related stuff. Let's move!"

The soldiers spread out to each side and disappeared through the doorways. Soon they began reporting back on their com links. The entries led to a series of chambers, most of which were storage rooms and what seemed to be alien crew barracks. A couple of spaces housed shipboard equipment as well, all of it nonfunctional. Nowhere did they see evidence of recent occupation, nor were any Knacker bodies found. It was as if the ship had flown itself out here alone to die.

Atom was about to call for everyone to regroup when a cry came over the com link. "Oh, no! Oh hell, *no...*"

The words were followed by the sound of retching, and another voice cut in sharply, saying, "Get it together, soldier! Do *not* vomit in your helmet! Eyes on me! Focus!"

"What's going on?" Atom barked, scanning the doorways around him. "Situation report!"

The voice of the unseen second soldier came through after a pause, sounding strained. "We—we seem to have found a...kitchen, I think."

"Then what is the problem?" Atom shot back.

"There are leftovers here, sir," the voice replied in lifeless tones. "Remains. They appear to be human."

The words momentarily froze Atom, and then he barked into the com, "All troops back into the corridor! Gunnarsson, find us a way up to where we need to be, and do it quickly. I'm already getting tired of this infernal ship."

The tall trooper appeared to shake himself. He consulted his readouts once more, aiming the scanner in various directions and adjusting the resolution. As he worked, soldiers began pouring back into the corridor from the surrounding doorways. After a minute of silent concentration, the sensor tech lowered his equipment, turning to the lieutenant. "There is a large shaft running vertically just ahead of us. I think it might be an elevator."

"If that's true, it won't be functional," Atom replied. "We'll need a stairwell or something similar. There must be alternate means of moving up and down in case of power loss. Do a detailed search of the area around the shaft."

Gunnarsson continued his scans while the troops reassembled. By the time everyone was in place and ready to move out, he had found what they were looking for. "I've got a sloped tunnel that appears to head up toward the next level," he announced, gesturing with a gloved hand. "It's just past the elevator shaft on the left. But there's something else."

"What is it?" Atom asked, catching the worry in his subordinate's voice.

"I'm picking up sporadic alien life signs. They seem closer than before, but I can't pinpoint them accurately. Either the ship's structure is interfering with my equipment, or the Crabs are using screens to shield themselves from detection."

"How close would you estimate?" Atom prodded.

"Anywhere from one hundred to three hundred meters' range," the soldier replied.

"Damn. They could be anywhere," the lieutenant fumed. "Everyone get ready to move out. Rearguard troops, do you see anything on your scanners?"

A handful of responses came in from the paired soldiers scattered back along their route. None reported any activity in their areas. The path of retreat seemed secure, but the further they ventured into this labyrinth, the more tenuous their connection to the outside would become. Atom's troops needed to move along to their target, and get out again, as quickly as possible. The longer they dallied, the greater the chance that they would be detected and attacked.

"Forward by squads," he commanded. "First unit, follow me. Corporal Gunnarsson, stay on my right."

They moved rapidly but cautiously down the corridor, past more open doorways that gaped menacingly on either side. The geography was ripe for a surprise attack, but Gunnarsson shook his head as he watched his screens; nothing living was detected in the vacant chambers.

Atom's squadron stopped when another intersection appeared, and when they had determined the side corridors to be clear, the second group leapfrogged them while they stood and provided cover. At the next intersection their roles reversed, and Atom once again took the lead with his team.

The troops from the second shuttle stayed just behind the two forward squadrons, acting as reserves, ready to move up in support if needed. They also continued to station soldiers at strategic points along the way, guarding their return route.

The squadrons soon came upon closed double doors on the left wall, which Gunnarsson identified as the access point to a large elevator shaft. Like everything they had encountered on this ship, the indicator lights over the doors were dark and lifeless. Ignoring them, they pushed onward, and a short distance further along they found the stairwell.

The left wall opened onto a large sloped passageway which angled upward in a sweeping curve. It was at least six meters in width, perhaps more. The dimensions seemed extravagant, but Atom knew from personal experience that the Knacker body type necessitated generous space allotments. This stairwell was just wide enough to allow the aliens to traverse the incline in both directions.

The passage curved out of view to the right within fifteen meters, and Atom worried about what might await them around the turn. Gunnarsson scanned ahead and pronounced the way clear. "This ramp leads upward past multiple levels, twisting around like a spiral staircase. Barring complications, we should be able to follow it to whichever floor the human captives are housed on."

Complications were what had Atom worried. Where were the alien crew members, and when would they make their presence known? The two lead squadrons proceeded into the stairwell, hugging the walls as they crept around the wide curve, eyes and weapons directed upward. The sloped metallic surface beneath their feet was formed into steps, but these were large and too widely spaced, making the ascent awkward. More than once Atom heard cursing as a trooper tripped and stumbled. "Stay in formation," he murmured. "Careful with your footing."

Back on the *Goliath*, Captain Dent and her bridge crew watched the camera feeds from the alien ship. Atom Granger's data stream was the most useful, as he had taken point and led the way forward. The viewscreen displayed twilight-gray images of oversized steps and curved walls sliding by for several minutes. No resistance was met, and finally the stairwell opened out onto a landing. It appeared the team had arrived at the next level in the pyramid.

When Atom's team approached the second floor junction, he held up his right fist, halting his squad. The landing on this level was more exposed than the one below. It opened onto a large intersection, with corridors stretching off to the left, right and straight ahead. This meant the enemy could come at them from any of three directions if they left the stairs.

When everyone was quiet, Atom motioned Corporal Gunnarsson to follow him. Together they stepped out of the stairwell and into the corridor junction. Dialing up the sensitivity on his external audio pickup, Atom held his breath, straining to detect the slightest sound. Hushed stillness was all that met his ears.

Countless doomed souls had trod these bleak hallways before them, leaving their legacy to weigh on the thoughts of the living. The empty corridors oozed silence; he could feel its oppressive weight like a soundless scream echoing down the vast spaces of this dead ship. Atom realized his heart was pounding despite the lack of physical exertion. He had faced down the enemy on multiple occasions without flinching, but it took all his will not to run back into the stairwell. He gritted his teeth and held his position.

After a handful of long seconds, Atom turned to the tall Norseman at his right. "Gunnarsson, talk to me."

The trooper nodded as he read the glowing screens held in his palms. "Life sign readings are coming in clearer now, sir," he said. "Humans, several hundred of them, clustered in a relatively small area, probably on the next level up. There seems to be a substantial barrier enclosing their location. Alien life forms are also registering, not as many as the humans, probably forty or fifty. Most appear to be above us, but a few may be down on this level."

"That's all?" Atom asked, perplexed. "No more humans or Crabs registering in this sector?"

"No, and that goes for the rest of the pyramid as well, lieutenant," the corporal answered. "Now that we're close enough for good readings, I think that nearly all the life signs are concentrated right above us. I see nothing anywhere else. There may be other Knackers scattered here and there; they don't read as well on our scanners. But it appears that all the humans, and most of the aliens, are clustered in a pretty small area."

"Why aren't there more?" Atom wondered aloud. "It makes no sense. If this was a loaded vessel returning to Xenopus III, as we thought, then there should be tens of thousands of humans on board, plus nearly that many Crabs. If they had died on board, then there would be bodies everywhere. Most of them must have been offloaded prior to our arrival, but then why leave these few behind?"

Gunnarsson was silent, as the answer to that question was a mystery. Just then, in the momentary lull in their conversation, something intruded. It was a sound so small that it might not have happened at all, but it cut across Atom's thoughts like a sword stroke. It lasted for just a second, a quick metallic ping echoing from far down the right hand corridor, like a piece of equipment bumping against a bulkhead. He whirled and squinted down the long tunnel, but could see nothing in the murky distance.

"Did anyone else…" he began, and Gunnarsson responded before Atom could complete his thought.

"I heard it too, lieutenant."

"What do you think?" Atom asked, not taking his gaze from the corridor.

"Well, it could have been structural noise, hull contraction for instance, but—."

"But?" Atom prompted.

"I'm getting sporadic readings of alien life forms on this level, and they seem to be originating from that direction. I'd advise that we get back into the stairwell, sir."

The words were stated blandly, but Atom knew his subordinate well enough to recognize that the man never "advised" a superior to do anything unless it was pretty damned important.

They backed toward the relative cover of the stairs, weapons covering the shadowy corridors as they retreated. When they had rejoined their squadrons, Atom said, "We're moving up to the next floor. Those in back, watch our rear. There may be Crabs here on the second level, and I don't want them coming up on us without warning. Most of the aliens are apparently waiting on the floor above us. That's also where our rescue targets are located. Be prepared for full combat."

The soldiers snaked up the staircase, plastered against the walls with weapons raised and scanners set to maximum. They were now spaced several paces apart, to allow full range of motion for their heavy plasma rifles, and to present less of a massed target to the enemy. Around the curves they ascended, inching up a step at a time, nerves taut as they waited for an attack to be sprung. Finally the third landing came into view, and they collectively exhaled as they came to a halt at the top of the stairs.

"Scanner report," Atom commanded.

No sooner had he spoken then Gunnarsson was there at his side, pouring over his instrumentation. The technician grunted with satisfaction, saying, "Readings are clear now, sir. This landing is similar to the last; several corridors intersect just outside the stair exit, leading to the left, to the right, and straight away. Beyond that, this level appears different than those below it. The entire floor seems to be a vast honeycomb of cells with similar dimensions. A network of corridors connects them. Each room within clear scanning range has a heavily constructed door. I think we've found a prison section of the ship."

"Where are the captives located?" Atom asked.

"Human life readings are concentrated down the left hand corridor, about one hundred meters away. There is a heavy bulkhead or blast door between us and them. Beyond that, there appears to be a short passage with multiple chambers along its length. That is our objective. I detect four large cells that contain human beings, each with a sealed entrance that will need to be opened."

"We've got our work cut out for us," Atom mused unhappily. "I'd have preferred a quick rescue and retreat, but so be it." After a brief pause, he spoke again over the com link, "Tomlich, move toward the front and be ready. We may need to make things go boom very soon."

A handful of heartbeats later the massed troops at the top of the stairs parted, and the explosives specialist came forward. His suit was loaded down with packs which contained the tools of his trade. The other soldiers gave him a wide berth; no one wanted to be near Tomlich if enemy fire came his way.

Atom waved him over and said, "Stay close; you'll need to blow that access door into the prison section, if Avery can't finesse it open."

"*Sir!*" Gunnarsson interjected. "*I've got alien—.*" His words were cut off as a brilliant blue flash lit the air. It cut through the night vision projection on Atom's visor, searing an afterimage into his retinas. The energy bolt also burned a clean hole through the center of the trooper standing next to Tomlich, and the man collapsed in a heap, dead before he hit the floor.

"Drop and fire!" Atom yelled reflexively, jumping behind the wall to the left of the stairwell exit. Troopers followed suit, scrambling for cover or falling to the floor to present minimal profiles. As they did so, hot plasma beams poured through the wide doorway, seeking human targets. Some struck home, and the com link was suddenly filled with the screams of those who had survived direct hits.

The soldiers under Atom's command were well trained, and within seconds they were aggressively returning fire. Dozens of yellow-white energy charges lanced out of their rifles, illuminating their surroundings with strobe light flashes. For a few urgent minutes there was no time to think, as the embattled troops fought for survival using pure reflexes and instinct.

The metallic walls sprouted glowing impact gouges as incoming energy rounds ricocheted crazily off the dense surfaces, zigzagging in the air over the prone troops. Smoke quickly hazed the atmosphere around them, and they would have been fighting in a blinding fog were it not for their night vision gear.

Trapped in the stairwell, Atom found his field of view limited by the doorway. When he hazarded peeks outside, he caught glimpses of ten-limbed creatures resembling giant suited spiders scuttling in the darkness beyond. The Crabs made sizable targets, and despite the tactical disadvantage of their cramped position, Atom's troops began taking a toll on their attackers. They were assisted by their suits' combat computers, which back-tracked incoming alien rounds to their sources, painting visual firing cues for the soldiers to aim at. Hot plasma bolts blew limbs off of Knacker warriors as the humans blanketed the corridors with heavy fire.

A soldier cursed over the com link. "The damned Crabs are carrying three or four weapons each! Even if you take off a limb or two, they just keep fighting!"

There was an edge of desperation in the man's voice, and Atom quickly barked, "Stay focused, troops! Crabs bleed just like us. Wound them and they'll soon fall from loss of bodily fluids."

And in truth a number of the Knackers were slowing, staggering clumsily as they hemorrhaged from stumps of severed limbs. Gunnarsson squeezed off a round that struck one of the forward aliens just above its row of eyes; the impact dropped the creature instantly to the floor where it lay twitching. The Norseman barked a laugh, adding, "If you don't want to wait, just hit 'em in the head."

Atom swung around the door sill and delivered another barrage of rounds from his smoking plasma gun. Return fire chased him behind the protection of the wall, where he took time to glance back at his troops. A half dozen were down, and medics had dragged the injured back out of harm's way to tend to them. Injections of pain blockers had stilled their cries, clearing the com links for tactical communications. "Status report!" Atom called out.

"Rear guard reports clear; no action here," the leader of the second squad responded promptly.

"The wounded are stabilized; three fatalities so far," the lead medic replied a moment later.

"Readings on the enemy forces?" Atom inquired.

Gunnarsson's voice answered, "They have concentrated in the central corridor straight in front of us, sir. Scans indicate about twenty-five Knackers still fighting. Some of those are compromised due to injury—ah, another Crab just went down."

"We've got the numerical advantage now; let's jump on them quickly," Atom said. "There are no external walls in this section, am I correct?"

"Yessir," Gunnarsson confirmed. "We're a good distance from the ship's hull."

"Then it's time to try out some new toys. *Tomlich*, to me!"

The munitions specialist had run for cover when the shooting began, but now he cautiously made his way toward Atom, sidling up to the wall adjacent to the main doorway and hunkering down next to his commander. "What have you got in mind, sir?" he asked, peeking around the edge of the door sill.

Atom said, "Tell me you've got some Hummingbirds."

Tomlich gave an emphatic thumbs-up. "*Yessir!* I've got a dozen of those beauties. I've been itching to try them in live combat."

"Well, here's your chance," Atom replied. "Fire a few at the Crabs and let's see what happens."

The specialist nodded, opening one of his packs. In a moment he extracted a device resembling a shortened grenade launcher. In essence that's what it was, with some major technical improvements. The sophistication of the weapon lay not in its compact size, but rather in the projectiles it fired.

The Hummingbird tracking grenades were a marvel of technology, packing sensor and navigation hardware that in past times would have been reserved for large-yield missiles. The devices could be programmed to seek out a specific life form, using bioenergy readings, infrared, and motion detection to home in on their targets. Once fired, they accelerated along a trajectory that could be altered in mid-air, using micro jets to steer. In flight they emitted a throbbing hum, similar to the sounds of small winged creatures found on some of the human core worlds.

Tomlich pulled out six of the finger-length tapered projectiles, and loaded them into the rear of the launcher. Snapping the ammo bay shut, he drew the weapon up, aiming its blunt muzzle forward. Crouched down, he shuffled to the door's edge, waiting for a lull in the incoming fire. His finger caressed the weapon's trigger like a musician itching to strum his strings.

When he moved it was with panther-like speed, whipping around the doorsill and sweeping the weapon from left to right, squeezing off all six rounds in a staccato barrage. The sharp reports of the launcher were followed by a deep *zzzzipppp zzzzippppp zzzzippppp* as the grenades sped away toward their targets. In the instant it took for the specialist to withdraw again behind the wall, the Hummingbirds were ripping into the alien troops.

The grenades carried a high explosive that was a distant descendant of the C-4 used on old Earth. It was vastly superior to its ancient predecessor, being more stable and yielding approximately ten times the explosive force for each gram of payload. Despite the small size of the projectiles, the result when they hit home was devastating.

Each grenade targeted a different Knacker soldier, and as the weapons impacted, the unlucky aliens literally disintegrated in a cloud of fragmented body parts and yellowish ichor. Any Crabs near the explosions also took major damage, leaving them mangled and hemorrhaging from multiple wounds. When the smoke cleared, over half of the remaining alien warriors had been incapacitated in a matter of seconds.

Elated cries erupted from Atom's troops as they redoubled the ferocity of their attack. Apparently demoralized by their sudden loss of numbers and the barrage of energy bolts assailing them, the Knackers who were still fighting retreated down the central corridor away from the stairwell. One after another fell as they went, and the survivors began to take refuge in the doorways which dotted the hallway. From these protected locations they continued to fire back at the humans, but their control of the corridor had been forfeited.

Atom saw his chance and yelled, "All right, troops! It's time to move! First squad, to me! We'll head down the left hand corridor to the prisoners. Keep your heads down and your guns lit! The rest of you, cover us."

The lieutenant charged out of the doorway and headed left, his troopers following close behind. As they ran they fired their plasma weapons nonstop toward the alien soldiers. Atom's second squad massed on the stair landing just inside the doorway, bringing additional firepower to bear on the depleted enemy troops. Within a few seconds Atom was entering the left hand corridor and out of the aliens' line of fire. The first squadron followed quickly, running bent over to present small profiles to the enemy.

They nearly all made it—but one trooper took a direct hit within meters of reaching safety. A high-pitched shriek sounded over the com link, and the small figure sprawled lifeless on the floor. From the burn mark on the soldier's chest Atom knew that the wound was terminal. He glanced at the insignia on the suit and cursed silently. It was Corporal Avery, the petite female tech who had opened the hatchways barring their passage. She would not see home again, but he was damned if he would leave her body in this place.

"We take our dead when we leave, is that understood?" Atom barked hoarsely into his com. Multiple assents sounded from the other soldiers, and he turned and led them stolidly down the corridor.

After seventy meters or so they came to the barrier Gunnarsson had warned them of. It was another large hexagonal doorway, and Avery was not there to coax it open. "Second squad, report," Atom said into his helmet mike.

A male voice answered over the com link. "We're secure here, sir. The Crabs are still returning fire, but they are contained in the central corridor, and we detect no other enemy activity near us."

"Good. Stay alert; there are more Knackers on this ship, I'm sure of it," Atom replied. He gestured at the slab barring their way. "Tomlich, blast this thing open."

"On it, lieutenant," the munitions specialist answered. He trotted up to the metal slab, eyeing it calculatingly for a moment, and then pulled out a flat metal disc. "A pancake charge should do the trick," he commented, slapping the device onto the center of the door. "It's a shaped blast, so there's minimal blow-back. Still, it would be wise to step back ten meters or so."

Recalling the thickness of the previous door slabs they had encountered, he adjusted the settings on the device to deliver a calculated amount of force. There was an art to using these munitions. Too little blast, and the door might scarcely be scratched. Too much, and collateral damage could be severe.

When Tomlich was satisfied, he stepped back to join the others, holding a remote trigger in his right hand. He lifted the device and pointed it at the door, barking, "*Live fire!*"

The charge on the door slab detonated with a loud concussion. For a brief instant the deafening report assailed their ears before the suits' sound dampeners hushed it to a distant murmur. A large puff of pale smoke billowed out from the slab. Momentarily the pulverized metallic dust obscured the view even with night vision.

As the air cleared, Atom saw that an irregular hole a meter wide had been punched through the dense material. It was large enough to let the soldiers squeeze through one at a time. The blast had been calculated perfectly. "Well done!" the lieutenant commended. "Gunnarsson, scan what's on the other side."

The sensor tech took quick readings, and replied, "The chambers holding the human captives are just past this portal. No alien presence noted."

"Good enough. Follow me," Atom said, and doubled over to ease his suit through the still-smoldering breach in the door. On the other side he straightened, plasma rifle at the ready, and surveyed his surroundings while he waited for the soldiers to join him.

What he saw was a short wide corridor, almost an elongated chamber, with two widely separated doorways on each wall. These were small by Knacker standards, maybe twice the size of an average human doorway, and rectangular in shape. Atom gestured at Gunnarsson, saying, "They're behind these doors?"

"Affirmative," the tech answered, watching his scanner screen. "Looks like nearly three hundred live bodies in the four chambers."

"We've got to get these cells open without injuring those inside," the lieutenant said. "Any ideas as to how?"

"Sir, come look at this!" Tomlich called from the nearest door-way on the right hand wall. "You won't believe it."

Atom approached the portal, and leaned in to inspect what the tech was pointing at. He blinked in surprise and looked again. "Is that what it appears to be?" he asked incredulously.

"As far as I can tell, sir," the munitions specialist replied in a bemused tone. "Extremely low-tech, but effective. My expertise won't be needed here, I think."

"Let's find out," Atom replied, and reached out his hand. He grabbed the handle of the simple sliding bolt which amazingly looked to be the only door lock. Cautiously he drew it upward, half expecting a booby trap. Nothing happened, and after the bolt was retracted, he took hold of the protruding door handle and pulled sideways. The sturdy slab rolled easily to the right, and the chamber within was revealed.

3.

Atom and Tomlich peeked inside the prison cell, with the other squad members pushing up behind them in an effort to see. They were appalled by what met their eyes. The door let into a large square chamber, maybe fifteen meters on a side. The space was mostly bare, lacking furnishings other than a row of structures against the far wall that resembled waste disposal devices. On the hard floor lay scores of humans, both children and adults, and their condition was deplorable. The prisoners were gaunt, filthy, clad in tattered garments that in many cases scarcely covered their bodies. Visual impressions assaulted Atom's brain: unkempt hair and beards, protruding ribs, thin gangly limbs, and skin pockmarked with sores.

He forced his gaze away from the inhabitants to the enclosure itself. Trays that might once have held food lay scattered near the doorway; only dried crusts remained in the containers now. Piles of what looked like human waste were dotted around the room's periphery, and Atom realized that any disposal systems were likely as nonfunctional as the rest of the ship's hardware. It was a small miracle that life support still worked at all. The thought made him check his suit readouts. The temperature in the room was livable, but quite chilly, especially given the scanty garb of its inhabitants. No wonder they huddled together in groups.

Most of the prisoners lay listlessly, but some nearest the front were scurrying backwards, eyes wide and unseeing. A few let out shrieks of fright at the noise of the troops' entry. Atom realized that to these terrified civilians the room appeared pitch black; they could not even see the outlines of the soldiers. For all they knew the Crabs were paying them a visit. Great Ares could only imagine what these people had been through at the hands of their captors.

Switching on his external suit speaker, Atom quickly spoke to the room at large, "It's all right, do not be afraid. We're human.

We're here to help." On the squadron com he added, "Let's bring up suit lights for these people. They'll need to see if we're going to evacuate them quickly."

Nine or ten troopers had joined Atom and Gunnarsson within the cell; several now lit their spotlights. The prisoners' cries had mostly fallen silent when they heard the disembodied voice speaking to them. Now exclamations of protest sprang forth as arms shielded sensitive eyes from the blinding light.

From the back of the cell a woman's voice arose, saying, "My God, they *are* human! Soldiers in space suits, come to rescue us! We're saved, *we're saved!* Thank you, oh thank you for coming for us, thank you thank you thank you…" The voice trailed off into sobs as the woman was overcome with emotion. Others arose to take its place, questioning, fearful, hopeful, all competing for the troopers' attention.

The strident chorus rose in volume until Atom overrode them, speaking forcefully with his external speaker at maximum volume, "*Quiet, people!*" The room fell silent as suddenly as if a circuit had been cut.

Into the stillness the lieutenant continued calmly, "We need to move you out of here right now. The Crabs still have soldiers on this ship. Organize yourselves quickly; those of you who are fit please help the infirm and injured. Adults need to get the children massed into compact groups. We'll assist you. Let's get moving; we leave in less than ten minutes."

"Lieutenant," Gunnarsson tapped Atom on the shoulder. "We await your orders. Should we begin evacuating the other cells?"

"Affirmative. Split the squad into four groups, one for each cell. Get the civilians ready to move out. I'll coordinate our actions with the second squadron. We'll need to minimize exposure to enemy fire as we evacuate. That won't be easy with three hundred people in tow."

"Yes, sir," the corporal replied, and he disappeared back through the doorway.

Over the next ten minutes Atom moved around the first cell, organizing the efforts to get the inhabitants moving, and checking in with the squadrons back at the stairwell.

"We've got the situation in hand here, lieutenant," the second squad leader reported. "The Crabs are pinned down, and we've got positional advantage. But I suggest you move fast. We're picking up additional alien life readings nearby, both on this floor and the one below us. They appear to be moving this way. Our window of safe operation may be closing soon."

"Understood," Atom said. "Keep alert, and watch your backside. We need an open line of retreat when we mobilize. We'll be coming fast; be ready."

Signing off, Atom turned and walked the prison cell from end to end, making sure everyone was able to travel. His troops had set up portable high-output lighting units to aid the civilians. These made it easy to navigate, but the room looked even worse when seen in color. The metallic floor was stained with unnamable fluids, and he had to sidestep mounds of more solid wastes on several occasions.

Near the rear wall he saw three prone figures and moved to assist them. Only when he drew near did he realize that they were beyond help; the bodies were in an advanced state of decomposition. He fought down the bile in his throat and turned away.

It was difficult to imagine how these people had survived with their sanity intact, lying in total darkness among their own wastes, awaiting a grisly fate with the putrefying corpses of their companions only paces away.

Atom was not easily impressed, but he felt something akin to awe as he surveyed the humanity around him. It gave him hope that they might somehow prevail in this war, no matter the odds.

Just then a pale hand grabbed the arm of his suit, demanding his attention. Turning, Atom saw that it belonged to a young woman. She was dark-haired and slender, and although she was smeared with grime and clothed in soiled rags, her face bore an expression of calm determination. He deliberately ignored the scanty nature of her attire, focusing instead on the words the woman was speaking as she looked up at him.

"Please, trooper, can you do something to help these children?"

She gestured behind her, where stood a large group of youngsters, who Atom guessed were mostly between six and twelve years old. Like the adults, they were filthy and thin, with stained clothing hanging limply from their slight frames. They pressed tightly together in an instinctive attempt to gain safety from numbers. Wide eyes like dark pits stared up at him from pallid faces.

The woman continued, "They're so terrified that I can't get them to move. Your appearance is strange to them, and they don't trust you. Perhaps if you showed your face, it would reassure them that it's okay to follow your soldiers. It would be best if we don't have to carry them out of here."

Atom hesitated, then spoke into the com, "Gunnarsson, are we still clear of hostiles?"

"Yessir," came the immediate reply. "The nearest aliens are contained in the corridor near the stairwell. I can't say how long we've got, though."

"Understood." Atom switched back to external speaker, and said, "Okay, miss. I'll take off my helmet and let them see me, and then we've got to move, okay?"

The young woman nodded and backed up slightly to give him room, turning and murmuring reassurances to the whimpering youngsters behind her.

Glancing once more at his external atmospheric readout, Atom hit the disengage control on his left arm, then reached up and unfastened the helmet coupling at his neck. With a faint hiss the headpiece came loose. He lifted it up and off, and the filtered environment of the suit was replaced with the reality of the outside world.

He scarcely had time to feel the chill bite of the air before the overwhelming odor hit his nostrils like a hammer blow. The stenches of human waste, of unwashed bodies, and most of all, of death, pervaded the cell, threatening to overcome his self-control. Thank the stars for olfactory fatigue; these people were probably so inured to this place that they had no awareness of how bad the air was.

He fought to maintain a normal expression, acutely aware of the gazes of the children as they scrutinized his exposed countenance. He must have been successful, for he saw relief mixed with the curiosity in their eyes.

Atom even managed a smile as he lifted his free hand and waved at them. "It's nice to meet you all," he said in a steady voice. "I'm Lieutenant Granger, and I've come to rescue you. I don't know about you kids, but I like my spaceship a whole lot better than this place. My ship has lights, and good food, and best of all, no Crabs! Let's all go back there together, shall we? What do you say?"

His question was met with ragged cheers from the cluster of children, and his grin widened as the young woman added her voice to the chorus. As her gaze met his, he could see the unspoken gratitude in her eyes. Atom nodded and winked at her before lifting his helmet back into place. He felt a profound sense of relief as the pressure locks engaged and cool processed air rushed over his face, calming his rebelling stomach.

Turning to survey his troops, he barked out orders on the com link, "All right, people, it's time to move out. Assemble in the corridor outside of the cells. Get the civvies organized into groups of about forty each. Put several soldiers ahead of and behind each group, to keep them organized and provide protection. We'll have to squeeze through the hole in the main door one at a time, which will slow us down. Once past the door, we'll reassemble and march at a quick walk toward the stairwell. These people are weak, and they'll struggle to sustain a quick pace. Be ready to help the stragglers. Now let's get out of here!"

Atom's squads were well trained, and in minutes they had the captives organized and ready to march. Each group of civilians was bunched compactly together, with the stronger adults at the periphery and the children and infirm protected in the center.

Those at the front began to move, following the soldiers' directions, with the spotlights of the spacers' suits illuminating their way. One by one they approached the main doorway enclosing the cell block, scrambling through the ragged wound in the hexagonal slab. Even moving quickly, it took time to get several hundred captives plus the troops past the barrier.

Atom was chomping at the bit by the time everyone was through, and he pushed them onward. "Reassemble, troops! Gunnarsson, stay toward the front and watch your scanners! I don't want any surprises. We'll march at a quick pace until we near the stairwell. We need to cross the open corridor intersection in order to reach the stairs, which will expose us to enemy fire."

As the soldiers herded the civilians back into organized units, the lieutenant called ahead, "Second squad, we'll be approaching your position at the stairs momentarily. What's your status?"

"We've got the Crabs pinned down," the reply came on the com. "Only a few are still returning fire. Looks like we've got them beat, sir."

"I don't trust it," Atom said. "They may be holding back and waiting for our return. Be ready to lay down heavy suppressing fire when we arrive. We'll be badly exposed and dragging civvies with us."

"Understood, lieutenant. On your signal, we'll let loose with all we've got."

"We're on our way." Atom turned his attention back to his squad. Behind him the corridor was filled wall-to-wall with the massed civilians. They had been organized into seven large groups in a rough parade formation, one after the other, with soldiers in between.

Even bunched tightly, the entire company of troops and civilians occupied nearly a fifty meter length of the hallway. It was going to be a challenge to get everyone moving quickly without tripping or falling, or worse yet, panicking and stampeding. Regardless, they had no choice. Satisfied that they were as prepared as they could be, Atom raised his right arm and swept it forward, saying, "Move out in orderly fashion. Follow me!"

4.

On the bridge of the *Goliath*, Taramay watched the images from the Knacker vessel with a mixture of hope and trepidation. Things seemed to be going smoothly, so she couldn't explain the persistent knot in the pit of her stomach. Maybe it was concern for her people who were stuck deep inside that alien horror. No, she'd been through plenty of missions before, and she was well accustomed to the stress of combat situations. This was something more.

Perhaps the pyramid itself was what bothered her. It felt wrong, somehow. It simply didn't make sense, finding the alien ship drifting out here alone, partially evacuated and then abandoned. If the crew and captives had been retrieved, why leave a fraction of each behind? Why hadn't the vessel itself been salvaged for the valuable materials it contained?

It wasn't like the Knackers to do a job halfway. Detestable though they were, she had to admit that the aliens were efficient and thorough. They would never leave a task unfinished, unless they had no choice. So, why hadn't they reclaimed this ship and the rest of its contents? It was almost as if they had been…interrupted.

Her heart suddenly in her throat, Taramay spun on her heels, her voice urgent. "Mr. Cotton, I want a deep scan of near space, out to a hundred thousand klicks from our location. Look for movement, energy emissions, life signs, metal detection, everything."

The tech officer looked puzzled, and he said uncertainly, "It would help if I knew what I was looking for, Captain."

"A Knacker vessel, probably a large one, possibly running in stealth mode," Taramay replied grimly.

Bruce Cotton looked as if he were going to ask another question, and then thought the better of it when he saw her expression. He nodded wordlessly, lowering his gaze to the task at hand.

"Who needs stealth out here among this mess?" he muttered,

as he set to scanning the first of eight pie-wedges of space in the region around their ship. This was going to be like searching for the proverbial mange mite on a Cerenese land-whale.

* * * *

Atom's squads herded the civilians down the lightless corridor as quickly as could be managed. Some of the erstwhile prisoners were little more than walking skeletons, and had to be half supported, half carried by their neighbors. This ship's situation must have been critical, for the Crabs to have let their potential food items reach such a pitiful state.

Within a minute they neared the corridor intersection at the stairwell. The troopers' suit beams highlighted their pitch-dark surroundings enough to enable the civilians to walk, but Atom continued to monitor his night vision and sensor readouts, distrustful of what the lights were showing him.

A bright flash lit the blackness just ahead, where the battle between humans and Crabs was continuing. Atom and Corporal Gunnarsson led their procession forward, slowing as they spotted a cluster of human figures in their path. The second squad troops had emerged from the stairwell to take up positions in the corridor. Soldiers were huddled behind the corners in the side passages, laying down suppressing fire into the central hallway where their enemy was pinned down. The Knackers' return fire had tapered off, and the humans were saving ammo, only discharging their weapons in response to incoming fire.

That all changed in a split second. On Atom's signal, the second squad soldiers rounded the corners of the intersection and began pounding the Knacker positions with plasma rounds. Some of Atom's squad added their weapons to the assault. Yellow-white ribbons of coherent energy crisscrossed the hall, bringing certain death to anything in their path. Enemy fire nearly ceased as the aliens were forced to withdraw into their doorway positions.

There was no time to waste, and Atom charged forward into the intersection, barking into his com link, "Everyone move! Stay in rank, and head for the stairwell!"

As he crossed the open space toward the beckoning shelter of the stairs, Atom glanced to his left, getting a glimpse of the central corridor wherein resided their enemy. The metallic walls were blackened and scored with impacts from hundreds of energy rounds. Alien bodies lay in untidy heaps scattered across the floor. The firefight pyrotechnics lit the scene with an eerie strobe effect, bursts of brilliant light dispelling the inky blackness long enough to paint the soldiers' movements in jerky stop-motion.

Then Atom was through into the stairwell landing, and he turned to watch the progress of the mass of humanity behind him. On they came, a tide of jostling, stumbling civilians in rags, guided by suited troopers who urged them on.

The first refugees poured into the stairwell, their mass clogging the doorway and blocking Atom's view of the corridor beyond. Soldiers quickly pushed them down the staircase, using their suit speakers to issue verbal commands: "Careful on the stairs; they're not sized for human feet. Help each other, do not rush. Continue past the next landing until we reach the bottom. Move along, move along."

Despite their traumatized condition, the ragtag group of civilians managed to maintain a semblance of order, and Atom felt a swell of pride for his species. For a minute or two the crush of bodies continued moving through the doorway and down the winding stairwell. He estimated that about two-thirds of the civilians had made it past him when bedlam erupted beyond the door.

Incoming plasma rounds suddenly sprayed the corridor outside the stairwell. Some impacted the wall over the crowd, while others slammed into the bunched humans waiting in the hallway. Screams erupted as the throng jostled and surged. Wide-eyed people pushed forward frantically, threatening to crush those in front as they tried to squeeze through the portal.

Over the uproar Atom heard the bellowing voices of soldiers issuing commands. They were telling people to drop to the floor to avoid being hit. But the crowd was too closely bunched, and only those on the periphery could comply. The rest were standing targets, caught in the press of packed bodies.

Com chatter flew back and forth as the troops holding the corridor tried to coordinate suppressing fire. Atom craned his head to see over the mass of panicked humanity, while helping his troops pull civvies through the doorway. "What's going on out there?" he yelled into his helmet mike, at the same time grabbing and almost throwing a rail-thin youth toward the stairs.

"The enemy is mounting a counterattack, sir," one of the squad leaders replied, his voice cracking with strain. "Looks like the Crabs want to stop the escape of their captives. We're trying to knock them back into their hidey-holes."

"Nail the bastards!" Atom spat in reply, feeling helpless. The crowd stood between him and the enemy; from here he could only exhort his soldiers on. Another burst of energy bolts shot out of the darkness, and more shrieks arose as the deadly rounds hit home.

Atom cursed vehemently, and shouted, "We've got to stop the incoming fire *now*! We're taking casualties!"

Just then a tall figure stepped up to Atom's left, and said, "Allow me, sir." Without waiting for his superior's consent, Tomlich raised his grenade launcher over his head, aiming its barrel out the doorway above the crowd. Locking his arms to keep the weapon steady, he depressed the firing trigger six times. His remaining half-dozen Hummingbird grenades buzzed the civilians' heads as they accelerated through the intersection toward the central corridor beyond.

Ignoring the humans entirely, the projectiles tracked the Crabs' life signatures and disappeared up the passageway in a blur. The first Hummingbird homed in on the nearest alien emanations; as it hit its target, the unlucky Crab was wiped off the sensor scans, so the second grenade tracked the next alien in line, and so on. Six rapid explosions rocked the ship, and flame and smoke belched out of the corridor. By the time the echoes had died away, the Knackers' guns had also fallen silent.

A moment later the human troops eased their fire as well, peering through the haze and watching their scanner readings for any sign of enemy activity. All was quiet, except for the shouts and wailing of the milling noncombatants still trying to escape the killing zone.

On the floor at the edge of the crowd lay ten bodies. A quick inspection showed that six were dead, and four lived but were seriously wounded. The energy beams had bitten their victims deeply, but they also partially cauterized the injuries, so blood loss was reduced. However, the wounded needed medical attention soon if they were to survive the day.

"Take the dead with us," Atom instructed his troops. "We may have to dump them if the going gets tough, but I don't want to leave anyone on this ship unless absolutely necessary."

"Understood, lieutenant," Sergeant Harriman's bass tones replied. "I'll see to it that we don't miss anyone."

The last of the refugees were coming through the doorway now. One of the final groups to pass was a cluster of young children, half of them sobbing as they stumbled along. At their center was a figure Atom recognized, the young woman from the prison cell. She was struggling to keep the youngsters together, as many were nearly delirious with fright. Seeing her difficulties, Atom moved to help her. Together they managed to contain the stragglers and get them headed down the oversized stairs.

The woman started to thank him, and then she saw his name insignia and smiled, saying, "Oh, it's you! My guardian angel! I should have known."

Atom realized she might not see him grinning through the faceplate, so he gave her a thumbs-up sign and gestured for her to follow the children down the stairs. He paused on the landing, waiting for the last troopers to exit the corridor. As they moved out he performed a quick scan of the area behind them. Nothing living registered on his readouts. With one last glance over his shoulder he turned to follow the soldiers down the stairs.

* * * *

Taramay paced on the command deck of the *Goliath*, her nerves taut as she watched the progress of the soldiers in the alien vessel.

"Come on, come on," she said under her breath. "Get yourselves out of there!"

For she couldn't shake the nagging feeling that her intuition was right, that there was a ship out there, hiding in the asteroid field, waiting for—what? If the Knackers had been interrupted while offloading the stricken pyramid, then why hadn't they attacked the human vessel? An alien destroyer was easily a match for the *Goliath*; could the Crabs have sent a simple transport out here instead of a warship? Were they waiting for reinforcements before showing themselves? Or was a hidden foe simply a paranoid product of her stressed mind?

She looked up into the star field floating overhead, but there were no answers forthcoming. A glance across the twilit bridge showed her tech officer still muttering to himself as he intently scanned his data screens. She shook her head; this situation had her doubting her own judgment.

Taramay knew that much of her frustration derived from her inability to act. Waiting was the hardest game to master. If only she could take some positive action, it would help settle her mind.

She turned to her com officer. "Ms. Stepanovich, hail the commander on shuttle one."

"Yes, Captain," Alena replied. In a moment the junior officer nodded and said, "Line is open."

"Shuttle commander, this is Captain Dent."

"Reading you, Captain," came the prompt reply.

"The squadrons will be arriving back at your ships soon, along with several hundred civvies. Be prepared; it's going to be a tight fit. Before they reach you, I want you to plant an A-M 33 antimatter charge on that pyramid. I don't plan on letting the Crabs salvage a single bolt from that monstrosity. Do it now."

"Yes, *ma'am*!" came the enthusiastic reply.

"Dent out," Taramay concluded the communication.

The words had scarcely left her mouth when the tech officer spoke up excitedly. "Captain, something is showing on the medium range scanner! Low level energy readings, originating from a large asteroid about two thousand klicks out."

"Or from something hiding behind it," Taramay replied. She quickly crossed the bridge to approach the scanner station. "Any indication of what it is?"

"Unclear at this time, Captain," the lieutenant replied, glancing up at her. "The rock has a high nickel content, like much of this asteroid field. This obscures refined metals to some extent. I'm working to compensate, but it may take a few minutes."

"Do it, Mr. Cotton. We have to know what's out there," Taramay commanded. "Ms. Stepanovich, hail Lt. Granger and both shuttle commanders; let them know that we may be running out of time. Advise them that they need to complete their extraction quickly."

To herself she added quietly, "Let's hope it's quick enough."

* * * *

Atom continued to bring up the rear as the humans on board the Knacker pyramid descended the stairs toward the base level.

While the civilians ahead of him shuffled along, he monitored the stairwell above and behind them, watching his scanner readouts for signs of movement or life readings. Gunnarsson was up at the front of the procession with his heavy sensor equipment, and Atom felt half-blind without the specialist at his side.

On down they went, past the second level landing. The last soldiers stationed there joined Atom at the rear of the pack. He stayed connected with the forward squads via the com link; the frontrunners had already exited the stairwell and were heading down the long passageway toward the exit.

He was about halfway down to the lowest level when a brief blip appeared on his scanner. It was there for just a second, and as quickly was gone. He froze, scrutinizing the virtual display in his helmet, but it showed clear. For a moment longer he lingered on the stairs, watching and listening. Nothing registered but the receding life signatures of the humans. Finally he shook his head and hurried to catch up to the tail end of the company.

They reached the bottom of the stairwell a minute later, and came out once again into the lowest level of the ship. Atom and his handful of rear guard soldiers turned right and headed down the corridor. From here it was a long straight shot to the exit where the shuttles awaited. Their scanners showed the route to be clear of hostiles.

Atom had just started to relax when the floor beneath his feet shuddered. He halted instantly, weapon at the ready, turning this way and that as he scanned his readouts for answers. Now a deep hum rose around him, seeming to emanate from the very structure of the vessel. It slowly climbed in pitch like a massive engine revving up, until his teeth gritted from the vibration. His readouts were jumping off the scales with incoming data as well.

Atom hissed into his com link, "Gunnarsson, status report! Are you seeing what I'm seeing?"

"Energy readings are spiking throughout the ship," the tense reply came. "It appears auxiliary power sources have been engaged. The Crabs may be up to something."

Moments later, a dim reddish glow began to emanate from a sconce high on the wall to his left. Atom could see similar fixtures coming to life at wide intervals down the hallway. They were enough to show the way, just barely, and he surmised that this was part of the ship's emergency lighting system.

A quick flash at the corner of his vision wrenched his gaze to the opposite wall. There a pair of crimson lights winked brightly off and on. They perched over large double doors, and their significance hit him with a jolt.

"Everyone move out, *fast!*" he barked into the com. "You soldiers with me, cover those doors! The elevators are functional!"

No sooner had the words left his mouth than the large twin panels began to rumble open. For a moment everything seemed to slow to a crawl. The widening gap between the doors yawned black to Atom's staring eyes, nothing visible within the shadowed interior of the elevator. Then his night vision gear detected movement. For a second or two the image was hazy and confused, before resolving into a massive clawed limb thrusting a weapon through the opening.

"*Drop and fire!*" he shouted, doing just that as brilliant lances of plasma erupted from the elevator. Multiple beams stretched out like glowing fingers, clawing toward the suited forms of the human soldiers. Those unlucky enough to still be standing were easy targets. In a few heartbeats three troopers went down amid bright flashes and dark puffs of smoke, their bodies riddled with flame-cauterized holes.

It was a testament to the skill and training of the SpaceForce troops that the remaining rear guard did not perish then and there. Atom and the three remaining soldiers with him returned fire from prone positions on the metal floor. Their barrage was concentrated into the small target area of the elevator entrance, and for a precious few moments the topography favored the humans.

For although the lift was enormous by human standards, able to hold a handful of large Knacker warriors, the partly-open door prevented more than one or two aliens from firing their weapons into the corridor at once. Their large body conformation simply didn't allow crowding into a small opening, either front-to-back or side-by-side. The Crabs' multiple prehensile limbs partially compensated: most of their initial salvos came from six weapons yielded by just a pair of Knackers.

But the humans had the early advantages of better visibility and angle of fire. The elevator took about ten seconds to fully open, and in that short time Atom's soldiers wreaked havoc among the aliens. The heavy door slabs partially shielded the Crabs, but they served even more to confine and constrict their movements. When plasma rounds were fired into that enclosed chamber, the solid metal walls and doorway deflected them every which way, creating a lethal crossfire from all angles. The aliens were sliced and skewered with nowhere to run.

By the time the elevator doors yawned wide, the enemy weapons had gone silent, and the open chamber within was a tangle of torn bodies and separated limbs. Atom rose shakily to his feet, barking commands to his companions to stay back and cover the corridors. His virtual display showed no live Knackers nearby, but then the scanners had also failed to warn them of the attack.

He approached the open car now, probing it with eyes and electronics. Blue smoke wreathed around the bodies within, and he squinted, trying to see clearly into the jumble. The interior was packed to capacity, and in their death throes some Knackers had ended up lying atop others. This could have served to shield some of them from incoming fire…

As the thought flitted across his mind, Atom saw the mass of alien corpses shift just a little. His pulse pounding, he panned his red-hot gun barrel across the elevator car, not daring to move closer. After a few tense moments, he slowly relaxed. No life signs registered; the movement had just been bodies settling.

He jumped as his com speaker blared with a sudden flurry of activity. The forward troops were frantically reporting that they were under attack. He turned toward his soldiers, opening his mouth to issue orders, when the body pile in front of him exploded outward. From its midst reared a live Knacker, multiple limbs churning as it burst from the embrace of its dead comrades. It moved fast, unbelievably fast, and it was upon Atom before he could bring his rifle to bear.

He had time to see the huge body charging, an environment suit hiding the details of its anatomy, all but the eyes, that row of six red eyes glaring at him through the wide aperture of its oddly shaped visor. Several of the alien's forelimbs were raised, weapons clutched in one or two of them. He glimpsed the short stump of a severed appendage leaking golden fluid as the Crab closed with him.

Disdaining use of its armament, the creature knocked Atom's

gun aside with casual speed. The heavy blow sent a numbing shock up his arm. He fell backwards, barely retaining his grip on his weapon. The alien rushed in, raising another appendage to smite him dead. Atom cringed as he flung one arm up in what he knew would be a useless defense—and in that moment his troopers let loose with their energy rifles.

The fusillade of glowing bolts struck the Crab in its right flank, piercing suit and exoskeleton alike. Atom was close enough to feel and hear the impacts. The harsh crackle of superheated plasma was overlaid with the sizzle of cooked flesh as the rounds bit deep. Mortally wounded, the alien staggered, its momentum carrying it forward as it fell directly on top of Atom.

The collision drove him heavily into the unyielding floor, knocking his breath out and bouncing his helmet hard off the surface. He lay stunned, pinned beneath the alien, while overhead a few more energy rounds pounded its dying body. As Atom's eyes focused, he found himself face to face with the Knacker.

Red faceted orbs glared into his visor from a mere hand's-breadth away. Atom's gaze was transfixed, unable to look away. Even this close he could read no expression in the creature's hard, chiseled features. As he watched, the life slowly ran out of those alien eyes, and they glazed over as thin membranous lids closed for the final time.

The weakly scrabbling limbs went limp, settling the full weight of the Knacker onto his prone form. He struggled to breathe, managing only a weak call for help on the com.

Within moments the dead body was pulled off of him, and strong hands hauled him to his feet. Atom stood bent over, hands on his trembling knees, fighting to get his wind back. When his lungs eased up, he straightened, still dazed.

It was then that he realized something was wrong with his vision. He shook his head, squinting to clear his sight. It didn't help. Everything around him was dark and murky, with only the dull ruddy glows from the wall sconces showing distinctly to his eyes. His soldiers were grayish smudges in the black. Even the larger bulk of the downed Knacker was barely visible from a few meters away. Strangely, he could read every detail of the heads-up display inside his helmet. As the cobwebs slowly left his mind, he realized what must have happened.

"I've taken damage," he spoke into the helmet mike. "The impact took out my night vision, but my scanners are operational. Are you getting this?"

"Loud and clear, sir" came the reply, and Atom felt a surge of relief. To be blind *and* deaf was a scenario he didn't wish to contemplate.

His eyes began to adjust to the dimness, and he cursed as he spied the inert bodies of the downed troopers. After a moment's silence, he said heavily, "We'll have to leave them behind. We can't remain effective while carrying three bodies." No one raised a dissenting opinion.

Recalling the reports of other Crab attacks, Atom sent a broad-link com message: "Forward squads, this is Lt. Granger. What's your status?"

The airwaves were silent for several long seconds, during which time his mind imagined a score of unpleasant possibilities. When the reply finally came, Atom recognized Torvald Gunnarsson's baritone. "Situation under control, sir. Several Crabs ambushed us. We returned fire, killing one, and the rest retreated. We took two casualties."

"Any idea of their current whereabouts?" Atom asked.

"No, sir," Gunnarsson replied. "They are not registering well on my scanners. Our previous estimates of Knacker troop strength may be erroneous. Still, I suspect relatively small numbers are aboard, based on our limited encounters so far."

"Agreed. But the danger is there nonetheless. How is the evacuation going?"

"The first civilians are nearing the exit now. We still have a long line straggling out behind. It's been tough keeping people together when the fighting starts."

"Understood. Keep them moving at all costs; we've got to get out of here quickly. Watch your backside, soldier!"

"Will do," Gunnarsson answered, and they signed off.

5.

On the bridge of the *Goliath*, Taramay was occupied with her own concerns. She paced the bridge deck, sipping on the tube of a spiced amino-juice pouch, restlessly waiting for events to play out. Abruptly Lt. Cotton looked up from his scan monitor and spoke to her. "Captain, I've got a clear profile of the energy source. You're not going to like it."

"A Knacker destroyer?" she asked, moving across the floor to his station.

The younger officer just nodded, his expression tense.

"Good work, Mr. Cotton. Now we know what we're up against," Taramay said as she leaned over to peer at the scanner console.

"I'm not sure I can take credit," Bruce replied in a low voice. "I've been running intensive scans, trying to clear out metallic ore interference, but it's been slow going. Then the readings suddenly intensified, allowing me to lock in and verify the source. That's got me worried, though."

"Explain," the captain said, holding the younger man's gaze.

"Well…the energy signatures suggest their main systems may be coming on line after having been mostly shut down. I think the Crabs are powering up their vessel."

Taramay straightened and glanced involuntarily at the main viewscreen. "Damn! That means they detected our scans. They know they've been discovered, and they're preparing for action."

"You mean battle?" Bruce asked, in a voice that suddenly sounded very small.

"Well, they're either getting ready to run or to fight, and Knackers don't like to run," the captain replied grimly. "Ms. Jónsson, power up the main plasma guns and energize the diffuser screens. Mr. DeBartolo, turn us to face the enemy. Set initial coordinates using Mr. Cotton's data. We may need to light that ship up quickly."

The tech officer called out, "Captain, I'm getting movement from the enemy vessel. It's rounding into view from behind the asteroid, and turning toward our position."

"Distance, Mr. Cotton?"

"Just under two thousand klicks. The readings are clear now; it's a Hades class heavy destroyer, and its weapons are hot."

"Battle alert, everyone!" Taramay called out. She surveyed her crew as the alarm claxon sounded twice and amber battle lighting bathed the room. "Forward diffuser screens at maximum density. Ms. Stepanovich, tell the away teams to get their butts back on board this ship, and double-time it!"

Just then the deck lurched beneath her feet, throwing her off balance. She grabbed the edge of Lt. Cotton's console to steady herself. A low rumble vibrated through the ship's hull and faded away, leaving a hushed quiet in its wake.

The members of the bridge crew were veterans of the war game, so no cries of alarm erupted; everyone quietly kept their attention fixed on their consoles.

"It's begun, people," Taramay declared. "Note for the record that they've fired the first salvo."

The *Goliath* had completed a ninety degree turn and no longer faced the giant pyramid. The human destroyer's prow now pointed directly at its adversary, though the alien warship was still too distant to detect with the unaided eye.

"Magnify view," Taramay commanded. "Let's see who we're fighting."

The forward viewscreen image swelled, making it appear that their ship rushed ahead at a breakneck pace. Distant asteroids grew from tiny specks to monstrous shadowy planetoids before vanishing past them to the left or right, as the telescopic viewer homed in on their target. Then a black form swelled out of the starry night, something that blotted out the stellar radiances behind it. No running lights showed on the forbidding shadow-vessel, and like its pyramid cousin, it was nearly invisible.

Unperturbed, the captain rubbed her cheek and said, "Enhance."

Lt. Cotton's hands darted over his console, and the image on screen was digitally highlighted with input from scanner readings. What was black became a lighter gray, and vague edges were defined. Within seconds the familiar blunt-nosed bulk of a Knacker destroyer emerged before their eyes. The bridge fell silent for several long moments, until the com officer finally said, "That thing looks… really large."

"Approximately 150,000 metric tons, give or take a few," piped up Greta Jónsson from her gunnery station.

"That's nearly twice the mass of the *Goliath*," Lt. Cotton croaked, his eyes a bit wide as he stared at the image.

"Yes it is," Taramay replied, "which is why we need to monitor its movements closely, *lieutenant*."

Abashed, the young officer snapped his gaze back to his scanner console. "Er… the Crab vessel is closing with us now, Captain, but at a slow rate of advance. Still over nineteen hundred klicks out."

As they watched, a glowing spot appeared on the bow of the alien ship. In a heartbeat it flared into brilliance, and a blue-white lance leapt from the Knacker destroyer, covering the distance between the vessels in an instant. The entire viewscreen flared white and the *Goliath* shivered from another impact.

The dazzling display lasted only an instant before the screen dimmed the glare, but the strobe flash left afterimages on their retinas. Blinking, Taramay said, "Damage report."

"No damage thus far, Captain," the first officer replied. "The new diffuser screens are working according to specifications. We were able to bleed off about twenty percent of the incoming energy into storage cells, which will reinforce the shields."

"Good," Taramay replied. "That gives us a larger margin for error…but we can't get careless. The enemy's weapons still outperform ours, and if they get close enough, they'll punch through the best screen like it wasn't there."

"Plasma cannons at full power," the gunnery officer said. "The enemy is in the outer envelope of our weapons' range. Do you want me to return fire?"

"Will it have any effect?" the captain asked her.

"Not likely. Their shields and armor will resist penetration at this range, even with the hyper-focused beam projectors that the *Goliath* was refitted with."

"Then hold fast, Ms. Jónsson. Let's allow them to believe we have standard armor and armament for now. If they get close enough, we may just surprise them."

* * * *

Atom Granger jogged down the midnight corridor of the alien ship, his three troopers close around him. Minus his enhanced vision capabilities, he could barely see. His companions had to lead the way. He had elected not to use his suit lights; their haphazard play of light and shadow would overlie the night vision images of the other troopers, reducing their ability to spot danger.

Proceeding lightless may have been wise, but Atom quickly found that being near-blind in hostile territory was nerve-wracking. The faint glows of the alien ship's emergency lights stretched down the corridor ahead of him, marking his path home, but their weak radiance revealed almost nothing of his surroundings. He found himself reaching time and again for the controls that would bring his spotlights to life. The floor was invisible beneath his feet, and he stumbled repeatedly over fallen structural debris as he pushed himself forward.

The side passages that intersected their path, already forbidding with their potential for ambush, now held untold menace in their impenetrable depths. Atom could barely sense the deeper dark looming to his left and right as they passed through the intersections. Even with his soldiers' assertions that the halls were clear, he felt a cold touch of foreboding as his anxious eyes probed those silent passages. Primitive animal fear pushed against his self-control, his instincts saying that a concealed monster would leap from the shadows at any instant.

During their fight with the Knackers in the elevator, Atom and his rearguard had fallen behind the civilian column. They now hiked alone, their footsteps echoing in the emptiness. As they hurried to catch up, they could begin to see flashes of clean white illumination far ahead. These were the suit lights of the soldiers escorting the civilians.

They closed to within about fifty meters of the main column, and then things went to hell. Without warning, Atom's scanners suddenly flared with alien life readings. Simultaneously a pair of Knackers burst from side corridors just ahead of them, visible as black hulks against the lights of the procession they were chasing.

"Crabs!" Atom shouted as he hit the floor. "Watch out for the civvies!"

The prone soldiers took bead on the aliens and unleashed a volley. The Knackers whirled and returned fire almost instantly. For a few seconds the air was lit with intersecting ribbons of light, then just as quickly the aliens disappeared back into the dark maze of the ship's passageways.

Flat on his belly, Atom squinted in vain through his visor. After a moment he spoke into his mike, "Status report!"

A trooper replied, "Scanners indicate that the Crabs are continuing to retreat down the side passage."

"What the hell?" Atom exclaimed as he rose to his feet. "Why'd they disengage so quickly?"

"Dunno, sir, but we should move while we can."

"Affirmative. Let's march," Atom replied. Half to himself, he muttered, "Why do we read the Crabs just fine when they're retreating, but not when they're coming up on us?"

No one had any answers.

The procession ahead of them had broken into a run when the shooting had started, and the troopers once again found themselves left behind. They hurried onward as fast as caution permitted, guns covering branch corridors which loomed and then vanished in the dark.

They encountered no further trouble, and in a few minutes they had caught up to the tail end of the civilian procession once again. Atom breathed easier as the glowing figures of the escorting soldiers loomed in his visor.

The rearmost troops greeted Atom and his companions eagerly. Their enthusiasm was tempered when they learned that three of their comrades had been lost. Together they resumed their march toward the pyramid's exit, following the civilian stragglers and providing fire cover for their retreat.

The com link continued to pick up communications between the troops escorting the civilians. Abruptly the chatter became louder and more urgent, and Corporal Gunnarsson's strong voice cut in, using priority override, "Lieutenant Granger, are you receiving this?"

"Granger here," Atom replied as he jogged along. "What's happening?"

"Crabs are hitting us hard from intersecting corridors; we've taken several casualties so far."

"What's your location?" Atom asked.

"We're currently moving past that decorated portal we encountered on the way in. I'm ordering a fast retreat toward the shuttles, but you may be cut off from the main body if we do so."

"Never mind us. Get as many troops and civilians out as you can. Try to keep everyone together, but cover your butts and retreat! We'll catch any stragglers."

Atom switched off from the command channel and added to his troopers, "Watch your scanners; the enemy is lurking up ahead. We've got to move quickly, or we may not get out of here."

* * * *

The bridge of the *Goliath* shuddered as another salvo from the alien destroyer broke upon their bow. "Damn!" Taramay swore. "If those soldiers don't get their carcasses in gear, we may have to leave them. Damage report!"

The first officer answered, "No structural loss, Captain. We are beginning to see energy bleed off of the main diffuser screens, however. If the incoming plasma beams increase in strength another five percent, we will start to get discharges hitting the hull."

"How much closer do they have to get before that happens?"

"Approximately two hundred klicks."

Taramay considered this for a moment, then asked, "Mr. Cotton, what is their rate of advance?"

"Relatively slow, Captain. They will be within lethal firing range in approximately five minutes."

Another blinding-white impact hit their ship, and the starscreen once again dimmed the image before fading back to normal view. The groaning deck pitched beneath Taramay's feet, and she automatically compensated like a sailor riding the seas.

"Ms. Stepanovich, what's the status of the away teams?"

"Boarding the shuttles as we speak, ma'am. But Lt. Granger and others are still within the pyramid."

"Put out a priority call," Taramay said through clenched teeth. "Let them know we will be *leaving*, and they'd better be on board when we do."

"On it, Captain."

Taramay turned her attention back to the big screen, where the ominous image of the Knacker destroyer continued to slowly grow in size.

* * * *

Atom's troops herded the last of the civilians along the corridor toward the exit. He swore as the *Goliath*'s summons came over the com. Urgency sped their feet, and soon the familiar lightning-flickers of weapon discharges began to split the darkness ahead of them.

Gunnarsson's voice followed moments later. "Lieutenant, my scans show that you're closing on our position. We're holding the corridor at the blast door, but I'm not sure how long we can keep the Knackers pinned back. I suggest that you hurry."

"Dammit, Gunnarsson, I told you to get out!" Atom fumed, picking up his pace and nearly running into the civilians just ahead of him.

"The majority of the civvies are boarding the shuttles as we speak. A small core of troops stayed behind to assist you. We're all that remain besides the last stragglers, mainly your group."

"We'll be with you momentarily, then," Atom replied, ending the communication.

The light strengthened as they approached the firefight. Atom could now discern the threshold of the large bas-relief doorway no more than thirty meters in front of him. Based on the energy beams spitting from the dark, the human defenders were nestled against the walls just on the other side of the portal. In the unsteady illumination it appeared that Atom's own party numbered maybe forty or fifty soldiers and civilians.

They only needed to get past this doorway, and then make a short run to the shuttle bay, and they should be home free.

"Coming up on you, Torvald," Atom announced as his troops neared the action. Switching to external speakers, he commanded, "All civilians on the floor, *now*!" As the non-combatants obeyed and dropped, he barked into the com link, "All soldiers with me, fire at will on enemy targets!"

Most of Atom's troops still had functional night vision and scanner inputs. Using these, they found the Knacker soldiers hiding in the mouths of the side corridors. The humans' weapons erupted almost as one, lighting up the night as they raked the enemy positions.

Within seconds their efforts drew return fire, and the soldiers hunkered down or plastered themselves against the walls, trying to present smaller targets as energy bolts snapped around them. Harsh cries echoed over the com link as two troopers were hit.

As the alien weapons fire was diverted toward this new threat, the front guard troops redoubled their attack, hitting the Knackers with everything they had. Plasma beams formed an almost continuous yellow ribbon writhing in the darkness, seeking out the enemy. Heavy concussions rocked the corridor as human grenades also found their mark.

The furious exchange continued for a handful of seconds, and then the enemy fire abruptly slackened and ceased. The humans eased up a few seconds later, and deathly quiet reigned.

"Talk to me, Gunnarsson," Atom spoke into his com.

"A handful of Crabs are down; the rest are retreating along adjoining corridors," Torvald's voice answered.

"*Again*? Why…?" Atom began, then stopped himself. "All right, let's move out quickly. Everyone through the portal; Torvald, lead the way with your troops. I'll bring up the rear."

The troops used their speakers to urge the terrified civilians to their feet and onward once again. The ragged band of humanity lurched forward, at first haltingly, then with renewed vigor as they realized that hostilities had ceased.

Through the blast door portal they jogged, the weaker individuals being half-dragged by their companions. Ten, fifteen, twenty went through, and still Atom's scanners revealed no sign of the aliens. Three-quarters of the procession were out the other side before Gunnarsson's urgent voice cut in on the com. "Lieutenant, I'm reading an energy surge at the doorway. The portal is being activated!"

The words had scarcely registered when Atom heard a grating rumble, and he saw the door slab began to move. There were only a small number of civvies and soldiers still waiting to pass through; without thinking, Atom began grabbing and pushing people toward the rapidly shrinking opening. Other troopers joined in, propelling civilians in and through to waiting hands on the other side.

For a frantic handful of seconds they worked, each soldier focused on helping those within reach. Atom assisted four or five civvies through the portal, then risked a glance around. The doorway was now three-quarters shut. Two children stood close to his right, and as the portal continued to narrow, he reached out and heaved the juveniles at the opening with a grunt and a prayer.

His aim was true, and both bodies hit the gap nearly dead center. Troopers on the other side yanked them through before they could be crushed. As the last child's hand disappeared from sight, the door slammed closed against the wall.

Deathly quiet settled over the corridor, and only then did Atom fully grasp his predicament. The *Goliath* was set to leave, time was running out, and his only escape route was now blocked. Heart pounding, he surveyed his surroundings, trying to take count of who was stranded with him. The suit lights of the civilian escort troops were gone, so darkness had engulfed him once again. His scanner readings showed several human life emanations close by. No Knackers registered within detection range, for what it was worth.

He spoke into the com link, trying to keep his voice calm. "How many failed to make it through the door?"

"You've got two troopers with you, sir," came the prompt reply, and Atom recognized the deep tones of Sergeant Harriman's voice. "There are also a couple of civvies huddled in the corner, to the left of the portal. Not sure if they're okay or not."

"I'm nearly blind in here; my night vision is out," Atom answered. "Check on the civvies while I find us a way home." Switching to the command channel, he said, "Corporal Gunnarsson, we're in need of assistance."

"Reading you, sir," the tech's voice replied. "The door is being controlled by the Crabs now; we can't override. I'm consulting the saved scanner data on the pyramid's layout; I recommend you do the same. It looks like an alternate route is available, which I have highlighted on the screen. Take the nearest corridor just behind you on the left wall. In about two hundred meters you'll reach an intersecting passage that parallels the one we're in; turn right and follow it until you reach another intersection; right again, and you should get back to our current corridor, but past the blast door."

"Got it," Atom replied as he viewed the images projected on his heads-up display. "We're on our way. Get your troops and the remaining civvies *out*, and I mean all the way. There's nothing you can do for us now, and there'll be hell to pay if I find you anywhere but onboard the shuttle."

"Understood, sir. Be careful."

The command channel went silent, and Atom switched back to the general com, turning toward those who remained with him. "Status report, sergeant."

A shadowy figure separated itself from a cluster of dimly-seen shapes near the corridor's end, and Harriman's voice replied, "We've got an injured juvenile and an adult civilian; we'll probably have to carry the child if we're going to make quick time."

"Let's do it, then. There's a way out, but we've got to go right now. We'll need to use the suit lights. There's no other way for me or the civvies to move fast. Light 'em, people."

Almost simultaneously, the three soldiers activated their thoracic light beams. The stark white illumination flared to life, beating back the darkness, and Atom got his first good look at his companions. Nearby stood the familiar tall bulk of Sergeant Harriman; behind and to his left, a smaller trooper waited with the two civilians. The civvies were both female; a dark-haired adult was crouched over a smaller figure lying on the floor. Atom blinked as he recognized the young woman from the prison cell; her injured companion looked like one of the children she had been shepherding.

He approached the civilians, switching on his external suit speaker. "How are you two faring, ma'am?" he asked as he knelt to examine the girl on the floor.

The distressed look on the woman's face was replaced by a weak smile as she realized who he was. "Coming to our aid again, lieutenant?" she asked, making a brave attempt at levity. Her expression turned earnest as she added, "I must say I'm relieved that you're here."

"How is she?" Atom asked as he glanced over the prone girl's body. The child was moaning softly and rocking side to side. On initial inspection he could see no sign of trauma, but then the woman carefully rolled the girl over, and an ugly black patch of charred and bloodstained cloth came into view on the back of the girl's lower left leg.

"She was hit during the firefight," the woman said. "She's been delirious and unable to walk since."

"Looks like a near miss, or maybe she caught part of a round reflected off a wall," Atom replied, squinting at the damage.

"Why do you think that?" the woman asked him.

"Because she's still got a leg attached below the burn," he replied. "She's lucky, but the pain will be intense, and that could drive her into shock." He touched a control on the back of his left suit glove, and a small pneumatic needle extended. Placing the blunt tip against the child's thigh, he clenched his fist.

A soft *thunk* sounded, as air pressure drove a micro sliver of concentrated analgesic into his patient. Imbedded in moist tissue, the dehydrated drug dissolved quickly, and in mere moments the whimpers of pain began to taper off.

Atom glanced over at the young woman, saying, "That's all I can do here; we've got to get her to the ship for proper treatment." The woman nodded and gave him a brief smile of thanks.

He shouldered his weapon, then reached down and carefully gathered the girl's frail body in his arms. Straightening, he broadcast through both his external speakers and his com link, "We've got to head out, *now*. Everyone stay close; we'll be moving fast and I don't want anyone getting separated."

The woman spoke up hesitantly. "I'm not sure I'll be able to keep up. I've made it this far on sheer will, but I'm not too steady on my feet. I don't want to slow us down."

Atom said, "We'll go at a slow jog; speak up if you can't maintain the pace, and we'll help you. Okay people, follow me."

He directed them down the left-hand corridor, thankful that the aliens had retreated in the opposite direction. Sergeant Harriman kept pace at his right shoulder, using night vision to help guide the way. The civilian woman and the other trooper were right behind them.

Down the empty passageway they jogged, guns panning to the left and right as they watched for hostiles. Atom's rifle was slung over his back while he carried the young girl, so he relied on his troopers to provide fire cover. They went as quickly as the civilian could manage, their pace bordering on reckless, driven by the knowledge that their time was running out.

6.

"Incoming fire!" Bruce Cotton called out from his scanner station. A heartbeat later, the fore viewscreen went supernova. The *Goliath* shuddered, hard this time, nearly unbalancing the crew members who were standing. The sound of the impact was different as well, no longer a deep rolling vibration, but rather a harsh resonance as if a massive gong had been struck with a hammer.

"*Ares blast it*!" Taramay exclaimed, her hands clenching the railing. "That one got through!"

"Affirmative, Captain," the first officer replied, glancing up at the command dais where Taramay stood. "We registered an energy hit on the forward section of the hull. The starboard diffuser screen was overwhelmed, and about twenty percent of the incoming strike got through."

"Damage?" the captain asked.

"The diffuser generators are functional; all defensive screens are still on line. However, several sensor arrays have been lost."

Taramay's gaze jerked back to the main viewscreen, where gaps had appeared in the forward view of surrounding space. "Compensate," she commanded.

From her other flank the tech officer answered, "On it."

Lt. Cotton's fingers danced over his control keys, and within moments the panorama on screen was made whole again. The alien destroyer once again dominated the sky, its powerful lines exuding ugly intent as it advanced.

"That's as good as it gets," the lieutenant said, sitting back. "Resolution is decreased by fifteen percent."

"We've got bigger worries," the navigator interjected. "The Knacker vessel is closing to lethal striking distance. Another hit like that and we could lose a screen generator. Then we're at their mercy. I just can't understand why they're advancing so slowly."

"And firing so infrequently," Lt. Cotton added. "Are they toying with us?"

"Knackers don't play with their food," Taramay replied grimly, "but I have to agree. Their pace of attack is most peculiar."

"Slow or not, they're coming into range, and we're in imminent danger," the navigator said. "We'll have to defend ourselves if we hope to hold this position any longer."

The captain nodded. "Agreed. Gunner, set our primary plasma cannon for a maximum strike. Mr. Cotton, what is the status of the aliens' defenses?"

"Their diffuser screens are running at approximately sixty-five percent of maximum intensity for that class of vessel," Bruce replied. His brows creased as his eyes darted over the data inputs. "Why are they not running full screens?"

"The damned Crabs think we're soft," Leofric growled.

"Always efficient, the Knackers are," Taramay said. "Based on our fleet's standard armament, sixty-five percent diffuser strength is all they need to repel an attack at this distance. Why expend energy when it's unnecessary? Ms. Jónsson, let's make them rethink that stance."

The gunner grinned and answered, "With pleasure, ma'am!"

"Select your target, lieutenant," Taramay said. "Assuming we can get a round through their defenses, where would you suggest hitting them?"

"Well, their propulsion systems are mostly aft. We've little or no chance of disabling those. I'd go for their main plasma cannon array; we've seen where it's located."

"Then target it, and fire when ready."

The gunner turned eagerly to her control board. "Targeting… and firing."

All eyes looked to the viewscreen as a narrow, sun-hot lance of radiant energy stabbed from the *Goliath*'s prow, covering the twelve hundred kilometers to their target in an instant.

The human destroyer had recently been refitted with prototypical armament. For the entire war, SpaceForce had struggled to match the aliens' offensive capabilities. Knacker battle tech was advanced, and their destroyers spat out highly modulated energy beams that were more stable, more coherent, than anything humanity could produce. This meant that Knacker plasma rounds suffered less bleed-off and diffusion over distance, so their ships' cannons had a greater reach than the big guns on human destroyers. The advantages were enormous: in naval engagements, human ships often took heavy damage before even coming into range for firing their own weapons.

SpaceForce had been working feverishly for years to improve its battle tech. So far the fleet had been unable to reproduce the aliens' energy stabilization techniques, but efforts to refine the human weapons had led to an alternate approach: focusing the plasma beam down to a fraction of its usual width, while retaining all the energy contained in a standard round. This somewhat reduced the degradation of the beam over distance, partially achieving the intended goal of increased range.

But there was another benefit, one which transformed this simple modification into an important weapons advancement.

Knacker diffuser screens consisted of interwoven sheets of force, magnetically bound to each other by alternating polarities. This increased the strength of the whole in a manner similar to that employed in a simple basket weave. Besides diffusing incoming energy effectively, the defensive screen could actually flex and deform while maintaining its functional integrity. This increased its ability to withstand heavy weapons impacts.

Such an energy field worked best against incoming strikes which were spread over a meter or more of its surface. This allowed a good portion of the screen to engage the incoming plasma, and minimized defensive breaches. The effect was much like a tough fabric sheet which could resist a strong man's punch without ripping.

But the hyper-focused beam fired by the *Goliath* contained nearly a million megajoules of energy, concentrated into less than one-tenth of the diameter of a standard destroyer round. The plasma's ultra-dense, narrow profile transformed its energy impact from a large "fist" into a sharp arrowhead, capable of tearing a hole in all but the most powerful diffuser fields.

When the human ship fired, there was no time for the Knackers to react, no chance to intensify their screens to repel the assault. The plasma beam flared against the layers of force cocooning the alien destroyer. For the briefest of instants, too fleeting to be detected by the human eye, opposing energies warred and crackled. Then the incoming round overwhelmed the defenses, and the Knacker ship's screens suffered a localized field collapse. The breach was small, and it was brief, but it was sufficient.

Nearly eighty percent of the *Goliath*'s strike made it through to the alien ship's hull. The round impacted straight on the enemy's main plasma cannon array, and the front of the Knacker destroyer was abruptly lost from view, obscured in a blinding flash of light.

"Direct hit!" the gunner cried, and Lt. Cotton called out confirmation of a hull strike as his scanners fed him the raw data.

Within seconds the impact glow began to fade, revealing the hulking mass of the Knacker destroyer still intact—but with an angry red crater pulsing on its prow where once had perched a weapons platform.

In another few heartbeats the alien ship appeared to leap toward them. Simultaneously its entire forward hull erupted with pyrotechnics, as multiple energy beams reached out toward the *Goliath*. A flurry of hits rained down on the human ship's defenses, and the hull resonated with a deep grinding rumble like a prolonged roll of thunder.

Taramay could feel the deck resonating under her feet from the percussions. They weren't as strong as the prior blows they had taken, but the volume of fire had surely skyrocketed.

"Looks like they're getting serious," the captain said worriedly.

Leofric glanced at her from the nav-station, and commented, "We've awakened the sleeping giant."

Greta Jónsson added, "They're firing all their secondary cannons at us in an effort to overwhelm our screens."

Taramay looked over at Bruce Cotton's station. "Readings on the enemy?"

"They've accelerated their approach, Captain. Enemy defensive screens now read full intensity. Their hull has lost no structural integrity; it appears they have full battle capability other than their main gun."

"So we've evened the playing field, but it's still anybody's fight," Taramay concluded. "We have to slow them down until our away teams are back aboard. Gunner, fire at will."

* * * *

Atom and his companions continued down the empty side passage away from the main corridor. They were heading in the general direction of the pyramid's damaged quadrant, and as they went, the floor became more clogged with fallen debris. Cracks and gaps began to show prominently in the surface finish of the walls and ceiling.

The spotlights of their suits jostled and swayed as they ran, casting bizarre shadows that jumped and stretched toward them as if alive. Atom's external suit mike began to pick up eerie sounds, like an animal mewling softly. After a moment he realized that the noises came from the child in his arms. Before he could react, the dark-haired young woman was at his left side, jogging in pace with him as she reached out and shushed the injured girl gently.

The woman was panting with exertion, the strain evident on her face, but her expression was one of grim determination. Under her touch the child soon quieted, and the woman glanced up at Atom's helmet visor, flashing a quick smile before falling back behind him once again.

They came to the anticipated intersection without incident, and turned right. Now they were paralleling the main corridor that they eventually needed to re-enter.

Within a handful of paces they began to encounter large hexagonal doorways which gaped blackly at intervals along both walls. This was prime ambush terrain, but they couldn't slow down to take proper precautions. Desperation pushed them onward without pause, hoping that fortune would favor the bold this day. With their nerves on edge, they passed a handful of entries safely. Scanners remained clear, and Atom began to watch for the right-hand passageway that would take them back to the main corridor.

Suddenly a large shadowy figure slid across the hallway just ahead.

"Down!" Atom shouted, dropping toward the floor as he tried to shield the child in his arms. The two troopers with weapons in hand fired at the vague shape ahead of them. Their target whirled and loosed a few blue-white plasma rounds toward the humans. In a flash it vanished into a doorway in the left-hand wall.

For a space of a few ragged breaths the corridor was utterly still, as if the apparition had been just a product of their imagination. Then without warning a hulking form filled the doorway. It extended a jointed arm around the wall and let loose with a plasma rifle, until the humans' return fire chased it again behind cover.

Atom took advantage of the moment, getting to his feet and yelling, "Cover me!" at his troops. When they acknowledged him, he ran crouched over with the young girl cradled in his arms, making for a doorway just behind them on the right-hand wall of the corridor. He was defenseless while carrying the child, and he worried about her taking a weapons hit if he drew fire. He had to get to shelter where he could lay his burden down and take up his weapon.

The portal loomed dark and menacing as he neared it, almost giving him pause. He gathered his resolve and ran headlong into the opening. Once inside, he stopped short, panning his suit light to the left and right, seeing the beam fade into the distant reaches of what was obviously a large chamber. Nothing moved in his field of vision, and a quick scanner check showed no life signs nearby.

He turned and gently laid the unconscious girl near the doorway, and then unslung his rifle. A flash of gunfire flared in the hallway, grabbing his attention. Turning off his suit spotlight, he approached the doorway and peeked around the sill into the hall.

His two troopers were each crouched down on one knee, side by side, suit lamps and rifles aimed at the doorway wherein their enemy hid. The civilian woman lay in the shadows a short distance behind them, face down with her hands clasped over the top of her head.

The Knacker extended a claw and fired a blind burst from its plasma gun. The humans returned fire instantly, and the limb withdrew behind the wall. A few seconds later the scenario repeated itself, and this time the troopers anticipated the height and angle of the alien's appendage. They fired dual bursts from their plasma rifles, and one well-placed round severed the Knacker's limb just above where it grasped the gun. The heavy weapon fell to the floor with a loud clatter. Yellow ichor spurted from the stump of the appendage before the injured Knacker yanked it back out of sight.

Momentarily the action paused.

Past experience told Atom that this was danger time: a damaged Crab sometimes went berserker on you. He carefully raised his rifle, taking aim from his hidden position.

"Stay ready, boys," he spoke softly into his com mike. His troopers held their positions in taut postures of anticipation. Five seconds passed, then ten, and he began to wonder if he had guessed wrong.

Even with tension-fueled adrenaline coursing through his veins, Atom was unprepared for the speed of the Knacker's rush when it came. The pain-crazed alien burst from the doorway into the middle of the hall, six of its ten legs pounding the floor, while its three still-functional forward limbs carried assault weapons. Such was its quickness that it was completely free of the doorway before the humans could begin firing. Even so, they beat the alien to the punch, raking it with plasma rounds before it could turn to get a bead on them.

Turn it did, even while two more of its limbs were amputated by the troopers' barrage. The damage threw the creature off balance as it brought its weapons to bear on the humans in the hallway. Staggering, it loosed a handful of plasma bolts that flew awry, missing high and to the left. The two troopers returned fire, hitting the torso of the alien as it struggled to right itself.

The Knacker's attention was focused on the pair of soldiers in the hallway, and Atom used this to his advantage, sighting carefully along his rifle before he squeezed off a quick burst of rounds. They struck the Crab where he intended, right above its row of eyes. The creature went down instantly, and just like that, the fight was finished. Atom kept his rifle aimed at the body in case additional shots were needed, but other than some random twitching, the Knacker didn't move again.

Relaxing slightly, Atom lowered his rifle and activated his suit light. Quickly he went to check on the limp figure of the girl. She appeared weak but stable. Nonetheless he knew time was running short for all of them.

Shouldering his weapon, he leaned over and unceremoniously snatched the child from the floor, carrying her back toward the doorway. Looking out, he saw his soldiers inspecting the alien's carcass; one of them gave a thumb's-up sign and began to walk toward him.

Atom's attention was so focused on the hallway that the small sound in the chamber behind him took him completely by surprise. He whirled, his heart pounding out of his chest, his spotlight beating back the darkness as he completed his turn.

There, not more than five meters from him, stood a fully armed Knacker warrior, its row of deep crimson eyes glinting coldly behind its faceplate.

Blast it, how had that damned thing managed to sneak up that close?

When his light hit the creature, its four forward limbs moved in a blur, whipping around to focus the barrels of four huge plasma rifles straight at him.

Even if he'd been holding his weapon rather than an unconscious civilian, Atom would have had little chance of winning this duel. As it was, he knew certain death when he saw it. When confronted with an armed opponent at close range, a Crab would always kill rather than be killed. His nerves frozen, he took a deep breath and waited for the end to come. And then—the most incredible thing happened. The Knacker hesitated.

He had but a moment to realize that he was still breathing, and another moment to wonder why, before a hot lance of radiant energy burned the air over his right shoulder and hit the alien in its faceplate. It fell backward, its limbs spasming. One clenched claw discharged a plasma gun, and the round zipped over Atom's head by a hand's breadth.

Then it was over, and he turned on shaky legs to behold Sgt. Harriman still sighting down his rifle from the corridor just outside the doorway. As the big man lowered his gun, Atom licked dry lips and managed to croak, "Thanks."

"Any time," came the deep-voiced reply.

After a few deep breaths Atom gathered his composure. Glancing around, he said, "We've got to get out of here. You take the girl; I'll check out the corridor before we move." He handed the child to the sergeant, and headed out to reconnoiter the hallway. The civilian woman was on her feet again, looking more than a little scared.

"Hi there," he said to her as he approached. "Are you all right?" When the woman nodded, he said, "Good. Before we continue, I want to clear the way ahead of us. Can you look after the injured girl until we move out? She's with the sergeant in the doorway there."

"Sure, I can do that," the woman replied with a small smile.

Atom watched her go, glad to get her moved into a relatively protected location. Then he approached the other trooper, a small framed man named Don Schilling. The soldier had taken up a forward position just past where the Knacker had fallen, and he was staring ahead down the hallway, his rifle clutched tightly in both hands. Atom turned his external speakers off, and spoke quietly on the com channel. "What do you have, corporal?"

The man turned his helmet to look briefly at him, before resuming his scrutiny of the corridor. "Nothing definite on scanners, sir, but a brief blip showed a moment ago. It's odd. Something was there for a second, then gone. I'm not sure if it's anything…"

"Where did you read it?" Atom interrupted, unslinging his weapon as his eyes scanned the darkness.

"Straight ahead of us, down this corridor, I think, sir," the corporal replied nervously. "I don't see anything on night vision, though."

Atom squinted as he tried to glean details from his murky surroundings. His suit beam shone brightly at close range, but faded to obscurity in the further depths of the hallway. "Damn. We've got to move; there's no time to waste. Let's form a tight group and we'll go. The intersection we need can't be far from here."

Atom started back toward Sgt. Harriman and the civilians. He'd taken no more than six or seven steps, when abruptly the corporal's voice shouted in alarm from behind him. "Crab straight ahead! Closing fast!"

He whirled and beheld a multi-limbed shape hurtling out of the darkness. Corporal Schilling let loose with his plasma rifle, and Atom followed suit a second later. The Knacker raised a limb and fired back, but no flash of energy erupted from its weapon. For an instant it seemed that nothing had happened, and then the world exploded.

Their adversary had eschewed plasma weapons and had instead launched a grenade. The alien's aim was rushed, and the explosive charge detonated on the floor in front of where the human soldiers stood. The corporal was closer to the impact point, and the blast knocked him clean off his feet. His suit protected him from most of the explosive concussion and shrapnel, but a high-velocity metal fragment impacted his face plate, shattering it. He fell in a heap on the floor, stunned.

Atom managed to stay on his feet, and he fired plasma rounds as fast as he could discharge his weapon. From behind and to his right, Sgt. Harriman's weapon chimed in. The impacts battered the alien, and it returned fire aggressively with two plasma guns, before scrambling backward rapidly. Its retreat was puzzling at first, given its headlong attack a few moments earlier. Then Atom heard it: sharp cracking sounds like the breaking of heavy tree branches, accompanied by an ominously rising squeal.

Understanding dawned, and he turned toward the downed corporal, shouting urgently, "On your feet, Schilling! Get your butt back here *now*! Hull breach imminent!"

His words galvanized the other man, and he struggled to his feet, but it was too late. Unbeknownst to the humans, their detour had led them too close to the damaged quadrant of the pyramid. While the corridor appeared intact, it lay at the bottommost level of the ship, with only the outer hull between them and raw vacuum. The exterior shielding had been mostly stripped off by the railgun blast that had disabled the pyramid. What was left was a thin metallic shell which was barely able to contain the corridor's atmospheric pressure.

The grenade blast had pushed the stressed structure past its limits. Small fracture lines grew into large fissures as air forced its way into and through the damaged area of the floor. The material creaked and popped as the instability worsened, and suddenly a small section of the floor was gone, sucked away into open space.

Atom felt a push at his back, the rush of air nudging him toward the enlarging breach. His suit speakers picked up a soft sigh that steadily built towards a howl. He struggled to keep his feet against the rising pressure. Even with his magnetic foot grips set at maximum, he knew he would not be able to hold his position if things got much worse. He looked around frantically, but there was nothing in the center of the corridor to grab on to. The bits of structural debris lying on the floor were too small to hold him in place, and in fact much of it was sliding toward the fissure as he watched.

Corporal Schilling was in worse straits. Five meters closer to the breach, and still fuzzy from the grenade detonation, he was swaying unsteadily on his feet as the flood of escaping atmosphere buffeted him. Atom bellowed, "Get away from there, Schilling!"

The soldier looked over at Atom, and the lieutenant could see the desperation in the man's expression. "I can't move, sir," the corporal gasped. "I'll be sucked away the moment I raise one foot off the deck."

Atom realized the truth of that statement, and he thought furiously, trying to figure a way to rescue the soldier. In that moment the hull gave way, and a meter-sized chunk tore loose with a loud rending sound. The rush of air instantly became a hurricane. Corporal Schilling's form bent over like a reed in the wind.

Now alarm claxons rang out, as the drop in air pressure triggered emergency containment actions by the alien vessel. Heavy metal panels dropped from the corridor ceiling behind and in front of the breach, isolating a seven or eight meter section of the hall.

Atom was just outside the near panel as it dropped; he could see Schilling's eyes, wide with fear, gazing back at him through the man's broken faceplate. It hit Atom right then: the soldier had no protection from the vacuum of space, and he was smack in the middle of the containment section. There was nothing Atom could do, nothing at all, except stand his ground with his comrade until the end.

As the panel slid toward the floor, Atom crouched over to see under its leading edge, maintaining eye contact with his man. The flooring around the hull breach groaned and buckled, and suddenly opened wide, yielding to the void beyond. Corporal Schilling screamed, his voice ratcheting up in pitch as the air evacuated the chamber, becoming inhumanly thin and reedy before fading out altogether. His suit-clad figure tore free and flew out into the open reaches beyond the hull. Atom caught a glimpse of naked space, velvety black dotted with the brilliant glitters of unfiltered starlight, before the containment shield slammed shut in front of him.

Instantly the flow of air stilled. In the sudden quiet, Atom stood upright without effort. The becalmed deck stood in stark contrast to the storm of his thoughts, where he could not shake that last image of the dying man's face. The corporal had been his soldier, his responsibility, and he had been powerless to help him.

He stood there, fists clenched, just staring at that closed panel. There must have been something he could have done, something…

"Lieutenant," a sharp voice reached him through the haze of emotion. Atom looked up to see Sgt. Harriman's large figure standing there, his arms full of limp civilian, and the young woman by his side. "We've got to get back to the shuttle, or we're going to be left behind," the sergeant declared. "Our way here is blocked, but my scanners show that the large room you were attacked in has several entrances. I think one of those connects to the passage that we want, the one leading back to the main entry corridor."

Atom focused on the sergeant's faceplate and managed to say, "Yes…good work, soldier."

He glanced back for a moment at the containment barrier, his mind's eye still elsewhere. Then he exhaled heavily and turned to the others, saying, "It's time to go. You lead the way, Harriman. Let's get the hell out of here."

7.

The *Goliath* fired a salvo from six of its secondary energy cannons, all aimed at the same point on the alien destroyer. The combined hits broke through the enemy's defensive screens. Debris sprayed off the Knackers' forward hull, graceful streamers of molten metal fountaining into space. Several smaller guns on that side of the ship abruptly went silent.

"Take that!" Lt. Jónsson growled, as a nasty grin lit her features.

She barely had time to gloat. A few seconds later, a bright flash and concussion rocked the bridge, and red lights lit up across the gunner's instrument panel. "Damn!" she cried. "We've lost our starboard diffuser screen! We're wide open for a hit!"

Taramay reacted instantly. "Turn us to starboard; present the port bow to the enemy!" The navigator had already reached for the controls before she spoke, and he hit the positioning thrusters hard, rotating the vessel to protect the exposed section of hull from another energy hit.

The captain then turned to the tech officer. "Distance to the Knacker ship?" she barked.

"Five hundred klicks and closing," Lt. Cotton replied.

Taramay swore softly. "We can't stay here without risking critical damage. We've got to move."

"And leave the rest of the away team?" the first officer asked, eyebrow raised.

"If they're not back here shortly, we may not have a choice," the captain replied. "But we're not leaving yet. Mr. Debartolo, back us up and swing around behind the pyramid; use it as a shield between us and the enemy. That will buy a bit more time."

"Affirmative!" the navigator answered, and his fingers put the captain's words into action.

* * * *

Sgt. Harriman led Atom back to the doorway on the right hand wall of the corridor. They entered it together, the civilian woman close between them. Both soldiers had their suit lights on, and they monitored their scanners carefully as they went.

The room beyond the doorway differed from any they had encountered on the pyramid. Its ceiling was lofty, so much so that it must have extended into the second level of the ship above them. They snaked their way through tall banks of unknown equipment, and past what appeared to be oversized work stations to the left and right. Some of the instrumentation was dark and dead, but portions were lit with tiny indicator lights which glowed steadily or winked on and off.

They neared the center of the room, and there they encountered a large rectangular panel rearing from the floor, maybe ten meters across and nearly as high. It was nonfunctional, and foreign in its design, but it was still recognizable as a viewscreen.

It was then that Atom realized what this room's purpose might be. "We're in a control center!" he exclaimed, panning his light around them. "This could even be the main bridge. If only we had more time!"

"But we don't, sir," Sgt. Harriman reminded him. "I'm reading an exit ahead and to our left; it appears to open onto the corridor that will take us back to the main passage. We've got to leave now."

Atom hesitated, and then said, "Yes, you're right, sergeant. Take the civilians, and get them out of here. Move fast and don't look back. I've got to stay."

The others began to protest, but he held up his hand, silencing them. "I've a task to do here; I won't be long." He grabbed the rifle off of the sergeant's back, and held it out to the civilian woman. "You'll need to use this if you encounter a Crab; the sergeant has his hands full. Keep your finger off the trigger except when you fire it, and don't point the gun at anything that you don't intend to kill."

"Sir, I don't think this is a good idea," the sergeant began, but Atom cut him short.

"Get out of here, and that's an order, sergeant. I'll see you on the other side."

The soldier hesitated, but he knew that his superior's tone of voice brooked no dissention. Sighing, he nodded, and said to the woman, "Follow me, ma'am. Stay at my side, so you have an open field of fire if we encounter resistance. Good luck, lieutenant."

And with that, they moved away through the banks of equipment, and within moments were lost to Atom's view.

He wasted no time once alone. Consulting his scanners, he moved through the area surrounding the large viewscreen. He was at the core of the cavernous room, and odds were that a primary control panel of some sort was located nearby. It didn't matter which one, be it navigation, communications, or general systems. What did matter was that it had a computer interface.

On the *Goliath*'s outbound voyage, Captain Dent had summoned Atom for a private meeting, and had given him specific instructions. "We're tasked with learning all we can from this alien vessel when we find her," she'd told him. "Much of that burden will fall upon you, lieutenant. Keep your eyes open at all times; record your findings whenever possible, and have your soldiers do the same. Retrieve artifacts if the situation allows. Above all else, find an opportunity to use this."

She had handed him a small device, the same one he now pulled from a pocket on the front of his suit. All he needed was to find a place to put it.

Eyes and scanner readings led him shortly to a large semicircular console. Its jet-black surface was dotted with controls and glowing indicators. The pale yellow symbols inscribed under the buttons and lights were inscrutable. However, for this mission he had been trained to recognize a computer input/output jack on the unfamiliar equipment. Soon he found one, near the left upper corner of the panel.

He extended his hand, holding the object that he had been entrusted with. The device had been created by SpaceForce scientists after months of research and development. It fit easily into his palm, a flat disc with a protrusion on one edge that could plug into the alien data receptacle. After a couple of tries, he got the thing properly oriented and it slid smoothly into the jack.

For a few tense moments nothing happened. Then the surface of the disc lit up, and intelligible words appeared on its face, one after the other: "Activating......interfacing......exploring records..."

Impatiently, Atom waited, fidgeting as he monitored his scanner and watched the progress of the device in front of him. Finally the word he was hoping for appeared: "Transferring."

The object he had inserted was basically an enhanced data storage device, carefully adapted to interface with the Knacker computer system and programming language. Captured alien equipment had given SpaceForce the requisite knowledge to access the enemy's info banks. The tiny disc's capacity was enormous; it could hold a quadrillion terabytes of information, each terabyte consisting of one trillion pieces of data. In theory, it might be enough to hold all of the memory contained in the pyramid's main computer, if he had time to collect it.

The storage device had been set up to run at extreme speeds, but time seemed to crawl as Atom stood alone in the heart of the alien vessel. He was a sitting target here, and his imagination ran wild as his eyes darted around the shadowy recesses of the vast room.

He switched off his suit light to reduce his visible profile, and instantly regretted it. As night engulfed him, a wave of anxiety surged through his mind. It shocked him with its intensity, threatening to break through his discipline and drive him running for the exit.

What in Ares' name are you doing, Atom? he thought feverishly. *Sitting alone in a Knacker pyramid with Crabs crawling everywhere, this is insane!*

Despite the urge to flee, he forced himself to remain immobile, letting his eyes adjust to the dim illumination. Gradually he could make out the faint bulks of the equipment around him, but little else. Across the way, in the direction from which he had come, he could see tiny lights of distant instrument panels glittering through the darkness.

The glowing readout on the data disc still said "Transferring," and he had no way of telling when it would finish. His finger fidgeted with the rifle trigger as he scanned the room yet again. The oppressive silence was unnerving. Maybe sending Sgt. Harriman on ahead had been a mistake.

He jumped when his suit com abruptly crackled and spoke in his ear, "Lt. Granger, do you read this?"

He answered softly, "Granger here."

"This is Harriman. We've boarded the shuttle; the path we'd

chosen was the correct one. You're the only human remaining on the Knacker vessel. Things are getting pretty hot aboard the *Goliath*; you'd better be coming soon."

"On my way shortly. Be ready when I get there; I may be moving fast and have company. Oh, and sergeant—do not let the shuttle leave without me!"

"I'm on it, lieutenant. Just get back here!"

"Granger out."

When the channel went dead his sole human contact was broken. Atom clutched his plasma weapon and looked around him, eyes wide as he tried to probe the darkness. It was no use. Minus his lights, he could barely see his own hand in front of his face, and the aliens had proven all too proficient at shielding their life signs from his scanners. If only he could detect them somehow.

An idea occurred to him then, one that he should have thought of sooner. This ship was a mostly empty hulk. Now that the humans had retreated, the only things moving besides Atom himself should be the aliens. He didn't have to rely on life sign readings to distinguish friend from foe; simple motion detection should be able to catch the enemy's movements. Of course!

Hurriedly he punched controls on his left arm panel, changing his scanner calibrations, and setting them to maximum sensitivity. Every living body causes changes in its environment, even if the object itself is shielded from direct detection. Alterations in air currents, footstep vibrations, sound resonations from a limb bumping against a wall or doorway, air temperature changes, all these could be measured and interpreted, forming a picture of an enemy's movements. Atom hoped it would be enough to warn him if a Crab got close.

* * * *

The *Goliath* had moved to nestle behind the derelict Knacker pyramid. Once again the giant harvest ship spanned the forward viewscreen, obscuring their view of the enemy destroyer as it approached. Their main guns were aimed just past the edge of the pyramid, where they expected their adversary to appear shortly.

"Four hundred klicks out and closing," Lt. Cotton announced.

"Any luck getting the starboard diffuser screen on line?" the captain asked, glancing to her left.

The first officer shook his head. "None. The damage is external, and we can't risk a hull walk in these circumstances. It's unlikely that we could effect repairs in the time we've got, anyway."

"I pretty much knew that," Taramay sighed. "We're going to remain vulnerable, then. Let's hope there's enough time to implement our plan when that ship gets close. We'll have little margin for error."

"It still sounds like our best chance for success," the navigator said. "Unless you want to disengage and run now."

Taramay shook her head vehemently, her expression resolute. "No, Lef. We need to give Granger every chance to get out. He stayed behind because he was following orders—my orders. I won't leave until we have no choice."

"If we wait until we're forced to vacate, running may no longer be an option," the navigator grunted.

"Thank you, Mr. DeBartolo," the captain said dryly. "I can always count on you for an uplifting sentiment."

"I'm just being realistic," her old comrade pointed out. "Sometimes the facts dictate a certain level of pessimism."

"Yes…but I prefer hope. I've found it to be a valuable ally, in times like these."

"Then let's hope your man gets himself on that shuttle."

8.

Atom whirled as a whisper of sound emanated from the darkness. He held his breath, pulse racing, eyes darting this way and that, but he could detect nothing moving. Had he actually heard it? Or were his nerves getting to him? He turned his external suit mike to highest sensitivity, and just stood, probing the vast room and adjacent corridors with ears, eyes and scanners. Emptiness met his straining senses. The thump of his heart and rush of blood in his ears were his only companions.

A tiny alert winked into existence in the left hand portion of his heads-up display. He jerked his gaze upward to stare at the crimson icon. Motion was detected a mere thirty meters from where he stood, and it was moving at right angles to his position. From what he could tell, it was coming slowly up the corridor that he and his companions had vacated, heading toward the entrance to this chamber.

Consulting his readouts, he located the approximate position of the unseen doorway, and aimed his rifle in that direction. His heart was pounding now. He could feel sweat beading on his brow, the moisture beginning to drip down his face inside the helmet.

He swore silently at his predicament. What was taking that damned disc so long to upload? Come on, *come on*! He needed to be gone five minutes ago; his time of safe operation was definitely at an end. Another soft sound reached his ears, a tiny scraping noise that was gone as soon as it had occurred. He could swear that it had originated from within the room.

His scanners flashed another alert, this one indicating movement from within twenty meters. It was just inside the entryway, across the room in the direction from which he had originally come. He stared helplessly into the gloom, still unable to see the danger moving toward him.

Then he caught a flicker of motion at the corner of his vision.

Turning his gaze slightly to the right, he caught the twinkle of indicator lights from a distant bank of equipment. Was that what had drawn his attention? He was about to look back toward the doorway, when something black moved between him and those distant points of luminescence, blotting them out.

For a moment he was paralyzed, unable to decide his course of action. Suddenly the data disc flashed at him from the control console, and he glanced down to see its message: "Transfer complete."

Relief warred with panic as he reached out and snatched the disc, stuffing it into a reinforced suit pocket. He glanced at his scanner readout to get his bearings, then back across the room toward the distant bank of instruments. Their lights shone clear and unobstructed once again.

Atom took a few deep breaths, tensing his muscles. When he moved it was with feline quickness. He activated his suit light, and its brilliance flared outward into the darkness, bathing the banks of alien equipment in stark clarity. In the same instant he burst from his sheltered position and made a mad dash for the exit that would take him home.

He had gone no more than a handful of strides when a tall pedestal just to his left exploded in a cascade of sparks. He glanced over in time to see a second plasma round punch a glowing hole clean through an instrument panel.

He didn't look back or slow down. Keeping his suit light aimed forward, he ducked and dodged between banks of equipment, trying desperately to put obstacles between him and any pursuers as he angled for the exit. Bolts of blue energy zipped and zinged about him, some of them ricocheting crazily off the metallic surfaces.

At his reckless speed he covered ground fast. His heads-up display showed the doorway just ahead now, with an open space to cross before he could reach it. Without hesitation he barreled into the gap, crouching over as he ran.

His right arm whipped across his body, aiming his plasma rifle back in the direction where he imagined the enemy might be. As he sprinted through the exposed area, he rapid-fired his gun blindly, not knowing whether he hit anything of importance. Maybe it helped; only a couple of return shots came flying out of the darkness, and both were wildly off target.

Then he was through the door and out, turning right to run up the passageway as fast as his fear-charged feet could carry him. He had nearly one hundred thirty meters to go before he hit the main corridor, and he sprinted hard, saving nothing for later. His light beam vacillated with each jarring step, but it lit his way enough for him to hurdle the debris piles littering the floor.

Multiple red icons began lighting up his helmet display, converging behind him, gradually closing the distance to their quarry. To Atom it looked like the hounds of hell were on his heels. He ran in pure panic mode now, not bothering to check the path ahead, nor the doorways that loomed and vanished as he rushed by. Nothing mattered but escape, and he strove with single-minded intensity for the way out of this place.

The main corridor came up so abruptly that he nearly ran past it. He turned hard left into the passage, skidding on the floor as he cornered at a full run. Now it was a straight shot toward home, and his feet pounded the floor, arms pumping, his breath coming harsh and loud within his helmet.

Far ahead he saw a glimmer of pure white, and he knew that this was the open shuttle bay entry. The sight energized him. He pushed forward, straining to reach his goal before he was caught from behind.

His scanner readouts were now showing motion in a side passage just ahead of him. The alien icons were moving toward his corridor, but he couldn't tell whether he or the enemy would reach the junction first. It was going to be tight.

Adrenaline was his savior, and his stride ate up the distance at a speed he would probably never duplicate again. He flew past the dangerous intersection with no Knackers yet in sight. The rectangular shape of the docking bay door loomed closer, its warm light beckoning with the promise of safe haven.

He panted into the com link, "Shuttle one, shuttle one, this is Granger. On my way in. Enemy in pursuit!"

Within seconds he saw human figures blotting out the light in the doorway ahead. He swerved to hug the right-hand wall, giving his troops an open line to fire past him. His scanner showed enemy icons closing on him, some less than thirty meters behind. Through a haze of fatigue he fleetingly wondered why the Crabs weren't firing their weapons. Did they want him alive?

Whatever the reason for the enemy's hesitation, the human

troops had no such compunction. They unleashed a vicious volley of plasma rounds down the hallway, carefully directing their fire around Atom. Now return energy bolts flew past him from behind, and he cringed in anticipation of the shot that would strike him down. He was so close, so close to safety.

Somehow the exchange of fire spared him, and he half-leaped, half-fell through the docking door into the brightly-lit bay of the shuttle craft. Welcoming hands grabbed and dragged him to the side, out of the way of incoming fire. Someone punched the door control and the airlock began to cycle shut. The heavy metal slab slid across the portal, just in time to intercept a flurry of plasma rounds which came flying out of the dark. They impacted harmlessly on the door's outer face, and the lock sealed closed with a heavy *thunk*.

Immediately the pilot's voice came over the wall speaker: "Shuttle bay sealed; prepare for acceleration."

The troops who had provided fire cover for Atom now scrambled to find handholds. Atom followed suit, slinging his rifle over one shoulder and grabbing a nearby support strut as he struggled to catch his breath. No time to strap into the acceleration chairs along the wall, and in any case these were already occupied by the most infirm of the rescued civilians. The remainder of the refugees packed the shuttle bay floor, sitting down to minimize risk of injury should their ship make any hard maneuvers. There must have been nearly one hundred and fifty civvies crammed into the compartment. This was going to be an uncomfortable ride.

The second shuttle had already loaded and disembarked, and was en route to the *Goliath*. Atom glanced around to be sure everyone was reasonably secured. Satisfied, he opened his com link and said, "Granger to pilot: we're ready for launch. Get us out of here!"

Scarcely had the words left his mouth when the roar of the shuttle's main engines shook the compartment. The airlock retracted as they began to move, severing the connection with the alien vessel. Normally care would have been taken to ensure that both ships' docking doors were sealed prior to disengaging. In this circumstance, no one wasted a moment's thought on the welfare of the pyramid or its crew, and the shuttle tore free before the alien ship's outer portal could be closed.

When the airlock seal ruptured, an explosion of outgassing air erupted from the Knacker vessel like a ghostly grey geyser. Such was the force of the jet that it pushed the human ship out and away from the pyramid's face. Chunks of solid debris came hurtling out of the alien hatch, clanking and pinging off the shuttle's hull.

A moment later the pilot's voice spoke excitedly from the intercom, "Whoooooweeee! A couple of Crabs got blown right out of their nest! Good riddance! Aw, now they're closing their hatch."

The news gave Atom a small surge of satisfaction. Even with environment suits, an unplanned trip into open space was often a death sentence.

Safely away, the shuttle kicked into heavy acceleration. Shrieks erupted throughout the cargo bay. These transports were basic utility vessels; as such, they lacked inertial dampeners to insulate the passengers from the impact of heavy maneuvers. Atom's troopers were hardened to the stresses of space flight, and partially protected within their suits, but not so the refugees.

The G-forces hit the civilians without warning, while their ears were assaulted by the deafening roar of rocket engines at maximum output. Even sitting on the floor, they were bowled over like dominoes. Bodies fell awkwardly atop each other as they slid toward one wall. The outcry quickly hushed as the pressure of acceleration squeezed air from struggling lungs.

Atom focused on keeping his thorax expanding and contracting at a steady rate, bracing his body to stand against the strain. The G's generated by the shuttle were not extreme, nothing like that of a high performance fighter. Nonetheless this was a heavy maneuver for this type of craft. His suit helped considerably, the magnetic grav-grips of his soles anchoring his feet firmly in place.

He watched the civilians with concern. They were fragile, and it looked like several of the weaker individuals had already lost consciousness. He wished he could see what was happening out beyond the hull. Time must be urgently short for the pilot to be hitting the throttle like this.

Up in the cockpit, the command crew had a clear view of their situation. Still accelerating, the shuttle shot quickly across the pyramid's face. In less than a minute they had cleared the far end of the giant craft. As they rounded the corner and turned to starboard, the lights of the *Goliath* sprang into view a half-klick away. They made straight for her, bearing down on the mother ship with their main engines burning hot.

The pilot watched the instrument readouts intently as their target grew in his sights. The *Goliath*'s prow was aimed almost straight at them. This meant they would have to fly lateral to the destroyer, and then swoop in toward her flank, to hit her main shuttle bay. It was normally an easy task for an experienced pilot. Not so when trying to perform it at high speed—hence the beads of sweat dotting the commander's brow. He had to cut acceleration at the last possible moment, spin the ship and reverse thrust hard, to slow them down in time. It was going to be a hair-raising maneuver.

In the docking bay, Atom heard the shuttle commander's voice through a haze of discomfort: "*Brace for deceleration.*" An instant later, the pressure on his body ceased as the main engines went dead. For a few glorious seconds his breath came effortlessly. He swayed as the deck slid sideways beneath his feet, and he knew that the lateral thrusters were turning the ship, presenting its stern to the *Goliath* as they bore down on the mother vessel.

Now the main engines roared back to life. The crushing force returned with a vengeance, but with its vector reversed. He was knocked half off his feet before he grabbed a support and held himself steady. A couple of unlucky troopers went tumbling across the floor, and the civilians began sliding in a new direction.

This time there were fewer protests as the beleaguered passengers simply hung on and endured. The deceleration was savage. Shudders wracked the hull repeatedly as their ship was pushed to the limit of its capabilities.

The pilot had been trained in high-g maneuvering, in order to handle exactly these situations. Monitoring the two ships' relative velocities, he cut the reverse thrust at the right time, matching the mother ship's drift nearly perfectly as they came alongside the *Goliath*'s open shuttle bay. Lateral thrusters did the rest, and only a few grinding bumps betrayed the haste with which he pushed them into the hold. They had barely cleared the threshold when he punched the com to the *Goliath*'s bridge and said, "We're in. *Go!*"

Taramay heard the shuttle commander's confirmation with a surge of relief, and instantly turned to her navigator. "Close the shuttle bay doors, and back us away from the pyramid, maximum acceleration! Mr. Cotton, monitor the alien destroyer, and keep our spotlights aimed at where she'll appear when she rounds the pyramid. Ms. Jónsson, be ready to hit the target with everything we have as soon as it comes into view."

"Affirmative, Captain," the gunner replied, alternating her gaze between the viewscreen and her instrument panel. Her fingers hovered over the firing controls of both the main and secondary weapons banks. Nothing would be held back now.

"Knacker vessel closing to within fifty klicks," the tech officer called out.

"Navigator, turn us twenty degrees to starboard; we need to protect the gap in our defensive screens."

"Implementing," Lt. DeBartolo replied. After a moment he added, "A firefight at close range will be nasty. We'd better hope that the Knackers steer their ship in tight to the pyramid."

"They will; it's the most efficient route around the obstacle," Taramay replied, but her words implied a confidence she didn't feel. Anxiously she tapped her fingers on her command console as she watched the pyramid receding in the viewscreen. Even at maximum thrust, their retreat seemed agonizingly slow. The massive harvest vessel still dominated the forward view; would they be far enough away from it when their adversary appeared? The seconds counted down toward the moment of truth.

Abruptly the alien destroyer's black prow nosed into view, rounding close to the pyramid. Seeing it up close, without the need for screen magnification, made its dimensions even more intimidating. For a moment the bridge crew stared, frozen, and then the captain barked, "Fire at will!"

The gunner needed no encouragement. Lances of glowing plasma erupted from the *Goliath*'s prow, lighting up the alien vessel's defensive screens in a brilliant cascade of colors. The Knacker ship turned as it came clear of the pyramid, and its guns fired in retaliation. The deck lurched sideways beneath their feet, and *Goliath*'s viewscreen flared with stuttering white flashes as plasma rounds impacted in succession. At this proximity, even the aliens' secondary weapons were brutally effective.

"Defensive screens nearing overload!" the tech officer called out. "We can't take much more of this!"

"Then let's not," Taramay growled. "Mr. DeBartolo, ready on my command."

"Trigger primed and ready, Captain."

Taramay squinted at the viewscreen, tracking the image of the alien vessel between flashes of incoming rounds. The huge destroyer was moving forward, flanking the pyramid. She watched, waiting until the two alien ships were side by side. *There!* She raised her arm and clenched her fist as she cried, "Detonate!"

Leofric DeBartolo's right forefinger punched a single button, and the universe went white.

The antimatter charge that the shuttle crew had planted in the alien pyramid was originally developed to obliterate large asteroids whose trajectories posed a risk to shipping lanes or to inhabited planets. The explosive force released by such a device's detonation could transform a five kilometer chunk of dense space rock into an expanding cloud of formless dust and radiation.

The Knacker destroyer massed considerably less than most asteroids, and had only its defensive screens to ward off annihilation. When the antimatter charge was triggered, the two alien vessels floated less than a half kilometer apart. At that proximity, the destroyer's formidable shields might as well have been nonexistent.

At the point of detonation, the doomed pyramid expanded for an instant, the hulking mass of metal splitting apart in a hundred places. Then it vanished, its matter converted into pure energy. The fireball expanded outward, instantly engulfing the second alien ship. Its shields delayed its destruction by perhaps one half of a second before it, too, succumbed, its demise punctuated by a second bright flash as its power plant went critical.

The plasma rounds pummeling the *Goliath* abruptly ceased, but the human ship was still in mortal danger. Now fifty kilometers out and accelerating away from the detonation, the *Goliath* was hit by a tremendous shockwave of heat and radiation. The entire ship shuddered and tilted as its defensive screens took the impact. The clash of opposing energies generated an intense electromagnetic pulse that in turn hit the ship's hull.

On the bridge, lighting flickered and died. Artificial gravity abruptly cut out, and suddenly-floating crew members were left grabbing for handholds and railings. Work station monitors and the domed viewscreen went black an instant later, plunging the bridge into impenetrable darkness. Taramay held her breath, fervently hoping that their vessel wasn't crippled, as she fumbled blindly to strap herself into her command chair. Right now they were helpless, sitting targets for any enemy ship that chanced to come along.

For a moment, the only sounds were the gasps and scuffles of the bridge officers righting themselves. Seconds ticked by, an eternity, and then the wan glow of emergency lighting came up around the room's periphery. The captain sighed deeply and relaxed her grip on her chair arm; her ship was still alive. Now control boards began to light all around the room as power flow stabilized. The destroyer's heavy plate shielding had deflected much of the EMP wave, and its radiation-hardened circuitry resisted most of the energy that got through. Still, it was a close thing.

Taramay took in the situation at a glance. Gravity was offline. Crew members held on to supports and belted themselves into their workstation chairs as they got their bearings.

"Status report, all hands," she ordered, tapping commands into her now-alive chair console as she spoke.

Lt. DeBartolo was the first to respond; his weathered visage appeared unperturbed as he read the reports of key systems. "Main propulsion offline; scanners and viewscreen offline; the central computer core was well protected and appears undamaged; key environmental systems mostly on line; communications offline, weapon systems offline." He looked up from his data screen and caught the captain's eyes. "Priorities?"

Without hesitation Taramay answered, "Scanners and propulsion. I want us out of here yesterday."

"Tasking crews to initiate repairs," the first officer chimed in from Taramay's left, as his fingers danced over his board.

One by one the other members of the bridge crew gave their reports. Lt. Cotton was working to bypass damaged circuitry where possible, and Lt. Jónsson was running diagnostics on her weapons systems in conjunction with engineers scattered throughout the ship. Communication and scanner malfunctions were both due in part to damaged exterior components. Engineers in environment suits were already headed out to the hull to begin damage assessment and repairs.

"Keep me informed of our progress," the captain instructed. "We need to get our ship healthy and move out of this region quickly. Otherwise our rescue effort could be for naught. We've risked a lot to get those people out of there.

"Speaking of which, does anyone know the status of the away teams and refugees?"

9.

Down in the shuttle bay, the soldiers and civilians were confronting their own problems. The shuttle's main engines had been powered down after the small ship had docked, so when the *Goliath* was hit by the EMP wave, artificial gravity suddenly vanished. Both the refugees and Atom's squads were left grasping for anything solid to cling to inside the shuttle, and those who hadn't found a handhold were now floating helplessly off the floor.

The soldiers were accustomed to zero-grav conditions, but not so the noncombatants. The children, in particular, were scared and thrashed around wildly, to no avail. Kicking and squirming in midair did nothing to propel one's body in a desired direction, but sent you into uncontrolled spins, further disorienting you. Combine the bodily gyrations with zero gravity's queasy effect on the abdominal organs, and nausea often ensued, with unpleasant results.

They were saved by the fact that the erstwhile prisoners had little or nothing in their digestive tracts, save small amounts of gastric fluid and bile. It could have been much worse. As it was, multiple stomachs expelled whatever they contained, producing globs of foul fluid which floated in the air, threatening to soil whatever they contacted. The sour odor did nothing to quell the stomachs of those around them. The acidic liquids posed some risk as well; they could short out electronic equipment on impact, or cause eye injury or choking if they hit someone in the face.

Atom braced himself with one hand as he assessed the situation. Then he calmly began issuing instructions via his suit speakers. "Squad members, help the non-coms find secure handholds. All you civilians, relax and stop moving! Zero gravity is distressing at first, but you can also hurt yourselves badly. Move slowly and carefully. If you're not within reach of a handhold, wait until you drift close or someone comes to help you."

He watched for a moment, and added, "Do not make rapid

movements! That will throw you off balance and cause you to spin. To move around, push off *gently* from a solid object, toward another target which you can grab. Do not attempt to get there quickly; you'll hit your destination hard and can sustain injuries on impact."

The volume and authority of his voice cut through people's fear, and forced them to pay attention. Within moments most flailing bodies had stilled, and soldiers carefully helped the stranded floaters to find secure positions. Long-handled absorbent pads were used to wipe the majority of the vomitus out of the air. Looking around, Atom nodded with satisfaction. The situation appeared to be stabilized for the time being.

As their initial fear waned, the civilians began to speak up, their voices strained and anxious. "Why don't we have gravity?" "When are we getting out of this shuttle?" "There is a mother ship, right? Does it have room for all of us?"

Atom had been trained in both the physical and psychological aspects of warfare. He knew that he needed to keep these people calm, especially while they were massed into a large group. Crowd behavior could be volatile.

He thought quickly, and decided to remove his suit helmet, so that he could address the civilians face to face. The move had a visible impact; numerous pairs of eyes met his, and facial expressions relaxed just a bit on seeing a human visage.

He spoke slowly and calmly, gesturing outward toward the room full of people with his one free hand. "First of all, let me say how happy my troopers and I are at being able to rescue you today. Many of you probably thought you would never see the human worlds again. You may have assumed that you were forgotten, written off as casualties of war. Well, we just couldn't let that happen."

Ragged cheers erupted from the crowd as Atom paused, and he waited for silence before resuming. "We are now on board the *Goliath*, a long-range human destroyer. The bridge has just informed me that we took on a Knacker warship and destroyed it, along with the pyramid you were imprisoned on."

Louder cheers interrupted him this time, and again he waited for the noise to fade. "We took damage in the battle, and repairs are underway. Artificial grav should be restored soon. In the meantime, we have to stay here, until medics can look you over. The sick and injured may need immediate attention, and all of you must be screened for disease before being released into the mother ship."

"What do you mean, disease?" a man in the middle of the crowd shouted out. Atom spotted the man's face, pale and gaunt, but set in a belligerent expression. This, too, he was prepared for. Traumatized people often masked fear with anger. It was a less distressful emotion for them to deal with, and made them feel like they had some control. But Atom couldn't let that emotion grow too strong; he needed to take a firm stance now.

"Contagious disease screening is a necessary and standard procedure; it protects both you and us from spread of pathogens," Atom stated firmly.

"We're all from Nueva Terra," the man retorted. "There've been no outbreaks of anything contagious there in over a century. This is a waste of time. We're malnourished, not plague carriers."

A chorus of assents rose from the crowd, and Atom raised his hand to quell the protests. "We're not worried about disease you brought from your home world," he replied, and paused a moment to let that sink in.

"What, are you suggesting the Crabs infected us with something?" the aggressive civilian spoke up again. "That makes no sense at all. They want us alive and healthy, not diseased and dying! If they wanted to kill us, their weapons could do that more quickly."

"Yeah, he's right, what are you holding us here for?" a second man shouted out, and other voices joined in. The rising chorus was becoming more strident, and Atom turned the volume up on his suit speakers to drown the crowd out.

"*Silence!*" he barked. The civilians were momentarily quieted, and he spoke quickly into the stillness. "Who said anything about a disease that would kill? You and I both know that the Crabs want healthy prey. You need to think like the enemy. Contemplate this: how about a slow virus, one that takes months to show itself, that can spread silently among the human worlds. A virus that robs us of our aggression, of our ability to resist, that makes us passive, makes us the perfect cattle for the Knackers to feed on."

There was no need to shout over the crowd now, as the hundreds of civilians stared at Atom in shocked silence. A woman hesitantly spoke up, her voice quavering, "Can they...really do something like that?"

"We believe that our enemy is fully capable of such technology, especially after having months to study us," Atom replied, nodding. "We also need to check for implants they may have installed inside you: spy devices, homing beacons, and so forth. These can be tiny, but quite dangerous. The Crabs held you captive for a good length of time; we do not want the enemy using you against your own kind."

"How long does all this take?" the original protestor spoke out again, his jaw set.

"We've got nearly three hundred refugees to process, and a ship that is damaged. We'll get you checked out and into temporary quarters in the cargo bay as soon as we can."

"Cargo bay? That's ridiculous. I'm a prominent citizen on Nueva Terra; I demand crew quarters at the least, and quick passage back to my home world. I'm needed there," the civilian stated emphatically.

Atom was beginning to dislike this person immensely. There always had to be at least one bad apple in every group, and he had little patience for self-important civvies during wartime.

"You'll get the same quarters as everyone else," he told the civilian. "A battleship lacks the space for extra quarters; every berth is already filled. And if you're in hurry to get back home, take a seat. Nueva Terra was overrun by Crabs. They've occupied that world; if we take you back there, you'll just end up on a pyramid again. Is that what you want?"

The civilian had no answer to that. Hearing his world's fate seemed to suck all the energy from him, and he sagged back to a sitting position on the floor, looking defeated.

Atom felt some pity for the man at last, and said quietly, "We're a long way from human space, anyway. Right now we're perched at the Cluster's outer rim, in enemy territory. Let's work together and focus on getting out of here, before we worry about the future. Your home world is occupied, but you'll find refuge on other planets, I promise."

"And what about our planet and our loved ones?" another civilian asked, his voice a hoarse croak.

"Eventually we'll liberate Nueva Terra," Atom reassured him.

"We took back Eden after the aliens overran it. We can do it again. But right now, we need to rest and heal. It's at least three weeks in hyperspace to get back to the human worlds. Use that time to help each other recover from your ordeal. We need to stick together to survive."

The man nodded silently at the lieutenant's words, his despondent expression easing a little. A woman next to him reached out and squeezed his shoulder, smiling at him. He glanced over and gave her a slight smile in return.

Atom took a slow breath. There would be more drama before this was finished, but for now he had done what he could. He looked up as the shuttle's port-side doors whisked open. A dozen suited troops with medic insignias floated through the entrance, moving skillfully from handhold to handhold as they spread out into the ship's hold. Help had arrived at last.

IO.

"Gravity coming on line in fifteen seconds," the first officer announced. "Take your positions!"

The bridge crew scrambled to get seated or have their feet planted firmly against the decking. Sudden transition from weightlessness to full grav could easily result in awkward falls and injury. They readied themselves and waited; finally a claxon sounded and gravity kicked in. Grunts and small thuds sounded as bodies dropped to their full resting positions, followed quickly by the clatter of previously-floating small instruments hitting the bridge floor.

It had taken nearly a full day of frantic repair work before the *Goliath* had begun to revive, and to Taramay it had seemed like an eternity. She was out of her restraint harness and on her feet the instant gravity was restored, swaying for a second as her balance reasserted itself. "Status report," she called out.

The tech officer glanced up from his console. "Diffuser screens repaired and at full capability, including the starboard screen. Sublight propulsion fully functional; scanners coming on line as we speak. Weapons and communications still down, and unfortunately the hyperdrive will be a longer project. Another day or two until we're fully mobile."

Taramay turned to her com officer. "Ms. Stepanovich, anything more you can add?"

Alena replied, "Com circuitry looks good; we're waiting on external antenna repairs to be completed. Should be soon."

The captain nodded, and turned left to look toward the gunnery officer. "Ms. Jónsson, weapons report."

"Weapons still offline, as Mr. Cotton stated. Primary and secondary plasma guns lost their power supply, due to line overload from that magnetic pulse. Power links are under repair and should be functional within the hour. Additional time will be needed to reset and charge the weapons to full capacity."

"How long?" the captain asked.

"Three hours minimum."

Taramay frowned and rubbed her brow. She could feel a headache coming on; it seemed like days since she had rested. "All right, keep me updated," she said. "Mr. DeBartolo, move us up close to one of the larger asteroids and hold us there; keep us in stealth mode, only essential systems powered up. We need to stay hidden until we can run."

Glancing around at the bridge crew, she added, "I'm off to grab a few hours of sleep; hail me if something urgent comes up. Otherwise, carry on." With that she headed off the bridge and down toward the lower levels.

* * * *

Early the next day, after a short but rejuvenating sleep, the captain finally found time to visit the refugees and the troopers who had rescued them. The medic staff had finished clearing everyone for contact, and the initial work of getting all the refugees bathed, clothed and medicated was nearly complete.

Atom Granger came to attention as the captain arrived in the cargo bay; the troopers with him did the same.

"At ease, soldiers," Taramay said, walking up to the lieutenant with a smile on her face. "It's good to see you in one piece," she commented, looking him up and down. "We weren't sure you were going to make it."

"Neither was I," the younger man replied with a wry grin. "To tell the truth, I'm still not sure why I'm standing here. It seemed like the Knackers had their chances to end me, and they didn't. I can't explain it."

Taramay regarded him for a moment, her brow knitted. Lt. Granger was an experienced fighter and knew the enemy's behavior well. If he had noted something unusual, it was worth exploring further. "Come to the main conference room tomorrow at eight hundred hours for a full debriefing," she commanded. "I want to hear more about what happened on that pyramid."

"Yes, ma'am," Atom replied, saluting.

The captain returned the salute casually, and said, "Now show me around the cargo hold; how are the refugees managing?"

"Pretty well, considering their condition," the junior officer replied, leading the captain toward the housing quarters they had set up in the hold. "Things have gone more smoothly since gravity was restored. We've assembled ten rows of two-tiered bunk beds, fifteen to a row. The last four rows are sequestered behind a privacy screen; that's where the women and children are bunked.

"We've opened several crates of water and juice pouches, and we're keeping the room warmer than the norm, as these people are prone to chilling. The mess hall delivers meals three times a day. A few civvies are still in the med bay, but most are stable."

"Good, good," the captain said, nodding as she glanced around. "I'd like to see some of the refugees if they're up to it."

"Sure. In fact, there's someone I'd like you to meet," Atom replied, leading her toward the screened section of beds. "She's the prisoner who was trapped in the pyramid with me. She showed a lot of courage, and she helped keep the children organized as we evacuated. From what people are telling me, it sounds like she was the primary caretaker for the little ones in her cell."

"That must have been a draining task," Taramay replied, shaking her head. "How do you keep yourself together in those conditions, and still find the strength to help children? And if you let yourself become attached to them, imagine the sense of loss when the Crabs come and take one away."

"I know," Atom said, glancing over at her. "My job seems real simple by comparison. I've got my troops beside me, and we meet the enemy on an even playing field, more or less. I've never been defenseless, and I've never been a prisoner without hope of rescue." He paused a moment, and concluded grimly, "I'd rather go down fighting, than experience what these people have been through."

They continued on in silence across the cargo hold. When they reached the women's section, Atom announced himself, and they proceeded down a corridor between the last two rows of bunks. Abruptly they stopped at a bed where a comely young woman lounged on her back, a digital reader in one hand.

She glanced up at them, and her face came alight with a broad smile. "Atom! I was hoping you'd visit! I've really enjoyed our chats." The civilian glanced toward Taramay, who stood watching with one eyebrow raised, and smiled again as she said, "Hello there, I'm Adara Knightsbridge, from Nueva Terra."

The woman began to stand, but Taramay waved her back to the bed. "No need to get up. It's nice to meet you, Adara. I'm Captain Dent."

The civilian took the proffered hand and shook it politely, looking a bit in awe. The captain grinned at her expression, saying, "Lt. Granger here has told me a little about you. He seems to be a big fan of yours." The latter statement came with a knowing look at her subordinate.

Adara blushed, and said softly, "The feeling is mutual. I'm in the lieutenant's debt; we all are. After so long, we had given up hope of ever getting free." Her expression darkened as she spoke, a haunted look briefly surfacing in her eyes before she masked it again. Taramay heard a small catch in the woman's voice as she continued, "I'm not sure we could have made it off that horrid ship without Atom's help. I know Eve and I wouldn't have."

"Eve?" the captain asked, looking from Adara to Atom.

"One of the children that Adara was looking after," he explained. "Eve Coventine. She was trapped in the pyramid with us when the blast door closed."

"Ah…" Taramay said as understanding dawned. "I heard about her. She was injured, yes?"

"Correct," Atom answered. "She was in physical and emotional shock when we brought her aboard. She's made good progress since then, however, and the medics expect a full recovery."

"I'm glad to hear it. That's a lot to go through at any age," the captain said. She looked to Adara and added, "Eve sounds like a resilient little lady. I'd love to meet her."

The young woman's face lit up. "Oh, she'd be so excited if you visited her! Eve is fascinated by spaceships, and she dreams about becoming an officer in SpaceForce. It's all she talks about." Adara paused then continued pensively, "Sometimes it has me worried; most kids her age would be focused on getting back together with their families. Eve rarely talks about her parents, and when she does, she's surprisingly subdued, almost detached."

Taramay nodded. "It may be a protective mechanism, perhaps burying a traumatic event that she witnessed."

"Maybe. I don't know," Adara said, putting her reader aside and standing up slowly. She steadied herself with a hand on the upper bunk for a moment, smiling at their concerned looks. "I'm fine," she said brightly. "I'm always stiff after sitting awhile, but every day I feel stronger." She let go of the support, and said, "See? No hands!" She took a tentative step, then two, and turned to them, saying, "Okay, let's go visit Eve. You will be the highlight of her day, I can promise you that."

They walked slowly along the row of bunks, stopping just short of the far end. In the lower bed to their right lay a sleeping girl familiar to Atom. Maybe ten years old, dark-haired and light-complected, the child lay face up on top of the bed coverings. She wore a blue shirt and shorts, exposing her left calf which was tightly wrapped in white bandaging. Despite her injury, she looked to be in far better condition than when Atom had last seen her. The caked filth had been washed from her slight frame, the tangled mass of her hair had been combed out, and most importantly, the pallor in her face had been replaced by healthier pink tones.

"Eve," Adara said, shaking the girl's shoulder gently. "Hey there, sweetie. Someone's here to see you."

The girl's eyes fluttered open. Her expression was fuzzy and confused momentarily, then her gaze focused and she smiled up at Adara. "Hi," she said simply. She glanced over at the other two visitors, doing a double take when her eyes lit on Taramay. "You're the captain!" she squealed. "I know your insignia!" She pointed at the emblem on the captain's shoulder, a golden double lightning bolt.

"That's right, young lady. I'm Captain Dent," Taramay said with a wide smile. "I'm very pleased to meet you, Eve." She gave the girl a formal salute, which took the youngster totally by surprise. Eve recovered quickly, though, and reciprocated the gesture with surprisingly good form, grinning from ear to ear.

The captain laughed out loud; this girl was quite delightful. Taramay knelt down beside the youngster's bed, and said, "I hear you've been very brave while recovering from your injury. How is your leg doing?"

"It's a lot better now. It only hurts a little. But they still won't let me walk much yet," the girl said with a pout. "I have to stay in bed almost all the time. It's boring. All I do is read and play digi-games."

"Well, I'm sure you'll be able to move around more very soon," the captain said.

Eve brightened immediately. "You think so? I hope you're right. It will be so much fun to see your ship." She looked up at Taramay hopefully. "When I'm better, could you show me the *Goliath*, and tell me about being a captain? After I grow up I want to protect people from the Crabs like you do. I'd like to be friends, when you're not busy. If that's okay," the girl added with a smile.

Normally Taramay would have nixed the idea quickly. She had little time to babysit a youngster, and a SpaceForce destroyer was no place for a child to be wandering around. But she found herself quite taken with the girl. Eve had a fragile waif-like aura that made Taramay want to hug her and tell her everything would be all right.

The strength of the mothering instinct that welled up inside her took Taramay completely by surprise. Early in her career she had made the choice not to have a family, once it had become evident that the Knackers were not going away. Despite a wistful daydream or two, she hadn't regretted her decision, not with the war steadily gathering momentum.

So why this sudden surge of protectiveness that she felt toward Eve? Maybe it was that innocent face and those large blue eyes; no one could deny the girl was quite fetching.

Almost against her will, Taramay heard herself say, "That would be a lot of fun! When you're better, I'll show you around the ship, and maybe you can even visit the bridge with me. Would you like that?"

"More than anything!" the girl exclaimed. "Thank you, Captain!"

"You can call me Taramay."

"Okay, Captain Taramay," the girl replied with a salute.

Once again the captain found herself chuckling. "That's twice you've made me laugh today, Eve. I can't tell you how much I needed that," she said, reaching out to brush the girl's long hair back from her face. The youngster's eyes widened at the unexpectedly tender gesture, and before Taramay could react, she suddenly found herself wrapped in a tight embrace.

The slender arms clung to her with surprising strength, and she could feel the girl's tiny body trembling as she hesitantly returned the hug. For a moment they stayed like that, Taramay stroking Eve's head softly. Self-consciously she snuck a peek up at Atom and Adara. The two adults were watching the exchange with interest: Adara with a tender smile playing on her lips, and the lieutenant looking more than a little surprised.

Finally she gently disengaged herself from Eve's grip, giving the girl a smile as she stood up. "I have to go now, but I'll come back to visit soon," she said.

"You promise?" Eve asked, her eyes shining as she looked up from her bed. Damn, it simply wasn't fair that any child should be so cute.

"I promise," Taramay replied.

* * * *

At eighteen hundred hours that evening the captain was awakened from another catnap by a high-pitched whistle from her wrist com. Groggily she said, "Yes?" as she rolled over.

"Sorry to disturb you, Captain," the first officer's voice came through the speaker. "We've got a situation that needs your attention."

The urgency in his voice made Taramay sit straight up, the remnants of sleep instantly dispelled. "On my way," she said as she reached for her clothes.

A few minutes later she strode onto the bridge, where the night shift officers were just showing up to relieve the day crew. She wasted no time. "What do you have for me, Mr. Caine?"

The first officer looked up from his console, his green eyes rimmed with red. "G' evening, Captain. Ms. Stepanovich notified me of an event that occurred late last night. It's quite concerning. I'll let her explain it."

Taramay's gaze snapped to the com officer, who nodded and said, "Communications were restored last night, Captain. Today I was doing a routine review of the com log, making sure no entries were lost when the system was down. I came across an unauthorized transmission."

"*What*?" The captain was stunned. "From this ship?"

"Yes, ma'am. It occurred around three hundred hours this morning, not long after the com was restored."

"What was sent? To whom?" Taramay asked.

"We don't know the message content," Alena answered, shaking her head. "No detailed data entry was saved."

"Well, what *do* we know?" the captain asked, exasperated.

"We have the basic com log, you know, time of day, type of signal, duration, direction. We do know it was a tight beam, it only lasted a few seconds, and it was directed…outward, toward the Cluster's rim."

"Outward!" Taramay exclaimed. She thought furiously, and then cursed as the inevitable conclusion presented itself. "We've got a mole, people. Someone on this ship sent a signal to the enemy!" She frowned in thought. "How much data could be carried in such a transmission?"

Alena sighed. "Plenty. If the signal was highly compressed, all the specs on the *Goliath* could be sent within a five-second transmission window."

"Those files are encrypted and require security clearance to access," the first officer pointed out. "It's doubtful that secure data were compromised."

"*Doubtful!*" Taramay spat. "It's doubtful that an unauthorized person could beam a transmission off this vessel, but it happened! I need to know how, and where, they did it. Not from the bridge, I assume?"

"No, Captain," the com officer said. "No one came on the bridge who wasn't authorized to be here. I've already played back security cam recordings for the past twenty-four hours."

"Then it was from another terminal," the captain stated flatly. "We need to find out which. Can we review security images of the computer access points throughout the ship? A skilled technician could send a signal from almost any of those sites."

"Unfortunately, we can't, Captain. The camera system outside of the bridge is shut down while the ship is in stealth mode. We have no recordings of the hallways and conference rooms from last night."

"Ares blast it," Taramay swore. "I want all security cams up and running as of this moment, and stealth be damned."

"Affirmative," the tech officer called out from his station.

"Strange times we live in," the navigator commented as he stood up and vacated his station to the evening shift officer.

Taramay shot him a glance. Leofric continued, "A security leak is…highly unusual. Any ideas who?"

"I've got some thoughts on the matter," she answered tiredly, running her fingers through her tousled hair. "Right now I'm off to get a change of clothes and some food. Barring any urgent developments, I'll see you, Lef, in conference at eight hundred hours. The rest of you, man your posts and stay sharp. We're not out of danger yet."

A chorus of assents met her ears as she exited the bridge.

* * * *

The next morning Taramay sat at the head of the table in the *Goliath*'s main conference room, organizing her thoughts as people filed in. To her right sat Leofric DeBartolo, and to her left was lieutenant Atom Granger with a second trooper, Sergeant Harriman. The table was rounded out with several medical staff who had evaluated the refugees during their stay aboard the *Goliath*.

"All right, people. Let's get this meeting started," the captain began. "I've waited to formally debrief everyone until we were out of imminent danger. Now that the Knacker ships have been destroyed and the *Goliath*'s repairs are well in hand, it's time to pool our findings and see what we have."

Taramay looked around the table. "I've read your reports, so I know the basic facts as stated. What I'm interested in now is hearing your thoughts, what do the data mean, and how do we interpret the events of the past two days."

She turned to Atom Granger. "Lieutenant, you had mentioned to me that the Knackers' behavior seemed out of character on board the pyramid; can you elaborate on that for us?"

The junior officer took a moment to respond, frowning with his hands clasped together on the table. When he spoke, it was slowly and deliberately. "Well, to begin with, let me state that I'm not sure what to make of the events aboard the Crab vessel. Several things struck me as odd, but that's a rather vague assessment, I know. I've fought the enemy on numerous occasions, and while their behavior is sometimes bizarre from a human point of view, it is nonetheless consistent. What I saw on the pyramid was divergent from the norm, which bothers me. I wish I knew what it meant."

Taramay was watching the lieutenant intently. When he paused, she said, "Elaborate, if you will."

Atom nodded. "I'll try. First of all, the Knackers were only there in small numbers. Why? They also left some prisoners behind, but not many. Again, to what purpose?"

Taramay interjected, "We may have interrupted the Crabs while they were evacuating their ship. If they detected our arrival, they could have elected to move their destroyer off a short distance, so as not to be caught vulnerable while offloading the pyramid."

Atom made a noncommittal noise, saying, "Perhaps, but there are things that still don't sit right. If they knew we were coming, why not mount a better defense? The aliens seemed to be scattered willy-nilly around the vessel. They could have made it a lot tougher on us if they had massed their numbers in strategic locations. Do you agree, sergeant?"

Sgt. Harriman nodded. "Yessir. They didn't converge on our troops during the fight to free the prisoners, nor did they really commit to cutting off our route of retreat."

Atom said, "Exactly. When they did attack, they quickly disengaged. Not at all what I would expect from the enemy. I know they want us alive when possible, but the Crabs are fierce warriors when facing armed opponents. The aliens onboard the pyramid acted...*soft*, for lack of a better word."

"They attacked and then retreated?" Leofric asked, looking bemused. "That is unusual, to say the least. I've never known Knackers to back up unless they were forced to."

"Yes, and they were using their stealth tech in an odd manner," Atom added, as the thought occurred to him. "We had a hard time reading them in general, and they surprised us several times because we didn't see them coming. That all fits, but it seemed that whenever they retreated, we could read them loud and clear. It's as if they turned their shielding off, like they wanted us to see them withdrawing."

Taramay tapped her fingers on the table, contemplating what she was hearing. "Atom, you mentioned when we talked before that the Knackers had chances to kill you, but they didn't do so. Can you detail the circumstances?"

"Yeah, that's not something I'm likely to forget," the younger man said. "A Crab snuck up behind me during a firefight. I mean it got to within a few meters of where I stood, don't ask me how. They're surprisingly quiet with those suits on. I turned around and there it was, with four plasma guns aimed right at me."

"And it didn't fire?" Leofric asked incredulously.

"Well, I'm here, aren't I?" Atom said with a grin. "Seriously, I don't know what would have happened, because one of my squad nailed the Crab between the eyes. But the point is, it hesitated, and I've never seen the enemy do that before. They're quick, with faster reflexes than humans. I should have been down even before I turned around to see it."

"Were you doing anything in particular that would have given the Knacker pause?" Taramay asked.

"No…I was just standing there. I had shouldered my weapon, because I was carrying a hurt civilian, so maybe it was trying to decide whether to kill or capture me. It just seems odd," Atom finished with a shrug. "I don't know if it means anything or not."

"Were there any other times you were spared?" Leofric asked him.

"Well, I got shot at plenty, so I can't say that they were overly friendly," Atom said, chuckling. "However, there was one other time I felt lucky to be alive—and I've learned not to trust in luck. Sometimes fortune falls your way, but when it happens more than once, I tend to question why."

"Explain," the captain prompted.

"After I downloaded the data from the pyramid's computer, I had to make a run of it to reach the shuttle. I had Crabs chasing me all the way, some of them not far behind. Not once did they discharge a weapon. Why? Did they want me alive? Dead should have been acceptable, if they'd wanted to prevent me from stealing their data. I'm not sure they even knew that I had accessed their computer, but in any event, why not shoot to disable me?"

"Maybe they wanted you to get away," Leofric said jokingly.

Taramay shot him a sharp glance, a contemplative look on her face. "What if they did?" she said after a moment's pause.

"I wasn't being serious…" the navigator protested, but she cut him off with a raised hand.

"The encounter with the pyramid has felt wrong to me from the beginning," the captain said. "Why had the Knackers not salvaged it by now? Why were only a few crew and captives aboard? And why would a Knacker destroyer back off and hide when we approached? They would have expected to handle us easily in a standup fight, especially when they seemed to have no idea of the *Goliath*'s enhanced capabilities. Why skulk around behind an asteroid, unless they wanted us to board the pyramid?"

"To what purpose?" Leofric asked. "They made no effective effort to ambush and capture the away teams, so why let us enter the shipwreck? Did they want us preoccupied so they could have an advantage in a firefight with the *Goliath*?"

"No, that doesn't strike me as the reason," Taramay mused. "Their destroyer didn't jump on us very quickly once we discovered its location. If anything, it seemed to be the opposite."

"You're right!" the navigator exclaimed. "Their ship advanced at an unusually slow pace; it made no sense at the time. Their rate of fire was leisurely as well—at least until we took out their main gun," he added with a wry grin. "That seemed to get them plenty annoyed."

"So what do we have?" Taramay asked, looking around the table. "The Knackers leave a stranded pyramid sitting out in the middle of nowhere, with a destroyer nearby, doing what? Offloading crew and human captives? If so, why leave some of them onboard the crippled ship? Why not tow and salvage the wreck, as is their standard procedure? Did we just happen to arrive during their recovery efforts? If so, why did they let us board the pyramid, and seemingly let us get out again?"

Atom Granger answered, "It almost suggests that they wanted us to complete our mission."

"Now hold up," Leofric protested, hand raised. "Are you saying that the Crabs wanted us to download all the data off their ship's mainframe? And let themselves be blown into space dust?"

"No. I doubt they anticipated that we would have time to hack their computer system, and I really don't think they expected to lose a destroyer," Taramay said thoughtfully. "But they could have wanted us to succeed in a rescue mission, and then send us fleeing before we could do any extensive study of the pyramid."

"That sounds borderline paranoiac," Leofric commented, with a glance toward the medical staff members. "Do you really think the Crabs would set up a ruse like that out at the Cluster's rim, so far from human space? What are the odds we'd even come out here?"

The captain frowned. "Well, this may be more paranoia, but the odds would be decent if the Crabs knew our tracking probe had detected the pyramid, and if they allowed the probe to survive and send back data that would entice SpaceForce to send a ship out. The probe had easily detected strong life signs, and yet we had a heck of a time finding that ship when we got out there. Perhaps the pyramid was still full of human captives at the time our probe encountered it."

Atom replied, "That was over three weeks ago. If the Crabs knew about the probe back then, and decided to let it transmit its findings, it means they also knew about the disabled pyramid. If so, then they had ample time to offload the crew and captives long before we arrived. So once again, we have to ask, why did they leave a few behind?"

"That's a lot of 'ifs'," the navigator declared with a scowl. "But let's say the Crabs did let us complete our mission; it's a wild theory, but it could explain their unorthodox behavior. Then we're left with the big question: 'why?' Any ideas?" He looked around the table, inviting a response.

"Perhaps the Knackers anticipated we'd download the pyramid's computer memory; in that case, it could be doctored with false data," Atom offered.

"We'll have to consider that possibility when the data are analyzed by SpaceForce, unfortunately," Taramay said. "It's a shame that events have cast some doubt on the viability of the information we stole. I'm still not convinced that the Crabs saw that one coming, so their purpose may lie elsewhere."

"Then what?" Leofric asked, his eyebrows raised in query.

"Well, if they didn't want us to collect corrupted data, then they may have wanted us to retrieve the human captives," Taramay offered.

"Why would they want that?" Leofric asked.

Taramay directed her gaze toward the three medical staff members who were in attendance. "Your examinations of the refugees found no evidence of latent pathogens or biotech implants, correct?"

A balding middle aged man wearing the red-and-grey smock of a senior medic spoke up. "None. As far as our technology can detect, the survivors are clean. No organic pathogens, and no foreign devices in or on their bodies."

"How about psychological manipulation?" Atom offered. "If not corrupted computer data, then maybe we retrieved… corrupted survivors?"

"That is a thought," the captain said with an unhappy look. "I hate to consider it, but those people were under the control of the Crabs for weeks. They could have been brainwashed, or behaviorally modified in other ways. The enemy has had ample time to study us, to learn our biology and the way our brains function. Crabs possess technology that human science cannot yet match; who knows what they could do with human captives?"

"If you're right, I'm thinking that this could explain the unauthorized transmission we detected," Leofric stated.

Taramay paused, eyebrows raised. "Of course! That signal was sent toward enemy territory. Someone we took on board may be spying for the Knackers, possibly without even realizing that they are doing so."

"There are nearly three hundred civilian refugees; it's going to be a challenge to figure out who is responsible," Leofric said.

"Well, it would have to be someone familiar with military computer interfacing," the captain responded. "Not everyone can access a shipboard terminal and send a directed tight-beam signal."

Leofric rubbed his forehead, saying, "We'll need to research the backgrounds of the refugees; it may be impossible to get detailed records with the Crabs occupying their home world."

"I've got one candidate to keep a close eye on," Atom spoke up. "I caught a male civilian wandering the corridors on the upper deck yesterday, and he couldn't give me a good explanation of why he was there. 'Just walking' was all he said. He was pretty defensive about it, too. Same idiot that was being difficult in the shuttle bay when we brought the civvies on board."

"Monitor his activities, as well as anyone he associates with in the refugee quarters. Whoever it is, our best chance may be to catch him—or her—in the act," Taramay said. "It's likely they will try to send more than one message, and unless they're ex-Space-Force, they'll have little knowledge of our security protocols. We may catch someone on camera if they try to interface with a computer again."

"I suggest restricting the civvies to quarters except when accompanied by a crewmember," the navigator offered. "If someone wants to sneak out unauthorized, it will make it easier to catch them. It also limits how much spying they can do, if they're not allowed to wander the corridors at will."

"Good point, Lef," the captain said. "As much as I want to catch the culprit in the act, we can't have sensitive intel being sent to the enemy. We'll inform the civvies that non-authorized personnel cannot wander about the ship. That's standard policy on military vessels, so it shouldn't raise any suspicions that we're aware of the security breach."

"I'll see that the passengers are informed," Atom assured her. "Should we lock the cargo bay doors at night?"

"No," Taramay said. "Let's leave the bay open. If someone wants to try an unauthorized computer interface, we'll give them enough leeway to reveal themselves. I'll have Alena program the com system to automatically record all outgoing messages, both their content and which terminal they originated from. If someone tries to contact the Crabs, we'll catch them in the act."

"There may be more than one mole," Leofric pointed out.

"Then we'll have to find them all. What choice do we have?" There were multiple nods from those around the table, and Taramay continued, "Start heightened security patrols until I say otherwise. Senior officers, keep close tabs on the status of ship repairs; I want hourly updates. Anyone who has new thoughts about what we're up against, contact me immediately. The stolen data we downloaded is useless until Space Command can analyze it, and we're all alone until we get back to the core worlds. We've got to use our wits to deal with this situation."

The captain paused, glancing around the table, and then concluded, "Okay people, back to work. Let's get our ship healthy and get home."

II.

"Give me some good news," Taramay called out as she strode onto the bridge the next morning. A full night's sleep had put strength back into her muscles, and she felt alert and energized.

"How about this?" the navigator replied with a grin. "Main propulsion is back on line; we're free to go."

"Weapons fully operational as well," Lt. Jónsson piped up from her chair.

"Excellent! Mr. Cotton, any sign of enemy presence in the area?"

The tech officer said, "No ships detected within scanner range, Captain."

Taramay nodded. "Mr. DeBartolo, maneuver us free of this asteroid field. As soon as we're clear, get us into hyperspace; set a direct course for home base."

"On it!" the navigator replied, and his fingers punched in the commands. On the viewscreen, the large asteroid they were hiding behind began to slide sideways, as the ship eased away from its protective cover.

"Ms. Stepanovich, send a tight beam message to Space Command; summarize the events to date, and let them know we're proceeding home. Estimated arrival time in twenty-two standard days."

"Yes, ma'am."

"Lef, I know our ship is barely patched together, but push her as hard as the engineers deem safe. I want us out of this sector as quickly as possible."

"Amen to that."

* * * *

Once in hyperspace, the *Goliath* raced at top speed toward home. Hour by hour the parsecs slid by effortlessly, as they left the rim worlds and headed toward the Cluster's core planets.

Two days into their return journey, they received an encrypted message from Space Command. It was brief, as trans-warp messages usually were. The *Goliath* was too far out to engage in real time dialogue, and being at war meant that long-distance communications were subject to interception. Usually they were limited to basic instructions or alerts, with minimal sensitive content. Alena logged the incoming transmission and called the captain to the bridge.

Taramay arrived a few minutes later, and immediately looked to Lt. Stepanovich. "Message on screen," she ordered.

"Message playing," Alena answered, tapping her keyboard. On the port-side wall of the domed viewscreen, a rectangular area of the star field was abruptly replaced by a blurry white background. The bridge officers watched as an image materialized and resolved: a woman clad in the uniform of a SpaceForce two-nova general sat behind a large desk. The circular seal of the Core Planets Alliance dominated the wall behind her.

She appeared to look directly at them as she said, *"Goliath,* this is General Naismith. Congratulations on your successful mission. We look forward to analyzing your data when you return. The civilians you rescued are to be transported to the planet Eden for processing; from there you shall proceed to Iliana IV for debriefing. Naismith out."

The message section of the viewscreen went blank, and in moments was replaced by the moving star field. The bridge was silent for a few seconds, and then the navigator spoke. "Well, that was short and to the point."

"As expected," Taramay answered. "They're taking no chances on giving the enemy anything to work with, especially with a transmission aimed outward toward the rim sectors. Too much risk of it being intercepted. Did you notice that they didn't even name Space Command, instead just said 'Iliana IV'?"

"Yeah, I caught that," Leofric said. "So we're dropping off our passengers first thing, it sounds like."

"That's fine by me. I'll feel better not having to worry about their welfare should we go into battle again," Taramay declared. "They'll be safer planetside. Then we can focus on delivering the data we obtained from the pyramid. We've got to get that to Command so it can be analyzed. Then, and only then, will our mission be completed."

* * * *

The next day Taramay sat on the bed in her private quarters, talking with Eve. With the danger of a surprise enemy attack receding, the captain had made time to befriend the youngster. The girl was perched on the bed's edge, legs swinging as she chattered on about the things she'd seen that day. Therapeutic energy wave treatments on her burned leg, combined with regenerative cell transplants, had worked wonders, and she was 70% healed.

In the morning, Eve had been cleared for unrestricted exercise, and Taramay had taken the girl on a tour of the ship. The highlight was a visit to the bridge which had the youth jumping out of her skin with excitement.

For a while Eve had stood and just stared in awe at the giant viewscreen, watching the rainbow orbs of stars sliding by in hyperspace amongst the colored streamers of dark matter filaments. The captain had introduced the girl to the bridge crew, and she had proven quite gregarious. She laughed and talked with each person, wanting to know what they did and how they liked their jobs, was it fun being in SpaceForce, what this display meant, what that button would do if you pushed it.

The youngster obviously had an agile and curious mind, and was mature for her years. The crew took to her right away. Taramay inwardly breathed a sigh of relief; visions of an excited child running amok on the bridge had flitted through her head beforehand. Afterward she had taken Eve for a frozen dessert in the mess hall, and then back to the captain's quarters.

Now they sat together just chatting, taking advantage of some down time between shifts. "So what have you been reading on your digi-pad?' Taramay asked the youngster. The hand-held screens had been provided for the colonists' entertainment, although there were far too few to go around. The children had received first priority, in an attempt to keep them amused and out of trouble. In an environment with few diversions, the devices had proven to be a big hit. It seemed that the girl always had hers in hand, her head bent as she studied the screen.

"Stories, mostly," Eve answered offhandedly. "Games, poetry, anything that sounds fun."

"Poetry, eh?" Taramay asked, her interest piqued. "I enjoy poems too. Tell me some you like."

"Well… I just read this one, it's pretty good," Eve said, tapping her screen and handing the pad over.

Taramay glanced at the screen and blinked in surprise. She wasn't sure what she had expected, perhaps a children's limerick about cuddly animals. What she saw instead was a notoriously dark work by a century-old poet, Demetrius, about the horrors of war and its lingering impact on those who waged it. She frowned as she scanned the opening lines. This one had always struck a chord with her, but it was hardly child's fare. She found it a bit disturbing that Eve was reading such things.

She mouthed the words of the first stanza as she read:

> *"I close my eyes and fade to black,*
> *each night to know the little death,*
> *Awaiting visions dire that haunt me*
> *all the days I still draw breath"*

Taramay thought she had spoken too softly to be heard, but to her surprise Eve chimed in with the next lines:

> *"Though waking thoughts may turn away*
> *from darker truths by light of day,*
> *Passion's deadly knife blade gleams*
> *in my dreadful darkling dreams."*

Hearing the words come from a young girl's mouth was disconcerting, but Taramay forced a smile and said, "That's very good. You've memorized this poem?"

"Memorized?" Eve asked, looking confused.

"You know, studied it until you know it by heart."

"No…I just read it. Now I know it. Why would I need to study?"

"You mean you remember all of it?" Taramay asked her incredulously. "It's nearly two pages long."

"Yes, Captain Taramay."

"Can you recite it for me? I'd love to hear it."

"Sure," the girl replied, giggling. Then she proceeded to narrate the entire rambling work, exactly verbatim, as Taramay followed along on the palm reader.

When the girl had finished, Taramay blinked and pulled her eyes from the reader, shifting her gaze to the grinning child. "That was really amazing, Eve," she said, and she meant it. "You recited that perfectly!" The girl beamed at the praise, and Taramay decided to test just how acute the youngster's memory was. "Do you have any favorite stories you can show me?" she asked.

"Let me have the reader," Eve responded, and the captain tossed it to her. After a moment's fiddling, she handed the screen back, this time displaying the title page of a popular fiction story.

"Althorn and the Unicorn. Hmmm, I've not read that one," the captain commented. "Do you know this story like you know the poem?"

"Of course," Eve answered with a snort. "I've read the whole thing."

"Okay, then show me how smart you are, girl," Taramay said, grinning. She flipped through the chapters on the reader, and then paused. "Tell me what is written on page fifty eight."

Eve squinted in thought, her head tilted sideways. After a moment she began, "It was a long trek down from the mountains to the valley, where the village lay shrouded in the shadows of the overlooking peaks. To this gloomy settlement came the herder to barter for supplies. He disliked the smells of civilization, the smoky pall of the outdoor fire pits, the stink of refuse in the gutters along the streets, so different from the clear cold air of the heights…"

As the narration continued page after page, Taramay shook her head in amazement. There was no doubt about it: Eve had phenomenal recall, so much so that the term "photographic memory" might apply, but regardless of what you wanted to call it, the girl possessed a truly rare gift.

After listening to ten pages of perfect recitation, Taramay held up her hand, laughing. "Okay, okay, you win! You've got the best memory I've ever seen, sweet girl. What a special lady you are!" She held out her arms, and Eve eagerly crawled across the bed to share a warm hug.

* * * *

Nine days into their homeward journey, Atom finished his evening shift, and before heading to the mess hall, he headed to the cargo bay to see Adara. Since their initial contact on board the Knacker vessel, they had discovered a mutual attraction that continued to grow as they spent time together. He found the young woman occupying his thoughts more and more as the days passed. It was way too early to tell if it would lead to anything long term, and in any case this was wartime; who could say what fate had in store? All he knew is that he enjoyed her company immensely, and he could tell that she liked him too. That was good enough for now. Without thinking he whistled a cheerful tune as he walked down the corridor.

He found Adara napping on her cot, and stood over her for a moment, appreciating the delicate lines of her face, the supple curves of her body under the thin blanket. When he had first laid eyes on her, she'd been a pale, underfed refugee with hints of a pretty countenance lurking beneath the grime. During her time recuperating aboard the *Goliath*, he'd watched her transform into a beautiful young woman, and now just looking at her took his breath away.

Although Atom enjoyed the physical attraction, her appearance was not what had turned his head. He was young himself, but had already learned the hard way that good looks didn't assure an amiable disposition. Adara, though, was sweetness personified, and under that gentle exterior resided a core of inner strength that he marveled at. She had endured things that would have challenged his will to live, and to all appearances had come through it with her spirit intact. Something within him responded to that, and he wanted more than anything to become closer to her.

Smiling, he reached out and brushed a lock of hair back from her face. She stirred at the light touch, and her eyes opened. Almost at once her face lit with a broad smile. "Atom! Aw, it's so nice to see you," she murmured, stretching languidly. "Were you watching over me, protecting me from harm again?" she asked in a teasing tone.

"Something like that," he laughed. He held out his hand, and she grasped it as she rose to a sitting position. She patted the bed for him to sit next to her, and he obliged. Even after she was upright, her hand remained firmly wrapped around his, and he felt a surge of pleasure at the warm contact.

"How are you doing?" he asked, looking into her eyes.

"Oh, I'm feeling so much better!" she said, smiling. "My strength is coming back, and everyone is being so nice to me. You have no idea how much difference a simple shower and a clean set of clothes makes. I actually feel human again."

"I'm happy to hear it. You're certainly looking well," Atom said, smiling. He squeezed her hand. "Hey, are you feeling strong enough for a walk?"

She arched her brows at the suggestion, a playful look in her eyes. "Are you inviting me on a date, kind sir?" she said coyly.

He stood and bowed with a flourish. "Let me show you the wonders of the universe, milady."

Adara giggled and rose from the bed to stand next to him. "I'm all yours," she said with a warm smile. "Lead on."

They walked out of the cargo bay together, and headed into a long straight corridor that ran lengthwise down the center of the ship. The cargo hold was situated in the lowest level, along with the shuttle bay and portions of the engineering section. This deck was not designed to include living quarters, and the décor here was strictly functional. Both floor and walls sported the basic military gray color scheme, with little adornment other than red stenciled signs on doors and hatches indicating what lay behind each.

Atom led them to an elevator in the left wall, which whisked them rapidly upward. Within just a few seconds the car halted its motion, and the doorway opened. They exited onto the third deck, and Adara slowed in surprise as she stepped through the doorway. The elevator had delivered them to a central hallway which was oriented identically to the one on the lower level, but the similarity ended there. Adara's eyes darted back and forth, excitedly drinking in the unexpected sights.

This floor sat approximately mid-ship, and included the quarters for the enlisted crew members, plus their dining and recreation halls. The *Goliath* was an extended-mission vessel, so efforts had been made to counter the tedium of long tours of duty. The interior designers had employed color and texture to provide visual variety, plus the illusion of spaciousness.

The floors were detailed in a colorful mosaic, reminiscent of antique tiles. Above their heads the ceiling was the deep blue of a sky near sunset, with pinpoints of light like stars dotting the heavens. But the walls—the walls were what captivated the eye. Up and down the hallway were arrayed glowing murals of rural vistas, gathered from human-occupied planets throughout the Cluster.

Prior to her abduction, Adara had never been off her home world, and she was enchanted by the floor-to-ceiling, three dimensional visions of alien landscapes. Atom named the scenes as they strolled past them: the teal clouds and cobalt cliffs of Ondarain IV, the night sky of Alta Luna with its twin ringed moons, the fabled ironwood forests of the planet Eden, sporting massive lavender and black trunks which reared incredibly skyward, topped by long trailing fronds resembling giant ferns.

"That will be your new home," Atom said, gesturing at the forest mural. "The Knackers invaded Eden, but we've liberated the population there. It's probably more secure now than many of the untouched human worlds."

"It's a lovely planet," Adara murmured, gazing at the image. "We're very fortunate to be able to settle there."

She stood quietly, saying nothing more, and after a moment Atom glanced over at her. The young woman's face was highlighted by the glow from the mural, and the light reflected off the moisture of tears running down her cheeks.

"Hey there…are you all right?" Atom asked, reaching out to touch her shoulder.

Adara looked up at him with red-rimmed eyes. When she spoke her voice was rough with emotion. "I miss my home so much." She lowered her gaze and continued softly, "I'm sorry. I know it's selfish. I should be happy to have somewhere to go, to just be alive. But all my friends and family are back on Nueva Terra. I don't know what's happened to them." She brought her gaze back up to meet his, her eyes glistening. "I don't even know if I want to know."

Atom's heart went out to her. The young woman had been courageous throughout her ordeal, and this was the first time he had seen her vulnerable. Instinctively he reached out and wrapped her in his arms. To his relief she didn't pull back, but returned his embrace without hesitation. They stayed like that for a moment, Adara's body trembling slightly as they stood pressed together.

Her head was nestled on his shoulder, and he moved his right hand up to stroke her hair. He spoke quietly, "You don't need to apologize for anything, Adara. I can't imagine what you've been through, but you're safe now. We'll protect you…I'll protect you. Things will be okay, I promise."

She laughed softly, but it was a joyless sound. "You can't promise that. No one can."

Atom reluctantly loosened his embrace, and pulled back enough to look Adara in the eyes. She was startled by the determination in his gaze, and there was something else there as well, something gentler. His voice was steady but urgent in its intensity. "I can promise to never give up. That's got to be worth something."

She nodded and smiled at him. "It's worth a lot. Thank you for being here, and for letting me cry on your shoulder." She wiped at her tears and grimaced ruefully. "I must look a fright, eyes all puffy and face streaked. Really lovely, huh?"

"Don't worry, you're still as pretty as the first time I met you," Atom replied with a grin.

Adara began to thank him, but then she saw his teasing expression and realized she'd been had. She sputtered, "The *first* time..?! Oh, I'll get you for that!"

Atom began back-pedaling as she came at him, and she said, "That's right, you'd better run! I'm going to make you beg for mercy, soldier."

They were both laughing by this point, and as it turned out, Adara could run forward faster than Atom could retreat. She caught him within ten strides, and a tickle fight ensued. Despite his best efforts, he quickly had to admit defeat at the hands of a more motivated opponent. He didn't mind at all. It was worth it just to see Adara's expression of delight as she lost herself in the moment.

Awhile later they stood together at the starboard observation port near the front of the ship, gazing out at the surreal panorama of hyperspace flowing by. "Are those globes of all different colors actually stars?" she asked him, her hand once again clasped warmly in his.

"Yes," he answered, smiling. "Their colors vary due to phase shifting from the warping of space around them, so I'm told. The mass and temperature of each sun affects how they look in hyperspace, as well as their distance and relative velocity compared to the *Goliath*. That's why some have deeper hues, while others are paler and hazier in outline."

"What about those rainbows?" Adara asked, pointing at a

writing multihued filament that stretched across the sky with no apparent beginning or end.

"Those are strands of dark matter. They're invisible in normal space, but here they appear luminous. Some can be hundreds of light-years in length."

"They're beautiful," Adara said in a hushed voice. "The entire sky is colored like a pastel painting, bluish up ahead, and then fading to pink tones behind us. I never knew that the universe could look so alive."

"Our senses limit what we can perceive in normal space; some say that hyperspace actually gives us a better window into reality," Atom stated with a wry smile.

Just then they heard voices approaching, and from around a corner came two female figures, an adult and a child. "That's Alena Stepanovich, one of the bridge officers," Atom said. He chuckled, adding, "It looks like she's made a friend, too."

The pair greeted Atom and Adara as they passed by, the little girl laughing and prattling on animatedly as she took in the sights. "She reminds me a little of Eve," Atom commented as he squinted after the receding figures. "Very cute and full of life."

"She seems to be quite fond of your officer," Adara chuckled as they turned back to look out the viewing port once again. After a moment she glanced over at Atom. "Thank you for showing me this," she said, smiling at him. "I'm happy to be doing something besides sitting around and worrying. This ship is so bright and cheery, it's wonderful."

Atom laughed. "I think that's the first time I've heard a Space-Force destroyer described as 'cheery', but I'm glad you like it."

"Compared to that prison ship, this is heaven," Adara declared, shivering. "Just being able to stay clean, and having light, and heat, food—simple things you take for granted until they're gone."

Atom hesitated, then asked gently, "How long were you in the dark on that ship?"

She shrugged, shaking her head. "I really don't know. Many days, maybe a couple of weeks even. When we were captured, we were stripped of all our tech devices, including time pieces. At first the pyramid seemed to follow a regular schedule, with the lights in our cell being periodically dimmed for sleep cycles. It felt similar to the day length on Nueva Terra, but I can't say for sure. We were fed twice each day-night cycle, and we kept count of the time in our heads. That is, until the light died."

Atom's eyes narrowed, and he said, "That pyramid looked dead when we boarded it. There was some reserve power, but most systems were offline. You were lucky to have life systems still functioning."

Adara nodded. "I don't really know what caused it, but around the fifth day aboard the pyramid, something big happened. It was during mealtime, and we were distributing the food trays in our cell when the whole room went sideways.

"We were knocked off our feet and thrown around pretty violently. The floor was shaking and bucking, and you could barely hear people's cries over the noise filling the chamber. I'll never forget that sound, a strange deep groaning that seemed to come from all around us, like the ship itself was alive and howling in pain. The lights went out briefly, and when they came back on, they were much dimmer than before."

"We think the pyramid took a strike from a powerful Space-Force weapon," Atom explained. "That occurred over Xenopus, a Knacker world which was the pyramid's original destination. The human fleet had surrounded the planet, and your prison ship was hit and had to make a run for it."

Adara listened intently, her gaze focused on his face. "That explains a lot," she said slowly, turning to stare out the view-port window as her mind's eye looked into the past. "We never got full lighting back after that. Eventually the cell went dark permanently. Meals became less and less frequent, and we had no way to measure the passage of time."

"It's lucky we found you when we did, or you might have starved," Atom said.

"Yes…but that would have been better than the fate many of us met," Adara answered in a hushed tone, as she glanced over toward him. "There were so many more in our cell at the start, but as time went on, the Crabs just kept taking people away. After the lights went out for good, it was almost a daily occurrence."

Atom nodded with a sigh. "I guess that makes sense. Usually the pyramid captives are kept alive until the destination planet is reached. Your voyage was interrupted by the attack on Xenopus. Eventually your ship was stranded, and the Knackers on board would have needed a food supply until they were rescued."

As the words left his mouth he caught Adara's expression of dismay. He immediately wished he could take them back. Holding up his hand, he stammered, "I'm so sorry! That was really thoughtless of me. My military training makes me tell things as I see them, and sometimes I forget that the truth can be pretty ugly. You didn't need to hear that. Please forgive me."

"It's okay," Adara said with a wan smile. "Supposedly it's better to talk about things than to hold it all in. I tell myself I should be able to discuss it like an adult, but it was just so horrible." She stared straight ahead, and after a pause, she continued in a lifeless monotone, "We would sit in that cell, blind in the dark, waiting, just waiting…and then the door would roll open, and those monsters would enter and grab two or three people in their claws, and drag them away screaming. Some of them I had become friends with. I wanted so much to help them but I was too scared to even move."

Abruptly she looked away, unwilling to meet Atom's gaze, as she continued in a small voice, "It wasn't just fear; each time they came and went I felt an overwhelming sense of relief that they hadn't picked me. How selfish is that?"

"What you felt was totally natural," Atom replied gently, touching her shoulder. "You were in a hopeless situation, and your survival instinct was all you had. We both know that self-sacrifice would have been fruitless. You simply would have died along with the others."

"But why should I be the one to live?" Adara exclaimed, her voice tortured. "Many of those people had families, children, loved ones who depended on them. When they died, it damaged so many lives."

"And *your* death wouldn't affect anyone?" Atom asked her, holding her gaze steadily. "Parents, brothers, sisters, friends?"

She nodded reluctantly. "Of course I have family…and friends, back on Nueva Terra. Mom and dad, my brother Stephan, my best friend Janille. If they're still alive," she finished quietly.

"The point is, we all matter to someone," Atom told her, holding both her hands now as he faced her. "We all deserve to live. Don't blame yourself for what you went through, and please don't feel guilty for surviving."

"It's not just the guilt. My home world has lost so much, sometimes I'm not certain if I want to continue on. For all I know, the Crabs may have taken everyone I ever knew," Adara told him, her eyes earnest as she voiced her greatest fear. "What if they're all gone? What's the point of living if you've got no one? In all the human worlds, what if there is no one left who would know or care if I died?" Her lips trembled as she stared into his eyes, searching for something to give her hope, to help her face the reality that had been thrust upon her.

"It matters to me if you live," Atom declared, meeting her gaze unflinchingly. "You are strong, kind, and beautiful, Adara, and I'm blessed to have met you. I don't know what fate has in store for either of us. I do know that I find myself happier now than at any time since this war began, and you are the reason why. Please don't give up hope."

Her eyes widened as he spoke, her hands gripping his tightly. By the time he had finished, her expression had softened and she seemed to shake off some of the malaise that had gripped her mood. A gentle smile began to play about her lips, and she disengaged her right hand from his, reaching up to slide it gently around the back of his neck. The heat of that contact sent his pulse racing.

A bit of Adara's usual spunk resurfaced as well, as she whispered playfully, "Well said, soldier. The feeling is mutual. Now, kiss me!"

Atom grinned. As he was commanded, he had to obey. After all, some things one must do for duty and honor.

12.

The next morning, Atom sat at his desk in the security ward office, trying to focus on the overnight reports his staff had saved to his computer. He hummed to himself as he worked. This was the part of the job he liked least, but it was a great day, and nothing could dim his spirits.

Such were his thoughts until just after sixteen hundred hours, when Sergeant Harriman and several troopers marched into the office. Between them trudged two ragged men wearing wrist restraints. Peeking from his cubicle along the starboard wall, Atom looked them over, one eyebrow cocked. "Are these the men you radioed in about? The ones you found upstairs?" he asked.

The sergeant nodded. "Yes, lieutenant. We caught them slinking along the upper deck hallway, keeping to the shadows. They had no escort and no good reason to be there."

"I see." Atom contemplated the captives for a moment. One of them was slight of build, shoulders slumped, with a sullen expression. He kept his gaze directed downward, avoiding eye contact. A quick assessment said that this person was psychologically broken, probably felt that he had nothing to lose. He would play the victim and be reluctant to engage in dialogue.

His companion though…that one had promise. The second man was tall, with a frame that looked like it had once supported considerable muscle, before the effects of prolonged stress and food deprivation had taken their toll. Even now he had an air of strength about him, and his head was held proudly upright, spine straight. He met Atom's gaze defiantly, not looking away even after several seconds. Yes, this one would speak up for himself. Whether he would be truthful, that was another question.

Atom sat back and let the silence extend uncomfortably while he sized up the prisoners. After a minute even the larger fellow was shifting his feet uneasily. When the lieutenant judged the time to be right, he finally spoke. "Would you like to tell me why you were out for a stroll during the sleep cycle?"

As he had expected, the smaller man simply shrugged, his gaze fixed on his shoes. The large civilian grimaced, and then blurted out defiantly, "Why do you think? We've been confined to that damned cargo hold for days, and we're going stir crazy. It's like we're still prisoners! We had our fill of confinement on that Crab ship; we don't need you all treating us the same way."

There was no apology in the man's tone, and the soldier couldn't really blame him. None of the erstwhile captives had had time to recover from their ordeal. Hell, some might never recover. Now they had time to sit and think about their situation, and not much but grey walls to stare at all day. This was a war ship, not a vacation cruiser; the amenities were slim to none.

Nevertheless there was security to consider, and a possible informant sending intel to the Knackers. Atom couldn't let the civilians break the rules, period. He sighed, and said, "I hear you. This ship isn't equipped to keep hundreds of passengers comfortably housed. I'll speak to the captain about trying to get more activities and entertainment options in the cargo hold. But I have to insist that you stay out of restricted areas unless escorted. This is for your own safety as well as the security of the ship."

"What's so dangerous about walking the decks?" the civilian retorted. "And for that matter, what security risk could we pose? Are you actually suggesting that we could be enemy sympathizers? *Us*? Great Ares, man, after what we've been through at the hands of those monsters, you're going to sit there and act like we are a threat to SpaceForce?"

The man's voice was rising in pitch and volume, and the soldiers at his sides tensed themselves for action should the man make a sudden move. He didn't, but simply glared at Atom and growled, "For words like those, I've a good mind to punch you right where you sit."

The lieutenant didn't flinch, nor did he respond with anger in kind. Instead he met the man's gaze levelly, and calmly replied, "The security risk is real, and it doesn't mean any of you is a traitor, not knowingly, at least."

"What the hell do you mean by that?" the man said with a scowl.

"I mean we've rescued people from the hands of the Crabs before this," Atom lied. "The last bunch included a few who had been brainwashed by the enemy; they attempted to sabotage the ship, to blow it up."

"Really?" the man said, taken aback.

"Yes, and the ship's crew remember it all too well. Some of those on security detail have itchy trigger fingers. I don't want you to run into someone who shoots first and thinks later. Hence my comment about your safety. Understand?"

The civilian nodded silently. After a moment he spoke again, more quietly than before. "Okay, we'll play by your rules." The man's eyes met Atom's, and his expression now held a grudging respect. He continued, "In return, I want some assurance that you'll work to improve the conditions in the cargo hold. Some of us are in pretty bad shape, both physically and mentally. We need something to pass the time, to take our minds off things."

Atom smiled and nodded. "I'll see what I can do, sir," he said. Looking to the guards, he told them, "Escort these men back to their quarters, and take the cuffs off before you enter the cargo hold. It won't help morale if the refugees see these men in shackles."

"Yessir," Sgt. Harriman replied, saluting.

As they headed for the door, the smaller civilian finally looked up, meeting Atom's gaze briefly. "Thank you," was all he said.

* * * *

Two days later, the lieutenant met with Captain Dent, to update her on the situation with the refugees. "I'm concerned about the civilians' emotional stability," he said as they sat in the officer's lounge. He took a sip of boroberry juice that originated, ironically, from Nueva Terra, squeezing the liquid pouch as he pondered the problem confronting them.

He swallowed and continued, "So many of the refugees are still struggling to cope with the traumas they've endured. It will be some time yet before they can move on and have normal lives."

"Whatever normal is during times like these," Taramay remarked, shaking her head. "Well, I've talked to the psych staff, and they suggested a couple of diversions that may prove helpful while we're in transit."

"Such as?"

"We've moved a video projector into the cargo bay, and we'll show at least two vids daily, mostly comedies, romances, or light action adventures, escapist stuff to take people's minds off their own troubles."

"Not a bad idea," Atom said with a grin. "I'd like to watch some of those too!"

"When you're off duty, perhaps. Just be sure that everyone on cargo bay detail pays attention to their jobs, and not the movie screen," the captain reminded him.

"Of course," he assured her.

"The medical staff are also organizing some participation games for the civilians."

"Nothing strenuous, I would assume," Atom said.

"Not at all; they're basically games of chance," the captain replied as she grabbed a handful of nuts from the bowl between them. "There will be a master of ceremonies calling out numbers as the civilians play along on their individual gaming boards. Winning combinations get a small prize."

"That sounds promising: get people interacting, entertain them, give them a reward to pursue, all positive things."

"Well, that's the hope anyway," Taramay said with a shrug. "Oh, by the way, I heard how you managed to defuse the situation with the two civilians you caught on E deck. I respect your ability to talk someone down without resorting to physical force. However, I'd ask that you refrain from being overly, umm, creative in your persuasion."

"Ah, yes. You mean the part about prior refugees trying to sabotage the *Goliath?*"

"Exactly," the captain answered, holding Atom's gaze with hers. "It may have been effective, but could just as easily backfire. If any of the civvies happen to mention it to a crew member who has no idea what they're talking about—it wouldn't look good. We can't afford to lose credibility with these people."

"Yes, you're right," Atom said, properly chagrined.

"Of course I am. I'm the captain," Taramay said, grinning to lighten the mood. "Now you must excuse me; I'm off to do more skipperly duties." To Atom's quizzical look she laughed and added, "I'm going to visit little Eve; she's quite taken with me, I think.

She made me promise to come see her today. I don't want to let her down."

"She's a strong kid," Atom commented with a smile. "It's good to see her recovering so well."

"Yes, she's a great little girl, isn't she? 'Bye," Taramay said over her shoulder as she strode out the door. There was a spring in her step, and Atom watched her leave with a calculating grin. The captain's upbeat demeanor reminded him of himself right now; he suspected that little Eve's infatuation wasn't a one-sided affair.

These civilians were certainly making life interesting. As for himself, he wasn't complaining. Not at all. Still smiling, he tossed his empty juice pouch in the recycler, and followed the captain out the door to begin his rounds.

* * * *

The following day the captain met with the head of the psych medics, to review how the refugees were faring. They sat down in the privacy of the medic's office, sipping hot tea from the ubiquitous squeeze pouches that were an intrinsic part of shipboard life. The room was cramped, as compartments on the *Goliath* mostly were, but the doc had found space to adorn the walls with color images of exotic worlds, both inhabited and inhospitable. His desk top was cluttered with digital patient charts and pocket-sized medical instruments, plus a handful of family photos.

Taramay knew that the doctor hailed from one of the human core worlds, which to date had remained untouched by the Knackers. This meant that the adults and children in the pictures likely still lived. Taramay found reassurance in those tiny images of normalcy, so at odds with the landscape of war that made up her own existence. She forced her attention back to the medic as he spoke.

"Most of the civilians are physically improving," Dr. Roman began, scanning a digi-pad that sat on the table between them. "Their mental and emotional states are more in flux, and some will be slow in regaining their ability to function productively."

"Any severe pathologies noted?" the captain asked. "We've had a few run-ins with civvies who were confrontational and borderline aggressive."

"No psychoses diagnosed, if that's what you mean," the medic said, shaking his head. "Lots of depression, anger, alienation, the usual. Ironically we're also battling some cases of anorexia."

"No kidding?" Taramay said in surprise. "I'd have thought that gluttony would be the issue, now that food is abundant."

"We've had some civvies taking full advantage of the chow lines," the doctor agreed, chuckling. "But the captives on the pyramid were underfed for weeks, and they had to ration food, with preference given to the young and infirm. That habit, coupled with a good dose of survivor guilt, has made it difficult for some civilians, particularly young women, to become comfortable with unrestricted food intake again. We're counseling them, and they're gradually improving."

"What a mess," Taramay said with a grimace. "Even the survivors can end up as casualties, one way or the other."

"Too true," Dr. Roman agreed.

"On another subject," the captain said, "I'm worried about the security breach we suffered soon after the refugees were brought on board. Have you found any evidence of subversive thoughts or actions among the civilians?"

The doc shook his head emphatically. "Not at all. There is a nearly universal reaction of fear and loathing whenever the subject of the Crabs is brought up. All the civilians answered the standard battery of security questions with physio monitors employed; we'd have detected any conscious deception on their part."

"How about subconscious?" Taramay pressed. "Could someone have been brainwashed so that they would commit such an act without being aware of it?"

"Yes, that is theoretically possible," the doctor conceded. "If one of the refugees did send that illicit message, then I think that's what you're looking for: a spy who doesn't know he's spying."

"Which will make it even harder to find the culprit," Taramay concluded grimly. "They'll not act guilty or suspicious if they don't know what they're doing."

"True. But there may be other markers of mental manipulation. I'd watch for unusual behaviors, even if they seem trivial or of little consequence. These might provide clues as to who's been psychologically altered."

"That sounds pretty thin," the captain said, scowling. "Have you or your staff noted anything odd so far?"

"Behaviorally? Sure, there's all sorts of 'odd' in that cargo hold right now, but nothing unexpected, given the history of recent trauma. Our psych evaluations stumbled upon an unusual talent, but that's about it."

"Talent?" the captain asked, her curiosity piqued.

"Yes, one of the children demonstrated remarkable recall, basically an eidetic memory. It's a very rare ability."

Taramay smiled knowingly and said, "You don't have to tell me. I've already seen that talent at work, myself. Eve recited most of a book chapter to me, word for word. She's quite the young lady."

"Eve?" the doctor said, frowning. "No, that's not the child I meant." He flipped through his digital log, muttering to himself. After a short search, his finger tapped the screen. "There. Yes, I thought I had it right. Alma Pindor, an eleven year old girl from Nueva Terra, orphaned from what we can gather. She was able to recite the *Goliath*'s entire book of regulations governing non-combatant passengers." The doctor looked up from his log, adding, "That's nearly fifty pages of rather boring text."

Taramay felt a small alarm bell going off in the back of her mind as she absorbed the medic's words. After a moment she brought herself to ask, "Just how rare is that ability, if I may ask?"

"Currently it's thought to occur in less than one in five hundred thousand humans, regardless of planet of origin," he answered. "Are you certain that Eve demonstrated this type of memory?"

The captain nodded silently, eyeing the doctor steadily.

"That is incredible," he said at last, shaking his head.

Taramay thought of something. "Is there any chance that the two girls are related?"

"That's a good question." The doctor consulted his records for a while, looking up both girls' medical findings. "No...there are few shared genetic markers between the two. That rules out natural heredity or cloning." He looked up at Taramay again. "The odds against this occurring naturally are incalculable. You do understand the implications here?"

The captain nodded reluctantly. "The girls may have been modified in some way."

Dr. Roman said, "Yes. The question is, by whom, and to what purpose?"

"I think we can guess who is responsible. But why..." Taramay bit her lip. She could imagine several possibilities, but she needed more information. "I want to know how many colonists have eidetic memories, especially adults. There must be some way of assessing that, without making people suspicious."

The doctor nodded thoughtfully. "Hmmm. We could add a memory game to our daily contests. That should identify those with good recall. I can devise other tests once we narrow the field."

"Then do it," the captain ordered. "I want answers before we reach our destination."

* * * *

At fourteen hundred hours that day Taramay marched onto the bridge, her thoughts in a jumble from recent revelations. As she scanned the room, Lt. Cotton motioned her over to his station. When she approached, the tech officer said, "I've been getting faint scanner readings sporadically, something far out, pacing us and shadowing our movements."

The captain grunted. "Ghost images?"

"That's what I thought, at first. Hyperspace scans are always prone to interference and ghosting. But I ran some diagnostic programs, algorithms designed to blank out phase shift reflections and other anomalies."

"Can you do that? I thought there was no way to rule out false imaging in hyperspace flight," Taramay asked, surprised.

"This is fairly new stuff, programs aimed at mathematically differentiating real data from artifact. We run deep space scans in different energy frequencies, which should produce varying anomalies, and cross reference them with analytic equations to eliminate those readings which do not repeat..." Bruce began.

"Okay, I don't need all the technical details; I trust you know your stuff," Taramay said, smiling. "If it helps us detect the enemy, I like it. So what are you seeing?"

"Well, for the past few days, I've picked up a very weak and sporadic signal contact with a possible object trailing us in hyperspace," Bruce stated. He tapped his fingers on his console, his brow furrowed as he illustrated reams of calculations on the screen. "It took me an entire day of analysis to rule out scanner ghosting with a decent degree of certainty. What remains is a 93% probability that the images are real."

"And the images show…?" the captain prompted.

"Best I can tell, the mass and energy signature is consistent with a Knacker destroyer-class vessel."

Taramay cursed under her breath. "Closing distance with us?" she inquired, reflexively glancing up at the main viewscreen, though it was a pointless effort.

"No, it is staying at extreme distance, just beyond normal scanner reception. We're lucky to have detected it at all; the *Goliath*'s scanners, like much of her equipment, are an upgrade over standard hardware."

"So it's shadowing us, then," she concluded with a nod. "Seeing where we're going, perhaps, or…" Taramay stood up straight as another thought occurred to her. "…or they're staying within range to easily pick up transmissions from our ship."

The tech officer looked surprised. "That's an interpretation I hadn't thought of—but I suspect you're correct, Captain. It would explain my findings better than anything I've come up with."

The captain clapped him on the shoulder. "Good work, Bruce. I'm learning that it pays to have young officers trained with the latest methodology. Keep it up, and call me if anything changes."

He grinned and nodded. "Will do, Captain."

As Lt. Cotton turned back to his console, Taramay wheeled and strode quickly to the bridge exit. She was tired of waiting for events to play out; some positive action was needed or she would end up climbing the walls.

As she walked the main corridor leading away from the control center, her mind spun with possibilities. What was going to happen next? And what could she do about it? She passed the open entrance to the officers' mess, oblivious to the lively sounds of laughter and conversation flowing into the hallway. On past the medical wing, rest rooms, and other doorways she went, heading toward the *Goliath*'s stern.

The echoes of life faded behind, leaving only the quiet hum of the ship and the muffled thuds of her shoes on the soft-grip flooring. She paused finally when she came to the main elevator. There she stood for a moment, indecisive, before thumbing the button and stepping into the lift. Once inside, she selected the lowest level and waited, her shoulders squared, face set in a determined expression.

The doors opened at the bottom deck, and she turned right toward the cargo hold. A cacophony of noise filtered out through the open doors as she entered the bay. It had been nearly two weeks since the refugees had first arrived. In that time some notable changes had taken place in their makeshift living quarters.

The sleeping section with its rows of cots was mostly the same, but tables were now set up in an adjacent open area. People were seated at many of them, apparently playing some sort of board games. A crew member stood at a podium at one end of the room, barking out letter and number combinations at intervals. "C-9!" he spoke as Taramay stopped and watched.

His pronouncement was followed by a flurry of activity and exclamations at the tables; everyone seemed to be playing the same game. The murmur of voices engaged in conversation filled the air, and the tones seemed amicable.

The captain smiled and glanced around the rest of the large room. A vid was playing on a large screen near the back, where lights had been dimmed to facilitate viewing. Quite a number of passengers were seated in chairs arrayed in front of the screen. Hands on her hips, Taramay nodded to herself with satisfaction; people were recovering from their ordeal slowly but surely.

She wound her way along the now-familiar path toward Eve's bunk, and found the youngster, as usual, stretched out on her cot, intently reading from her digi-pad. But the girl dropped it the moment she saw her visitor, squealing with delight, "Captain Taramay! I've been waiting for you to visit!" The girl bounced up to a sitting position and snapped off a military salute.

Taramay laughed out loud and returned the gesture, saying, "How's Corporal Eve today?"

The girl grinned hugely. "I've got a promotion?! I was a private last week!"

"Well, I think you've earned a raise in rank, based on good behavior and how much you've learned," Taramay replied, smiling.

"I've been studying all about Eden, that's where we're going to live now," the girl stated in a serious tone. "It's a pretty place, and has lots of people and cities and spaceports and stuff. Big forests with wild animals too! Some are ferocious and dangerous."

"Yes, I've heard about them. Big black creatures, deadly hunters, what are they called…?"

"*Groons*!" Eve answered enthusiastically. "They're one of my favorites!"

"As long as you don't meet one in person," Taramay warned, holding up a cautionary finger.

"Oh yes, they'd be very scary to see up close!" the child agreed, nodding emphatically. "But they're fun to read about!"

"Say, do you want to go for a walk on the upper levels?" the captain asked. "We can see out into hyperspace, and go to the officers' dining hall; the food is different than what you can get down here."

"Yes, ma'am!" Eve replied with another salute.

"Okay, c'mon then!" The girl didn't need any more encouragement, and she quickly slipped into her shoes and skipped across the cargo bay ahead of the captain.

They spent the afternoon touring the sights on the upper decks, and eating dinner and dessert in the officers' mess. After their meal they made their way to the captain's quarters, where they lounged on the bed talking. "Wow, I'm really full!" Eve proclaimed, rubbing her stomach. "That chocolate mountain mousse was bigger than I expected!"

"You finished it, though," Taramay observed.

"Yeah, it was too good to waste any. I haven't had chocolate since I left Nueva Terra."

Taramay's ears perked up. She had been waiting for an opportunity to broach the girl's past life, but it had to be done carefully. If Eve was sending information back to the Crabs (which the captain personally didn't believe), then any suspicious line of questioning could reveal to the enemy that humans were aware of the spies.

At the same time, Taramay needed to learn all she could about Eve and any other humans with unusual abilities. Were they the source of the security breach? Or did they know something about other refugees that might help identify the culprits? She had to find out.

"Did you get to eat at restaurants much on Nueva Terra? Or did you mostly eat at home?" the captain asked casually.

The girl's expression darkened and she hesitated before answering, "Mostly at home."

"That sounds nice! Were your parents good cooks? Did they

make chocolate desserts for you?"

Eve nodded silently, her features working. Taramay watched the emotions warring on the child's face, the fleeting smile at the mention of desserts quickly overshadowed by anguish. It looked like Eve was close to tears. The captain felt a rush of pity for the girl, and altered her line of questioning.

"How about school? You're a smart lady. I'll bet you had an easy time in class."

The child's response was unexpected. "Nah, I never liked school much. It was fun making friends, but I hated classwork, having to learn all that stuff, studying for hours, doing homework instead of playing or reading something fun."

Taramay fought to hide her surprise, saying, "Well, I was much the same way when I was in school. I learned a lot of important things, but I sure didn't like the work it took!"

Eve smiled at the shared sentiment, and she held out her hands for a hug. The captain obliged, and they snuggled like that for a minute. Once she felt the girl's body relaxing, Taramay gently prodded once more. "You can talk about your family if you want, Eve. You know you can tell me anything. I'd love to hear more about your life, and what it was like growing up on Nueva Terra."

Eve tensed up once again, and she was silent for a long run of seconds. Taramay wished she could see the child's face, but it was hidden, buried against the shoulder of her uniform. Finally, Eve spoke, but the captain had to strain to hear the words. "I don't like talking about my family. It makes me sad."

"Because they're gone?" the captain asked quietly.

No reply, just a gentle movement as the child nodded.

Taramay hesitated, then continued, "How did you survive? Were you somewhere else when the Knackers came?"

"No! I was right there," Eve blurted out. "The Crabs came to our house, and we hid in the basement. They found us anyway. You can't hide from them." Her small hands were now clenched in Taramay's uniform, gripping tightly.

"They took your family captive?"

Eve's voice became very faint. "No…when the monsters came, papa said it was better to die than be taken by them. We had guns. We fought. And the Crabs killed mama and papa. I saw it. I saw it…."

Tiny sobs racked the girl's body now, and Taramay felt moisture on her shoulder where tears soaked the fabric. She held on as Eve let out her pent-up grief, wishing she could purge it all, pull out the sorrow and the terrible memories and make the girl whole again.

Sadly, the reality of the human mind was not that simple, and Eve might never be who she once could have been. Taramay could only hold on and ride out the storm, murmuring soothing sounds in Eve's ear. She stroked the child's head, softly, slowly, until gradually the cries tapered off and faded to silence.

Finally Eve pulled back and looked at Taramay. Her little face was smudged and tear-streaked, but her expression was calm, almost blank. She said dully, "I think I was supposed to die too; papa said he would make sure the monsters didn't get me. When they came, he pointed his gun at me, but he didn't shoot right away, and the Crabs killed him before he could do anything. I'm—I'm not supposed to be alive. I'm supposed to be with my family."

Taramay cupped the girl's face in her hands, saying, "No, no, Eve, you're supposed to live, do you hear me? That's why your father couldn't kill you. He only wanted to protect you. And that's what my job is, to protect people from bad things. This whole ship is built to do that. It's very powerful; it's what allowed me to rescue you from that Crab pyramid."

She leaned in and kissed the youngster on the forehead. "I'll protect you, Eve, because I care about you very much. You're my little angel, and I'll watch over you."

Eve looked up at her, and her face now held a glimmer of hope. She spoke just one word. "Always?"

Taramay hesitated only for a second. Gazing into those elfin eyes, with Eve's expression so vulnerable at that moment, there was no way she could deny the child. "Always, I promise."

13.

The strident sound of her personal communicator woke Taramay out of a sound sleep. She swam upward out of a half-remembered dream and pawed for the source of the noise. A glance at her wrist com said the time was just after three hundred hours in the morning. She groaned; this had better be important.

She licked her lips and swallowed, trying to lose the cotton in her mouth, and croaked into her com, "Yes, what is it?"

"Captain, this is Lt. Atwater on the bridge. We have an urgent situation."

Taramay blinked and sat up in bed. "Fill me in."

"Another unauthorized transmission just occurred, on the lower deck."

"Did the security cam catch anything?" the captain asked, her pulse racing.

"Yes…the perpetrator."

"I'm on my way. Give me five minutes. Captain out."

A short time later, Taramay stood on the hushed bridge with the night shift officers, watching a security video playing out on the viewscreen. Her navigator and first officer from day shift had also joined them.

The camera view was aligned down the main passageway on the lower deck, not far from a wall-mounted computer relay terminal. This access point allowed crew members from the lower levels of the ship to interface with *Goliath*'s main system functions, including the communications array.

The vid was recorded during the ship's night cycle, so the lighting was muted. For a minute the dark corridor stood empty, then a ghostly figure appeared in the distance, slowly moving closer. The individual seemed to be clothed in a pale sleeping suit, and wasn't making any attempt to be stealthy. Indeed, the hazy form moved straight down the center of the hallway. As it neared they could see that it moved with an odd shambling gait, arms limp at the person's sides.

"Wow, that is creepy," one of the officers commented in hushed tones as they watched.

Now the figure moved near enough for them to make out details, and Taramay gasped in surprise and dismay. There was no mistaking it; the person on camera was Eve.

The captain could feel eyes on her as the crew came to the same realization. She clenched her jaw, resolutely fixing her gaze on the viewscreen. Onward the girl shuffled, until she was only a few meters from the camera. She halted, then slowly turned to face the wall terminal.

"How does she know the protocols to access our systems?" Lt. DeBartolo wondered aloud.

Taramay found her voice. "She's got an eidetic memory. I suppose she could learn anything she was allowed to read, instantly."

"But look, she's not even using the touch screen. Her hands are at her sides," another officer interjected.

Sure enough, the small figure just stood there, staring at the terminal, then leaned forward until her head touched the screen. Like a tilted statue she remained in that position, arms dangling, motionless.

After maybe a minute she pulled back, and turned to shamble away down the corridor toward the cargo bay. The video went blank a moment later.

Collectively the officers on deck released their held breaths and pulled their gazes from the viewscreen. Inevitably most eyes came to bear on the captain. Silence reigned for a moment, until Taramay cleared her throat. She drew a deep breath, and kept her voice firm as she said, "The transmission came from that terminal, at exactly that moment?"

Lt. Atwater said, "Yes, we confirmed it."

The captain sighed, and looked around at the night crew on the bridge. "Now we know," she said. "The Crabs have used the youngest, the most innocent of us to do their bidding. This is unacceptable. I want a full meeting of all top officers today, at twelve hundred hours. Make sure our intel and psych divisions are represented. We have a lot to consider."

"Should we confine the girl to quarters?" the first officer asked.

"No. No, I don't want to give away the fact that we know what's happened," the captain said. "We'll prevent all refugee access to sensitive areas of the *Goliath*, especially the bridge and engineering. If asked, say it's just standard procedure. Do not discuss ship operations around any civilians. Any further plans will be formulated at the security meeting."

Taramay paused, wearily rubbing her eyes. A thought struck her, and she added, "I want the chief medical officer at my quarters in ten minutes; I've got some tests I want the doc to perform before the meeting. After I meet with him, I'm heading back to bed to get some sleep; I suggest the other day-shift people do the same. I want you fresh and alert when we conference. Night crew, as you were."

The bridge officers saluted the captain as she left for her quarters.

* * * *

At precisely twelve hundred hours the captain sat in the conference room, with ten of her high level staff arrayed around the long table. Besides the day shift bridge officers (and some of the night crew as well), other notables included Atom Granger, as the acting head of security; the chief intel analyst, Maraya Ahman; and the chief psych clinician, Eli Roman.

"Let's begin," Taramay said, looking around at the assembled staff. "We all know what has occurred in the past twelve hours, and we know what's at stake. To summarize, we've now had two security breaches in the form of unauthorized pulse transmissions. Both occurred after we rescued the human survivors from the alien pyramid.

"The signals were directed back toward the Cluster rim, which we believe is Crab territory. Mr. Cotton has informed me of a probable scanner contact at the limits of our detection range, suggesting an alien destroyer pacing us. I suspect that ship is keeping its position in order to intercept these rogue transmissions from our ship. Last night, security cameras caught a young refugee girl apparently interfacing with a lower deck computer terminal. The timing of that event coincides with the latest transmission."

"So we have identified at least one perpetrator," Lt. Granger concluded.

"Yes. A summary of pertinent data from various departments has been uploaded to your viewscreens. What I need now is your input and discussion. There are a lot of questions needing answers. We also have to form a plan of action. I'm open to ideas from any and all."

"I have one question," the navigator spoke up. "I understand that refugees could be manipulated by the enemy to be spies. What I want to know is how? How can a little girl interface with our computers *and* get through security protocols to send a transmission? How did she do so without even using her hands? I've seen a lot of crazy things during this war, but that video…what I saw was really bizarre."

A chorus of assents arose from around the table. Taramay looked to the chief medic. "Dr. Lott, did you get the tests run as I ordered?"

He nodded. "I obtained a brain scan on Eve this morning, using a hand-held portable unit. She didn't even have to leave her cot."

The captain asked, "Were you careful to hide your agenda?"

"Yes, I also did a whole-body scan on Eve plus a handful of refugees in the same row of bunks, under the guise of general check-ups."

"What were your findings?"

"Well, the routine security scans had already shown no tech implants in any of the refugees. But this scan was aimed at detecting soft tissue anomalies in the brain, and—we found one."

Murmurs erupted around the table, and the captain held up her hand for silence. "What was it?" she asked.

"There is a mass, approximately 1.5 centimeters in diameter, situated between the pons and hippocampus."

"In English, doc," the navigator piped up.

The medic scratched the grey stubble of his military haircut. "Well, the…growth, for lack of a better term, sits in the lower, more 'primitive' area of the brain, a region not associated with conscious thought. The structures it lies adjacent to are interesting. The pons is associated with sleep regulation, and the hippocampus is involved with learning and memory."

"It looked like Eve was sleep walking on that video; is it possible she wasn't conscious when the event took place?" Taramay asked.

"Possible, yes," the doc nodded. "I can't say for sure. Can you play the video in question?"

"Mr. Granger?" the captain said, glancing toward the security chief.

"One moment…here it is," Atom said as he tapped controls on the viewscreen set into the table surface in front of him. Similar screens were arrayed around the table for the attendees to access, and within a few seconds they all lit up with the video images of the previous night. The doctor leaned forward with interest as Eve came into view and approached the camera.

"Yes…see how she walks, very simple movements, no use of nonessential muscle groups such as her arms. Can you freeze the image there?"

Atom's fingers flew, and the vid halted with a frontal view of the girl facing the camera.

"Good," Dr. Lott said, nodding. "Now zoom in on her face, if you would."

Atom complied, and Eve's countenance swelled in the view field until she appeared to be gazing directly out of their viewscreens.

"Yes! Yes, look at her eyes and face," the doctor proclaimed excitedly. "No expression, no muscle tone at all, just like her arms. She looks like a person hypnotized. Dr. Roman, any thoughts?"

The chief psychiatrist nodded. "I agree. Her condition right then was likely very similar to somnambulance, er, sleepwalking. I suspect she has no recollection of the events of that night."

"Okay, so she did this unconsciously, I can accept that," Lt. DeBartolo said. "But how did she interface with our systems?"

"That's a more difficult question to answer," Dr. Lott said, shaking his head. "You'll notice that she put her head in direct contact with the computer terminal. I suspect that this mass of abnormal tissue in the brain, besides allowing a hypnotic state, also is able to generate some sort of electromagnetic field which interacts with our circuitry."

"How do you mean?" the captain asked, looking bemused.

"Well, she may be able to *think* her way into the computer, in a manner of speaking," the doctor answered.

"What?" Leofric snorted. "How could she do that? Interface with a completely foreign machine intelligence?"

"I'm not sure, not sure at all," the doctor admitted. "Please understand that this is beyond anything our technology can achieve, and as such, my interpretations are strictly hypothetical at this point. One possibility is that she has been taught specific protocols in order to evade our security algorithms. The Crabs have had ample time to study our computer tech via captured equipment. Memorizing digital data bundles would be very challenging, but an eidetic memory would make it easier to achieve. Or, Eve may interact with the computer more instinctively, by feel, and somehow convince the system to let her in."

"Well, however it was accomplished, there's no doubt that it happened," the captain concluded. "I'm curious; do you think her enhanced memory is also related to the brain mass?"

"Yes, I do," the doctor answered. "The abnormal tissue is adjacent to, and conjoined with, the hippocampus, a structure involved in learning and memory functions. Eidetic memory occurs naturally only in rare cases. In those individuals, the talent is often accompanied by certain genetic markers, similar to those associated with some forms of autism. In the children we've identified so far with eidetic memories, none have had the predictive genetic codes one would expect to see. I think the enhanced memory was created, not innate. All in all, it's a very elegant piece of bioengineering."

"Of course! That would fit with what I've observed with Eve," Taramay exclaimed. "Now it makes more sense."

"Explain," Dr. Lott said.

"Well, I was asking Eve about her life on Nueva Terra, trying to see if she had regular childhood memories, or was she a blank slate," the captain explained. "She was able to tell me about her family and about school. What surprised me was that she didn't find her education easy; in fact she hated the amount of effort and studying that it took. She sounded just like a normal kid, who had to work hard to learn the materials. Not at all what I'd expect from someone with perfect recall."

"True," the doctor agreed. "The question is, what does that mean? It could be that these children were created in a lab, artificially grown for a purpose, and implanted with false memories to make them seem normal. You may have stumbled upon an oversight, wherein the Crabs were so concerned with their creations appearing 'average,' that they implanted memories inconsistent with the child's true abilities."

"Do you really think that the children are…artificial?" Taramay asked, dismayed.

"No," the doctor replied. "It's possible, but that's the pessimistic view. In my opinion, it is more likely that Eve began life as a normal human and has been modified. In that case, she wasn't always who she is now, either in ability or emotional state. The latter goes without saying, I suppose. As with all the refugees, trauma has likely taken its toll on her to some degree."

"That much is certain," Taramay sighed. "Damn. There is a lot to consider here. Let me know if you learn anything more about what was done to the children. I need to know as much as I can. Right now I'm not even sure how to feel about them. They seem to be sweet kids, but if they're weapons grown in an alien laboratory…I just don't know." Her voice tapered off as she shook her head in frustration, looking down at her hands on the table.

An uneasy quiet reigned for a handful of seconds, finally broken by someone clearing his throat. Pulling herself together, Taramay looked around at the assembled officers. Somber gazes met hers, but none held any answers. They were all waiting for their captain to lead.

She gathered her thoughts, and forced herself to say, "Okay, we know Eve has sent at least one message, likely to the Crabs. Let's discuss our next concern: do we know its content?"

The com officer, Lt. Stepanovich, spoke up. "Yes, we do. It was a compressed transmission, but easily decrypted. The data it contains is odd, mostly a mix of still images of viewscreens and shipboard equipment, plus recordings of conversations. Surprisingly, officers are featured much more than the refugees in the cargo bay, despite her spending most of her time with her peers. It seems that her experiences were edited somehow, focusing on interactions with people in positions of power. How the Crabs accomplished that, I can't say. There's quite a bit of footage from her visit to the bridge."

"Ah yes, that's on me," Taramay admitted sheepishly. "I trusted her; who would suspect a harmless little girl?"

The psychiatrist interjected, "This may be precisely why they chose children; you'd never have allowed an adult you barely know to wander the bridge. Instead we have fresh-faced youngsters who are innocent and vulnerable. In addition they all possess attractive facial contours, and slightly larger than average eyes, traits that tend to foster positive emotional reactions in adult humans. This includes a parental nurturing instinct, the desire to protect the child."

Taramay felt a pang of dismay as she recognized that exact response within herself. The emotion quickly turned to anger. The idea that her feelings had been manipulated, even if that was only a small factor in her relationship with Eve, made her feel violated. Along with everything else the Knackers had done to humanity, she could now add their callous use of these young innocents as additional motivation. She would make them pay for this, even if it cost her own life to see it happen.

She forced her attention back to the conversation around the table. "...know the content on the viewscreens when Eve observed them?" Lt. Cotton was asking. The tech officer had been one of those with whom Eve had spent considerable time during her bridge tour.

"Nothing critically sensitive," the first officer replied. "No star maps of our home systems, no detailed specs on our ship. Mostly just scanner readouts, maintenance reports, things of a routine nature."

"Maybe we're okay then," Lt. Debartolo said, "but we should play through every conversation Eve picked up, every image she recorded, in case someone let important information slip."

"How about the other children?" Lt. Stepanovich inquired. "Could they be sending messages as well?"

"We don't know," the first officer replied. "Security cams were down during the first incident. It's hard to say who sent that one."

"Well, I can say it probably wasn't Eve," the captain stated.

"How so?" Lt. Granger asked.

"Because at that time she was laid up with a major leg injury, and could barely walk."

Atom smacked his forehead in disgust. "Yes, right, I knew that."

"So that means at least two children have actively participated in the espionage," Lt. Debartolo concluded grimly.

"Yes, Lef, and more may soon join in," Taramay replied. "Dr. Roman, how many have you found so far?"

The doctor ticked off names on his fingers "So far we know of three children with superior recall, namely Eve, Alma Pindor, and a young boy we just identified via the memory contest we set up. His name is Jozeph Karnell." He lowered his hands and added, "No adults have demonstrated enhanced abilities to date."

"It's a good start," Taramay commented, "but we need to find every person who's been compromised. The crew tell me that not all the refugees participate in the memory games. Any other ideas for detecting modified civilians?"

"Well, obviously tissue-scanning them, as I did today with Eve," Dr. Roman suggested. "I did most of the children on her row today; I can prioritize juveniles and get most of them scanned in the next 48 hours."

"Excellent," Taramay said. "Do it, but carefully. Avoid suspicion at all cost."

"Why be stealthy?" Lt. Stepanovich inquired. "We're going to deny the children access to our computer terminals, right? So what does it matter?"

The navigator knew the captain better, and he grinned slyly. "You're up to something, aren't you?" he asked, looking straight at Taramay.

She gave him a faint smile in return. "Maybe, Lef. For now I want to keep all our options open. Including sending false intel to the Crabs in the future. That could prove invaluable to us. But if they think the children are compromised, that option is lost."

"False intel…you want to use those kids as weapons?" the com officer said, aghast.

"Only if I can do so without harming them, Alena," Taramay assured her. "Their welfare matters to me, as you should know." Noting her subordinate's look of anxiety, the captain narrowed her eyes, and said, "Tell me, why the sudden concern? You've never paid much attention to civilians we've rescued before, regardless of their age."

"There's one in particular she's concerned with, I think," Atom stated, recalling the child he had seen walking the corridors with the com officer.

Alena blushed, and said, "Yes, well, I've become friends with one girl, and she's very sweet and kind. It makes me feel for all of them, and I don't want to see them used any more, by us or the enemy."

"I understand fully," the captain told her. "I will not let them come to harm."

Dr. Roman spoke up. "Just out of curiosity, what is the name of the girl you've befriended?"

"Lexa Bandon," Alena replied.

The doctor consulted his notes, muttering, "Twelve years old, orphaned…have you scanned her yet, Dr. Lott?"

The other clinician shook his head.

Dr. Roman looked at Alena and said, "I'd request that you play some memory game with little Lexa, or perhaps ask her about something she's read in the past, a fun book for instance. See how acute her recall is. I don't think she's participated in the games in the cargo bay as of yet."

He looked around the table. "Have any more of you been making friends with refugee children? Be honest; this could be important."

Two other officers slowly raised their hands. "Ah, good," the doctor said. "Give me their names after the meeting is concluded; I want to investigate a bit further."

"What are you thinking?" Taramay asked, frowning.

"Nothing certain yet, just a hunch. Based on the profiles of the children we've discussed, I've got some ideas that may help detect our little spies. But I need more data to be confident in my analysis. I'll let you know when I know."

"Fair enough," the captain replied. "Now that our first order of business has been covered, I want an update on the intel from the Knacker pyramid. What have we gleaned from our analysis to date?"

Lt. Maraya Ahman straightened in her chair. Her lustrous black hair hung straight but short in a regulation cut, framing a petite oval face set with expressive dark eyes. Her olive skin tones complemented the green of her Intelligence Division smock as if it were a planned stylistic choice.

She consulted her screen momentarily, then began, "We've not attempted to read the files downloaded from the pyramid's main computer. Space Command will do that once we've returned.

"However, we've been able to collate the scanner data and personal observations of the troops during their time aboard the alien vessel. It's allowed us to analyze the Knacker movements in response to our incursion. An unusual pattern of behavior was detected, which did not fit the enemy's typical combat protocols."

"I thought as much," Atom commented, nodding.

"Can you draw any conclusions from the analysis?" the captain prompted.

"Yes. Several findings stood out as peculiar. First, the aliens made no attempt to attack our troops when they entered and explored the pyramid, until they reached the section where the prisoners were held. One could argue that the Crabs were unaware of our presence until then, but this seems unlikely. Their destroyer was waiting nearby and alert to our presence, and their soldiers' scanner technology is at least the equal of ours. They had to know we'd boarded, but they waited a long time to respond.

"Secondly, the aliens were spread out haphazardly through the pyramid, not in good defensive positions, other than the small contingent near the holding cells."

"Any idea why?" the navigator asked.

"Yes, lieutenant. The most logical interpretation of the data is that the Crabs were positioned to minimize unwanted incursions into other areas of the pyramid, while allowing us to access the prison cells."

"Then why did they have a contingent guarding the cells?" Taramay wondered aloud.

"To maintain the appearance of resistance, most likely," the intel officer answered.

"If you're right, then our guess was correct and they wanted us to rescue the civilians," the captain said. "However, trickery isn't the Knackers' usual *modus operandi*. How certain are you about this?"

Lt. Ahman shrugged. "All the data support this conclusion. Once the prisoners were acquired by our troops, the Knackers made token attacks to keep us moving, but quickly withdrew each time, even when they had a positional advantage. Our soldiers' line of retreat was never cut off. Instead, the aliens actually seemed to be funneling us back to the shuttles and off the pyramid. Just enough pressure was exerted to keep us in a defensive mode and prevent a thorough examination of their ship. The intent was never to defeat us."

"No time to think, no time for us to deviate from the Crabs' agenda," Taramay mused.

"Exactly. Their destroyer's slow-paced attack on the *Goliath* also fits this model, not crippling us, but keeping us rushed and off-balance, and forcing us to leave as soon as the refugees were in hand."

"That explains why they chased my butt off the ship but never shot at me," Atom chuckled. "I thought I was just lucky."

"You were," Lt. Ahman asserted. "Almost certainly they were unaware that you had hacked their mainframe computer. If they had known, you would have never been allowed to leave."

"Unless the stolen info was false, and they wanted that re-trieved as well," the first officer threw out.

"Unfortunately, that's a possibility we can't ignore. However, I think it's unlikely to be falsified," the intel officer responded. "The Crabs pushed our troops into a hurried retreat; they probably never anticipated anyone having the time or ability to download their data banks."

"They forced us to detour when they shut that damned blast door," Atom growled. "Sounds pretty deliberate to me."

Lt. Ahman shook her head. "That door was closed during your retreat, probably to keep your squads from heading back into the pyramid. It was just blind chance that a few of you were trapped on the wrong side of the barrier. That obliged you to take a side route which led you to the ship's control room. I don't think the enemy could have predicted that eventuality."

"Speaking of the detour, I still don't know why I survived my encounter with that Knacker warrior," Atom said, shaking his head. "It had me dead to rights. I was an armed soldier, even though I wasn't holding my weapon at the time. Crabs usually fire first when up against a human combatant. It's simple self-preservation."

"Yes, I found your report intriguing," the intel officer said. "I wanted to ask you more about that incident. You say you weren't holding your weapon at that moment. Why not? What exactly *were* you doing?"

"Hmmm. I had slung my rifle over my shoulder, so that I could pick up an injured civilian. I was holding her when I turned to face the Crab..."

"Was the civilian in question," Lt. Ahman glanced down at her screen, "Eve Coventine?"

Atom sighed. "Yes, that was her."

The intel officer spread her hands. "I think this is another affirmation of the Crabs' agenda. They wanted us to rescue the captives. More specifically, they wanted us to rescue *her*. And the others who are like her. They had invested considerable effort in engineering those children. Killing one with a plasma rifle would have been…counterproductive. Hence your life was spared."

"We've been puppets doing the masters' bidding all along," the navigator commented sardonically.

"Not entirely, Lef," Taramay reminded him. She looked around at the dismayed countenances of those at the table. Grinning, she wagged her finger and said, "Don't forget, we got a massive load of data from their ship's mainframe. Ms. Ahman here seems to think it's the real thing. And we blew both the pyramid and a Knacker destroyer into stardust. Not a bad bit of work for puppets, eh?"

Lt. Ahman spoke up once more, "Oh, I forgot to mention: the scans we made of the alien destroyer during our firefight showed no human presence aboard. That ship hadn't taken any captives from the pyramid."

"Then we didn't interrupt the Knackers while they were retrieving their spoils," Taramay said. "They had offloaded their soldiers and prisoners long before we arrived. The destroyer was simply waiting for us."

"Yes, Captain, so it would appear."

"Well, now we know what we're up against," Taramay declared. She shook her head, saying, "I never would have thought the Knackers would get this devious. They've always seemed to rely on numbers, and superior military technology, to achieve victory."

"Our recent successes against them must have pushed them to get more creative," the intel officer suggested. "These children— they are an entirely new sort of weapon in this conflict."

"A *weapon*," Leofric muttered to himself, frowning.

"Mr. DeBartolo, you have something to add?" the captain asked.

The navigator slowly looked up with a dumbfounded expression. "An idea just came to me," he said. "You recall our mission parameters?"

"Yes, of course. Why?"

"What was the final, highly-classified directive you revealed to us?"

"Space Command wanted us to gather any intel we could on a possible new secret weapon the enemy was developing…" Her voice trailed off as the realization hit her, and she stared back at the navigator. When she spoke it was barely more than a whisper. "We've found it, haven't we?"

14.

After the conference ended, Taramay took Atom Granger aside to a corner of the room, where they could converse in relative privacy. "Lieutenant, we really need to identify all the refugees who have been altered by the Crabs," she began. "I know you have spent time with Adara Knightsbridge. Do you think she is trustworthy?"

"Yes, I'd stake my life on it," Atom replied.

"I trust your judgment. Unfortunately, we now know that someone could be genuine and still be unconsciously aiding the enemy. But I had Dr. Lott scan Adara along with Eve, and she had no visible brain anomalies. I think we're going to have to take a chance here, and ask for her help."

"What did you have in mind?" Atom asked.

Taramay said, "I seem to recall you mentioning that Adara had looked after the children in her prison cell."

"Yes, she did." The lieutenant raised an eyebrow as understanding dawned. "Do you think she might know something that can help us?"

"Possibly. She spent a lot of time with them, so she may have noticed if they exhibited any unusual behaviors or abilities. I want to meet with her and see what she can tell us."

"I'd like to be there," Atom said. "She knows me and will be more comfortable if I'm involved."

"I agree. Let's meet here at fifteen hundred hours," the captain decided. "Use discretion and be sure Adara does the same. We don't want any other civvies to be aware of what's up."

At the appointed time Atom brought Adara to the conference room, where the captain awaited them. Taramay had decided to handle this without other officers present, as it might make the civilian more relaxed and cooperative.

"Hello again," Taramay greeted the young woman informally

as she sat down at the table. "You're looking well; how do you feel?"

"Much, much better," Adara said with a smile. "I can't thank you enough for your hospitality. When Atom said I might be able to assist you, I thought it was the least I could do."

"Well, I hope you can help," the captain said. "We've got some problems that need solving. Mind you, this is classified information, and we don't want this conversation leaving this room."

"I understand," the young woman said. "You can trust me to keep it confidential."

They proceeded to lay it out for her, the unexpected deep space transmissions, and the discovery that children were the instruments of the espionage. They even played the footage of Eve sleepwalking. When they had finished, Adara looked dazed as she tried to process it all.

"It's a lot to absorb," she said finally. "I've spent long hours in close quarters with those kids, under the worst conditions imaginable. They showed more humanity than many of us adults, bonding together, helping each other survive. I can't believe any of them would knowingly work for the Knackers."

"We don't think so, either," Taramay said gently. "They've been modified medically, and they don't know what they're doing. I've grown close to Eve during her time on this ship, and I would have personally vouched for her. Yet you saw the video. She's been used by the Crabs, and that is a tragedy."

"What can I do to help?" Adara asked. "I don't know anything about mind control or spying; I feel out of my league here."

Atom replied, "We've discovered that the children in question have enhanced memories, to the point of nearly perfect recall. Have you witnessed anything like that while you were with the youngsters in the pyramid?"

Adara's eyes widened, and she said, "Yes! In fact, there were two different children who amazed me with their abilities."

"What did they do?" the captain asked.

"Well, we often told stories sitting there in the dark. Once the lights went out for good, there was nothing to see and nothing to do for days on end. The sensory deprivation was awful; you're alone with your thoughts, and the fear just weighs down on you. You become desperate for human contact, and without eyes, our only refuge was our voices.

"We sat together, sometimes holding hands, and told tales to pass the time. I wasn't very good at it; mostly I just made stuff up. But Eve and Marla could recite entire novels they had read in the past. I didn't have the texts to compare, of course, but it sounded like they recited them verbatim. They told some stories more than once during our time together, and I remembered phrases that were repeated exactly the same as the prior telling."

Taramay looked over at Atom. "This is very interesting. I seriously doubt the Knackers gave them books. Which means they were recalling stories they had read prior to being captured."

"Didn't we conclude that the children weren't born with photographic memories?" Atom said, frowning. "How are they recalling things from their past with such accuracy?"

"Good question. They say the brain remembers nearly everything a person experiences, at some level," the captain mused. "The modifications the Crabs made may have triggered enhanced recall of some prior events as well as current ones. Either that, or the Knackers did give the children reading materials while they held them, perhaps to keep them occupied or to test their recall skills."

"Either way, we have two kids from your cell to focus on," Atom said to Adara. "We know Eve was one; who was the other?"

"Marla Crestor," she replied. "Ten years old and alone; both her parents were presumably killed when the Knackers overran her home town."

"That's a new name added to our list," Taramay said, nodding with satisfaction. "No one else you can think of?"

Adara shook her head. "Of course we were only one cell; the other prisoners were unknown to us," she said. "And...not all of the children told stories. Some were quiet and shy, and just listened. So I can't say whether their memories were average or superior."

"We've got one name to investigate at least. For that we're thankful," Atom told her.

"Glad I could be of help," Adara replied. "Hey, I just thought of something. I don't know if it's relevant at all, but it involves the children, so maybe?"

"Anything you can think of is worth mentioning," Taramay declared.

"Okay, well, after the cell went dark, the prisoners couldn't even see each other, so we had to rely on voice and touch. The Crabs would come and take someone away, and we often didn't know who it was. Their lights were so blinding when they entered, and they snatched people so quickly…so we started doing roll calls to keep track of who was still with us."

"That makes sense, I guess," Atom said. "Damn, I never stopped to think how difficult daily life was on that ship."

"It was a nightmare. We would call out our names in the dark, and every time the Crabs had visited our cell, there would be a couple of voices that had gone silent. We would never hear from them again. Later, when food stopped coming, we had some deaths from malnutrition as well."

"Yes, I saw the bodies when I was there," Atom said quietly.

"I'm sorry, I digressed," Adara apologized. "The thing I wanted to mention was that sometime during the dark days, a handful of new children were added to our cell.'"

Atom and Taramay both straightened in their chairs. "How many? What were their names?" Taramay asked intently.

"There were six in all. We didn't even know what they looked like until we were rescued; I only knew them by name and voice."

Adara paused, brows knitted in thought. Lifting her gaze to meet Taramay's, she slowly recited, "Eve Coventine, Jozeph Karnell, Marla Crestor, Alma Pindor, Lexa Bandon, and Nia Kourtoukas." Looking over at Taramay, she concluded, "We assumed they had been moved from another cell for some reason, but in truth I don't know where they came from. That's all I have to offer. I'm sorry I couldn't give you more."

"You've done more that you can imagine," the captain told her excitedly. "You just named four people who we already know have eidetic memories. The other two are highly suspicious by association. They all came in to your prison cell together, long after the Crab ship had left Nueva Terra."

"Planted there for us to retrieve," Atom finished for her. "This might be the break we've waited for! With luck, these six juveniles could comprise the entire spy corps."

"We can only hope," Taramay replied, fingers tapping on the table as her thoughts ran at light speed. "I'll have Dr. Lott scan our three new suspects right away. Hopefully all the young refugees can be examined within the next few days, and the adults soon after that. Then maybe we'll have a handle on the situation."

She stood and offered her hand to Adara, smiling. "My thanks once again. You are a resilient young lady. Atom was accurate in his glowing assessment of you."

The young woman blushed at the compliment. "My pleasure, Captain. Let me know if you need me again."

Atom ushered the civilian to the door, and Taramay noted his hand on the woman's slender waist as he walked beside her. Smiling to herself, she shook her head and walked out behind them.

* * * *

A day after her meeting with Adara, Taramay met with Dr. Lott and Dr. Roman. She was eager to hear the results of their examinations of the refugees.

The chief medic had performed most of the physical assessments, so he spoke first, "As we suspected, the six juveniles who were brought into the prison cell separately are confirmed to have abnormal masses in their brains. We've scanned all the other refugee children, and no anomalies were found."

"Excellent," the captain said. "How about the adults?"

"We're working ten-hour days, and so far we've finished examining approximately one fourth of the adult civilians. All tested completely normal."

"Good. Keep at it, but I suspect we'll find that the adults are not compromised," the captain said. "Dr. Roman, do you have anything to add?"

The psychiatrist pursed his lips and said, "I found some behavioral correlations between the children. Believe it or not, their psychological profiles are ideally suited for the roles the aliens chose for them."

"How is that?" Taramay asked, surprised. "They seem to be sweet kids, not hurtful or dishonest."

"A pleasing demeanor is actually an asset for a spy," Dr. Roman pointed out. "…as well as being intelligent, resilient and open to new experiences. And their emotional needs as orphans make them easily manipulated by our enemy. They all seem to seek out authority figures as parental substitutes; in this case, high ranking officers in positions of power. Such individuals satisfy the child's instinctive need for security and safety. They also happen to be the best sources of classified information."

"Great Ares!" Taramay swore, her eyes smoldering.

"Yes, it makes perfect sense," the doctor continued. "Just as with hypnosis, it's difficult to make someone do things that they're innately opposed to. The children fear and loath the Knackers; they would never choose to help the enemy. The psychological alterations that would have to take place to override their natural resistance would likely leave them damaged. The individual might be able to pull off basic tasks as directed, but wouldn't be capable of maintaining a normal appearance as a healthy, functional child. That would in turn raise suspicion."

"So instead, the Crabs make use of the children's needs for love and protection," Taramay said. "We in turn befriend them. Via interacting with us, they are exposed to sights and conversations full of useful information. The children subconsciously record what they experience, aided by enhanced memory which makes it all effortless. Then when they're in a dream state they do what they're programmed to, and report to the enemy."

"Essentially, yes," Dr. Roman said, nodding. "It would be interesting to know what the children remember of their sleep periods. Do they dream, and if so, what do those entail? It might give us clues as to how they function. Maybe we could break their programming through hypnosis or other techniques."

"All right," the captain said. "That's something to pursue in the future. For now, you've given me plenty to work with. Finish your scans of the refugees and report when you're finished—or if you find another anomaly."

* * * *

The *Goliath* sped apace toward the human core worlds, with the suspected Knacker vessel still trailing them. They were now only nine days out from their destination. Before long they would be deep into human-occupied space. Taramay suspected their pursuer might soon break off and fall back, in order to avoid an encounter with SpaceForce ships. If she were going to implement the plan she had been forming, she would have to do it quickly, as it required the alien destroyer's participation.

Three additional clandestine transmissions had been logged in the prior forty-eight hours, each by a different child. No damaging data had been sent, so the captain had given orders to continue allowing the children's activities.

On the bridge, the captain handed a small data disc to the com officer. "Lieutenant, I want you to send the contents on a tight beam transmission directly to Space Command. Highest compression and encryption possible."

"On it, Captain," Alena said, turning to her console.

"Oh, and Ms. Stepanovich," Taramay added.

"Yes, ma'am?"

"Let me know the moment you receive a reply. It will be brief and won't make any sense, but I need to know their response immediately, regardless of time of day."

"I'll handle it."

"I'm going below to check on the refugees. Mr. Caine, you have the bridge."

The first officer nodded and saluted. "Captain."

Taramay resolutely made her way down to the cargo hold to see Eve. She felt torn between her duties to SpaceForce, and her promise to an unfortunate child who had looked to her for help. Eve had become a pawn in a struggle between forces far greater than she could imagine. Taramay could not bring herself to abandon the child.

When Eve saw the officer striding down the row of bunks toward her, she shouted "Captain Taramay!" and came running. The girl leaped into the captain's arms and hugged her fiercely. "I was hoping you'd come!" she gushed. "It's been two days since you visited. I worried that you'd forgotten about me."

"I could never forget you, sweet girl," Taramay said, wrapping the eager child up in her arms. "I've just been really busy. But I found time to come see my favorite crew member." She set the youngster on her feet, and grinned, saying "I'll bet you want to get out of here. Let's go for a walk; I'd like to show you more of the ship."

The girl squealed and hopped around in excitement. "Can we see the engines? Can we?" she pleaded.

"I'm the captain; I can take us wherever I want," Taramay told her. "Let's go look!"

They had exhausted most of the limited recreational offerings of the *Goliath* in past outings. Today Taramay wanted to show Eve some of the more technical wonders of the ship. The girl had an active and curious mind, and wanted to follow in the captain's footsteps someday. Although recent revelations had cast doubt on that future, Taramay wanted to encourage her dreams.

Breaking from their previous routine, they left the cargo bay through the rear exit, and proceeded down the central corridor toward the *Goliath*'s stern. Despite the casual appearance of their outing, Taramay was alert and focused. She planned to closely control what Eve was allowed to see. As long as no sensitive information was revealed, the risk was manageable.

She had another motive as well. If enough interesting sights were seen, the captain hoped that the girl would be triggered to report her experiences. Assuming that SpaceForce approved Taramay's plan, she needed Eve to send a transmission. And she needed it soon.

They reached the blast door enclosing the power plant and engineering section. It was heavily reinforced and disproportionately thick, comprised of nearly a meter of solid composite metals in cross section. The entrance it occupied resembled a tunnel more than a typical door sill. Eve marveled at the massive portal, asking, "Why is this so big?"

"It protects the rest of the ship in case the reactors ever fail," the captain told her.

"You mean explode?" the child asked, wide-eyed.

"Yes."

"Does that happen often?" Eve asked, looking worried.

"No, it almost never happens," Taramay assured her. "It would require heavy damage to our safety systems, which probably means the ship was attacked and badly hurt. By then we'd have bigger worries than the reactors."

The child stood silent for a moment, staring at the entrance as she contemplated the captain's words.

Taramay broke the mood, saying, "Let's take a look inside. It's perfectly safe. The main engines are in here, c'mon!"

Hesitantly the girl followed her through the entrance. Once inside Eve's fear faded away as she gazed around in wonder. They had emerged into a vast room dominated at its center by a glowing azure dome rearing at least ten meters off the floor. The sky-blue surface was streaked with fine white discharges, like miniature bolts of lightning that flickered into and out of existence almost too fast for the eye to follow. A deep hum of power resonated in the air and could even be felt through the floor beneath their feet.

"Wow! What is that giant ball?" Eve exclaimed, pointing.

"That is the hyperdrive field generator," Taramay replied with an amused grin. "It's what allows the *Goliath* to move from normal space into hyperspace, so we can travel at great speed."

"It's beautiful!" Eve exclaimed. "Is that electricity on the surface?"

"Not exactly. The small flashes are plasma discharges, a very potent type of energy…and they're not on the surface. The dome is transparent; you're seeing what's happening on the interior. If you watch closely, you can see that some of the sparks are deeper inside than others, and some are coming straight out at us. See?"

"Yes! I see it now!" Eve replied, mesmerized by the display. "There are lights all through it!" She watched for a while longer, before wrenching her gaze away to look at Taramay. "So this is what makes the ship go? But there is only one. I thought there were three engines."

"You are correct, clever girl. There are three. The field generator doesn't propel the ship forward; it simply gets us into hyperspace. The main engines do the pushing."

"Like a blimp, then," Eve said.

"What?" Taramay asked, puzzled. "How is it like a blimp? That's a very primitive flying machine."

"Well, with a blimp, the gas inside makes it float, so it can get off the ground and fly, but it takes an engine to move it forward."

The captain blinked in surprise. The analogy was accurate and showed more insight than she had expected. She smiled with approval and said, "You are exactly right, Eve. I'm impressed."

The youngster grinned from ear to ear and looked intently around the room. "So where are the engines, then?"

"Can you figure it out? You know how many there are."

After a moment, the girl gestured across the chamber. "Those?"

She referred to three hulking blocks of grey metal arrayed along the back wall. They were dully unspectacular compared to the field generator, but their girth was substantial. Each roughly cubical structure reached nearly as tall as the central dome. Black power conduits the thickness of a man's torso snaked down the back wall into the tops of the units.

"Yes, those are the main engines," the captain confirmed. "They are fusion-powered, same as in our fighter ships, but a lot bigger."

"They don't look like much," the girl said with a disappointed tone. "You can't see anything."

In truth there wasn't much to observe. The metallic exteriors were mostly featureless, broken only by inset rectangles that might have been access doors. The flat faces lacked ornamentation other than a control panel low on the front of each unit. A technician was standing at the far right engine, taking notes from the glowing displays.

"Can we go look at what he's doing?" Eve asked.

"No, he's busy with important work," Taramay replied. "We shouldn't interrupt him."

In reality, the captain was concerned about exposing her young companion to detailed information about their main drive units. The technology itself was commonplace; both SpaceForce and the Knackers utilized fusion engines in their ships. The aliens actually possessed superior propulsion systems, so no major technical advances would be leaked here. However, detailed information on the specifications and capabilities of the main engines would be useful to the enemy. This was especially true with an upgraded vessel such as the *Goliath*. It was best not to show one's hand until absolutely necessary.

Seeing the disappointment on her young charge's face, the captain offered an alternative. "Say, would you like to see what these engines are really doing?" she asked the girl. "There's a special viewing port where we can see the jets."

"Yes! I want to see that!" Eve said with an enthusiastic nod.

"Come with me," Taramay said, and she didn't have to ask twice. She led them to their right, past the glowing hyperspace generator. As they passed within a few meters of the dome, they could feel a static charge growing in the air. An odd tingling crept over their skin, and the hairs on their arms stood stiffly erect. In a moment the captain heard Eve giggling.

Glancing over at her young companion, she saw the girl grinning back at her and looking very amused. The youngster pointed at Taramay's head, saying, "Your hair, it's sticking up like you're under water!"

Eve's hair was longer than the captain's, so the effect was even more pronounced on her. When Taramay pointed this out, the girl momentarily looked dismayed, raising her hands to feel her own head. But then she caught Taramay's teasing grin and they both broke into open laughter.

Still chuckling, they continued on past the generator, angling between two of the giant engines until they reached the rear of the room. There a staircase led sideways up the wall. It ended at a small platform halfway to the ceiling.

"Hold on to the railing," the captain cautioned. "It's a long way up, and the ship could change momentum unexpectedly."

Upward they climbed, their shoes clanking on the corrugated metal stairs. When they reached the platform, Taramay gestured toward a small viewing port set into the wall. "Go ahead, take a look," she told her eager companion.

Eve plastered her face to the window and peered through. What she saw made her gasp in wonder. "It's amazing!" she squealed. Taramay joined her, and they stood side by side, gazing out the *Goliath*'s stern.

The view from here was unlike any other on the ship. Long metal projections stretched gracefully outward from the hull, pointing back in the direction from which they had come. These were scanner and communications arrays. Their slender lengths were vividly highlighted against the swirling background of hyperspace. But the origin of the illumination was what transfixed the gazes of the two passengers.

Erupting from three separate ports, the fusion drives jetted blue-white plasma in graceful trailing streamers that stretched hundreds of meters into the distance. Totally silent in the vacuum, the sheer magnitude of the light show still bespoke of tremendous power being unleashed. Its entrancing beauty was an unintended side effect. No words would have done it justice, so they just stood there, sharing their appreciation of the view in silence.

Later that evening they ate dinner in the officer's mess, chatting about the day's adventures. "That was a lot of fun, seeing the engines and the big hyperspace dome and all of it," Eve enthused. "Thank you so much for taking me."

"I enjoyed it, too," Taramay replied. "I spend so much time

working aboard the *Goliath*, sometimes I forget to stop and appreciate the little things."

"Mmm-hmmm," the youngster mumbled around a mouthful of food.

"How is your dinner?" the captain asked with amusement. From the looks of it, there were no complaints.

"It's all really good," Eve managed between attacks on her food. "What is it?"

"Let's see." Taramay surveyed the child's plate. "The meat looks like Dire Buck."

"That's from the planet Eden, where I'm going!" Eve exclaimed. "I've seen pictures of them!"

"Yes, that's right. The fruits are seaberries; they grow in the inland lakes of Alta Luna. And the vegetables look like a lettuce hybrid. I'm not sure where they're from."

"It's fun to try things from other planets," the youngster said with a bright smile. She gestured around her. "There's so much to see and learn here. It's all so different from where I grew up. Sometimes it seems like a dream."

Taramay saw an opportunity and took it. "Dreams are fun. Sometimes I have dreams about really strange things that make no sense at all. Do you have any good dreams when you sleep?"

To her relief, the child seemed unperturbed about the question. "Sometimes. I tend to have the same dreams a lot, so it gets boring actually."

"Really? What do you dream about?"

Eve cocked her head. "I often have a dream that I'm going to my grandma's house. I'm visiting her so I can tell her all the interesting things I've done. She loves to hear my stories."

"Sounds like a nice dream," Taramay said. "Do you tell her about things long ago, or things more recent, like our spending time together?"

"Mostly things that just happened. In my dream grandma always wants the latest gossip. Just like in real life." She paused with her fork halfway to her mouth. "I don't know why she makes it so hard to get into her house, though. That's not at all like her."

"How does she do that? Does she lock her door?"

"Yes, and she's got more than one lock. Some require number combinations to open, or I have to say a password. It's a lot of work just to get inside where I can speak to her."

"That's a funny dream," Taramay said, fighting to keep a calm demeanor. Inside she felt a huge surge of excitement at the child's words. This almost certainly was Eve's dream recollection of interfacing with the computer. The doc had been right; the Crabs had used the child's own inclinations to provide a pleasant cover for her nocturnal activities.

"It's a bit weird having the same dream so often. At least I get to see grandma, so I guess it's okay," Eve said.

"Well, I can think of much worse dreams to have," Taramay said.

The girl pondered her words for a moment, then said hesitantly, "Sometimes I have bad dreams, too."

"Like what?"

"I don't remember exactly. Maybe I don't want to; it's scary."

"Do you dream about the Knackers?" the captain asked softly. The child nodded slowly. "Like when they came to your house?"

To Taramay's surprise, Eve shook her head. "No, it's not about anything on Nueva Terra. It's in a strange place I don't know, a big room with lots of shiny machines. The room with the blue lights. The room where bad things happen."

The child's voice had started to waver, and her hand was shaking so hard that she couldn't stab her lettuce with the fork. Giving up, she dropped the utensil and covered her eyes with her hands.

The captain hesitated, and decided to push just a little more. "What happens in that room? Do they hurt you?"

"Yes," Eve whispered. "I don't remember what they do, but sometimes it hurts a lot. I don't want to remember." She looked up at Taramay, and her cheeks were streaked with tears. "I want to forget all of it! Please don't ask me anymore."

"Okay, little lady, don't worry. I won't ask about it," the captain assured her. She reached out and touched the girl's hand, catching Eve's gaze with hers. "Remember, it's only a dream. It didn't really happen. Dreams can't hurt us, only scare us a little."

"Or a lot," Eve retorted, but her expression had lightened a bit.

"You did really well with dinner," the captain commented, trying to put the conversation back on a better track. "Your plate's nearly empty. Would you like some dessert?"

"Oh yeah! Can I have some chocolate? Please?"

Mood successfully upgraded, Taramay thought to herself. *At least that part was fairly easy*. She got up and headed for the food processors along the far wall. When she returned with a big slice of chocolate cake, the child eagerly dove in.

Taramay smiled indulgently. It might not be the healthiest dish, but it was the least she could do after making Eve revisit a terrible episode. For she suspected that the recurring nightmare was based in reality. Was it possible that the girl actually retained fragmented memories of the procedures the Crabs had performed on her?

Even if it were true, it was unlikely that many details could be gleaned by delving deeper. As she watched the girl contentedly eating her cake, Taramay made the decision to not report this discovery. For Eve to continue healing, any recall of Knacker horrors was probably best left undisturbed.

After she had seen the youngster back to her bed for the night, Taramay returned to her quarters for some much needed rest. Despite her fatigue, she found sleep to be annoyingly elusive. She tossed restlessly as her mind grappled with the day's events. Worse, she urgently needed a response from SpaceForce, and time was running short. The night dragged on endlessly before she finally fell into a fitful slumber.

15.

At six hundred hours the next morning the captain's wrist com buzzed. Fumbling to answer the call, she mumbled grumpily, "Why is it always when I'm sleeping?" A moment later she spoke into the com link, "What is it?"

"Captain, sorry to disturb you," a voice said. "This is Lt. Karmel, the com officer for this overnight shift. Ms. Stepanovich had instructed me to inform you when we received a message from Space Command. One just came in."

Her eyes snapped open wide, all traces of drowsiness gone. "Open it," she commanded. "What does it say? Don't worry about what it means; just read it verbatim."

"That's easy. It's very brief. The message says, 'Approved.' Nothing more. Does that make sense?"

"Perfectly," Taramay answered as she leapt out of bed. "I want a meeting of the senior day officers, plus Dr. Lott, Dr. Roman, and Lt. Granger, at eight hundred hours. The night crew may need to cover the bridge for an extra hour or so."

"I'll notify everyone," the lieutenant said.

"Make it happen. Captain out."

At the appointed hour, the staff assembled in the main conference room. Taramay wasted no time getting to the business at hand. "I've brought you all here to discuss an important development," she began, scanning the faces around the table. "We're within days of reaching the human core worlds, and time is short. For most of our return voyage, we've had a vessel trailing us, probably a Knacker warship. We suspect it's there to intercept transmissions from our young spies. Speaking of which, how are the civilian examinations progressing?"

Dr. Lott looked up and replied, "All of the refugees have been brain-scanned, both the children and adults. Other than the six juveniles we'd already identified, everyone checks out normal."

"As I had hoped," Taramay said. "Excellent. Now we know the situation aboard our ship. It's time to take action." She glanced around the table, and said, "I submitted a plan to Space Command en route, and they just gave us their stamp of approval. We need to move on it now if we're going to implement it."

"What does it entail?" Lt. Debartolo asked.

She looked to her right to meet the navigator's gaze. "I want to plant information with one of our young informants, Eve Coventine," she answered. "False intel, to be precise."

Murmurs sprung up around the table. The first officer was the first to speak up. "To what purpose?" he asked.

Taramay frowned and said, "Throughout this conflict, we've been handicapped by not knowing where or when the enemy would strike. Their fleet is larger than ours, and we're unable to gather our forces in advance to strongly repel an attack. It's time we changed that dynamic." She paused for effect, and then declared, "I want to draw a Knacker fleet to a specific point in space, a place of our choosing. Then I want to annihilate them."

There was a brief moment of total silence as surprised faces absorbed her words. This was quickly followed by eager nods and grins around the table, along with a chorus of approving voices: "*Yes!*" "I like it!" "Let's do it!"

One island of calm cut through the clamor. Greta Jónsson raised a hand and said, "I'm all for hitting the Crabs where it hurts. But nearly every time SpaceForce has gone against them head-to-head, we've lost. How do we turn the tables in our favor?"

The gunner's question got everyone's attention. Eyes turned back to the captain, and the expressions were now intently serious. Taramay nodded to herself; this was the frame of mind she needed in her crew.

"Okay, let's look to our data screens," she began. "You'll see a diagram of the Tantori star system. It lies within the region of space controlled by our core worlds, but contains no habitable planets. There is, however, one significant installation located in that system."

The picture focused on an area just beyond the system's third planet. A dense asteroid belt occupied that region. The view zoomed in closer, to target a particularly large rock at the periphery of the debris field. It far out-massed its neighbors, with its bulk holding enough gravity to have shaped it into an irregular oval. A graphic appeared next to the asteroid, and Lt. Debartolo grunted in recognition.

"*Clandesta*," he said, nodding thoughtfully. "I remember when this was a big deal. It never panned out though; I'm not sure why."

"Logistics, Lef. That's why they abandoned the project," the captain said.

"What is Clandesta?" Lt. Cotton piped up, looking totally lost.

"The Clandesta project was top secret, which is why many of you haven't heard of it," Taramay said. "It was intended to be a hidden base of operations for our war effort, separate from our inhabited worlds. A place where the Knackers would never think to look. The asteroid was excavated, and extensive facilities were built underground. But the project was abandoned prior to completion."

"Sounds like a good idea," the com officer commented. "Why was it never finished?"

"Because, Alena, what sounds good in theory doesn't always work in practical application," the captain replied. "The asteroid was chosen because it has some positive attributes. It's big enough to hold a sizable habitat plus defensive installations. The dense nickel-iron composition can shield the underground compound from casual scans, and it provides some physical protection from attack. Construction could rely heavily on native materials, rather than having to ferry everything in from other worlds. The location was also deemed optimal, being outside of any inhabited planetary systems, but not too isolated."

"So why change direction mid-stream and abandon it?" Leofric asked.

Taramay pursed her lips. "The primary advantage of such a facility is secrecy. The concept is seductive, when considered in isolation. In reality this proved very difficult to achieve. Any installation that houses a large number of people needs infrastructure to support that population. Without a hospitable planet, there is no readily available supply of food, water, or atmosphere. These and other essential items must be transported regularly to the facility. That means ships need to come and go with some frequency. Combine that with deep space transmissions necessary to coordinate SpaceForce operations, and you have traceable clues pointing to the location of the hidden installation."

"Did the Crabs ever find the base?" Lt. Cotton asked.

"We don't think so. After a supply ship detected a Knacker vessel tracking their route, it was obvious that Clandesta would be discovered before long. Then it would be an easy target. They discontinued the supply runs and abandoned the project, even though it was ninety percent completed."

"Couldn't they provide protection for the base?" the first officer asked.

"They could have, but that would defeat the purpose of creating a hidden facility. Basically it would be like another planet to defend, and with fewer natural resources to justify the effort. Habitable worlds are valuable beyond just the populations that live there. This sterile rock had little worth defending except the base itself."

"Still, after all that effort to build..." Lt. Cotton shook his head.

"The Knackers were attacking multiple human worlds at will, Bruce. SpaceForce was already spread too thin. Taking military resources away from inhabited systems to protect this base didn't make good sense. They mothballed the installation and left it intact, in case it was needed in the future."

"So how does Clandesta factor into your plan?" Leofric asked, sitting back in his chair.

The captain folded her hands and explained, "I want to plant information for our young informant to send to the enemy. Information that shows Clandesta as an important, operational Space-Force installation. Taking a lesson from our recent success, we'll mine the asteroid with high explosives, plant artificial life-signal generators to make it appear populated, and wait for the Crabs to attack it. A SpaceForce fleet will be waiting nearby, a short hyperspace jump away. When the base is attacked, we'll ambush them and blow the asteroid. With good planning, the explosion will take out much of the alien armada. Our fleet will do the rest."

Leofric nodded slowly. "I like it. If it's done right, this could strike a major blow against the enemy. But we've got to tailor this operation as precisely as we can."

"What do you suggest?" Lt. Granger asked.

The navigator pondered his reply for a moment. "The Knackers will allocate resources based on their appraisal of the situation. They prize efficiency. If the target is small, they'll send fewer ships. A large important target will draw a much stronger response from them."

Taramay nodded. "We need to decide how many enemy warships we can handle. For this effort to pay big dividends, we need to destroy a lot of the enemy's fleet. But we don't want to lose the battle by going up against a vastly superior force. I need input from everyone as to what we can plan on achieving."

Leofric said, "Normally I'd want a two-to-one ratio in favor of our ships. The enemy destroyers are too powerful to defeat without numerical superiority."

Lt. Jónsson countered, "That may not be as necessary here. We have the advantage of surprise, plus the mined asteroid. If we use antimatter charges of sufficient power, we should be able to wipe out a lot of Crab ships instantly. We just have to make sure that they are in close proximity before we detonate."

Taramay added, "If we can anticipate the attack, we can also muster extra help, such as Lampreys. Our super-dreadnaughts can take on any warship the enemy has. We just don't have many in operation, and they're scattered throughout the human core worlds. Gathering them at one site will require good coordination."

"How do we anticipate the number of ships the Knackers will bring to the party?" Lt. Cotton asked.

"We'll have to estimate that based on how large our fictitious base is," Taramay said, "and how important it seems. We'll present it as a major military command center. I want our logistics and intel people to come up with approximate numbers of Knacker ships that could be mustered for a quick assault. I suspect the Crabs will jump on the opportunity when they become aware of it."

"Even if we estimate their forces correctly, how will we know when they'll attack?" Lt. Cotton asked. "Working from normal space, we can't reliably detect ships approaching in hyperspace."

The captain shrugged. "We won't have to wait long, I suspect. But as you say, there is no exact way to be sure."

"I have a thought," Leofric interjected. "We might be able to estimate both enemy numbers and movements by watching the forces we are already aware of."

"Explain," the captain said.

The navigator tapped commands on his viewscreen. "Looking

at the star system charts, we can see that the Knackers are currently occupying Nueva Terra, and are attacking two other core worlds within reasonable striking range of Clandesta. If they are to mount an aggressive assault on the asteroid, they will likely pull ships away from those planets. Observing exactly when they do this, and how many ships they call up from those other exercises, could help us predict the timing and strength of their attack."

"That's a good thought," the captain replied. "We'll include that recommendation as part of the final plan we send to Space Command."

"Are we formulating the strategy?" Leofric asked. "Doesn't Command usually make those decisions?"

"We can't chance any communications being intercepted," Taramay answered. "We're being tracked by an enemy ship; any messages directed at us would be picked up by the Crabs. I sent my proposal to Space Command via tight beam, and requested that they only respond 'yes' or 'no' so that nothing would be given away."

"Then it's up to us? We're running the show?" the first officer asked.

"Yes, Mr. Caine. It's our engagement to coordinate, at least until we're no longer being shadowed."

"Well then, we'd best get our part of this in play quickly," Leofric declared. "What's our next step?"

Taramay looked to the tech officer. "Mr. Cotton, I want to prepare a special show for Eve to witness. I'll give her another tour of the bridge soon. I need you to produce some falsified displays to show on a viewscreen when she's there. Data that show Clandesta as a primary command center, with a listed population of, say, two hundred thousand people. That should get the Crabs' attention."

Bruce nodded thoughtfully. "Yes, I could create a star chart showing the system's location, plus a schematic of the base. Can you give me any of the actual specs on the facility? It would be best if my data reflect reality, so that any scanner readings the enemy makes will not expose our ruse."

Taramay nodded. "I can access the necessary files and send them to your console. Let me know when you have something put together. I'll review it, and if it looks good, we're set to proceed. Time is crucial. I'm not sure how much longer the enemy ship will shadow us."

Leofric spoke up, "Maybe we should plan some conversations to discuss when Eve is there. You know, some reference to the base, to be sure she focuses on the information we wish her to observe."

"Excellent thought, Lef," the captain said. "We'll rehearse something after this meeting is adjourned." She looked around the table. "Any other thoughts? No? Okay, if no one has anything else to offer, we need to compose an action plan and send it to Space Command. Use our meeting notes as a framework. Mr. Caine, can you put that together?"

The first officer nodded. "Consider it done."

"Okay, people, we've got little time. I'll expect finished projects from Lieutenants Caine and Cotton by fourteen hundred hours today. That's less than six hours from now. Let's get to it!" She pushed her chair back and stood. "This meeting is concluded; everyone back to stations. Mr. Debartolo, let's discuss our upcoming stage performance."

They sent their detailed strategic summary to Space Command later that day. Taramay reviewed Lt. Cotton's falsified display pages, and approved of his basic designs, with one or two minor modifications. He would fill in the detailed specs before his shift ended, and load the images onto the navigator's console. Everything seemed to be coming together as planned. The captain told the bridge crew to finish their preparations and be ready for implementation the following day.

* * * *

The next morning the captain strode onto the bridge brimming with nervous energy. It was time to set their scheme in motion. The day shift officers were already at their stations. Looking around the room, she could read the tense anticipation in their gazes.

Taramay cleared her throat and said, "Okay, everyone, it's time for action. I'm going to bring Eve up to the bridge. Everyone needs to behave normally. Be friendly to her, as you were on her last visit. Mr. Debartolo and I will handle the important conversations, and he will have his screen displaying the appropriate images when Eve heads his way."

She looked to the navigator. "Have you tested the falsified data readouts on your console?"

Leofric grinned. "It displays perfectly, just like a real navigation screen. Mr. Cotton is a true artist."

Taramay nodded. "Okay, it looks like everything is set, so I'm heading to the cargo hold. I'll be back shortly."

She started toward the bridge exit, then paused and turned back, saying, "We need to be careful. The enemy will likely be pouring over every image Eve absorbs, looking for any signs of trickery. We can't seem too eager to show her classified information. Lef, once you're sure she's scanned your screen, blank out the images. Make it seem like you didn't mean for her to see it. Above all, we need to remain calm. Understood, everyone?"

Taramay gazed around the bridge and was met with nods. Satisfied, she headed for the lower decks and her date with destiny.

The captain entered the cargo bay a few minutes later. Her pulse was racing as she approached the row of bunks wherein Eve resided. She had rehearsed this scene over and over in her mind, and she still wasn't sure if she could pull it off. *Relax, Taramay, just relax*, she told herself. A moment later she was greeting the smiling youngster, and from that point she relied on instinct to carry her through.

Taramay had decided against openly suggesting the visit to the bridge. Rather, she wanted to subtly lead Eve to make the request. If the child thought it was her idea, then this might allay any suspicions of a setup.

"Hi there, little angel!" the captain greeted her small friend effusively. "I've missed you!"

"Me too!" Eve replied as she hugged Taramay. After a handful of seconds the girl loosened her embrace and looked up reproachfully, saying, "You didn't visit me yesterday. I've been bored to death down here." Her lower lip pouted. "Can we go for a walk and see something new? Please?"

"I don't know, Eve," Taramay replied, looking regretful. "I'm really busy today. I wanted to see you, but I didn't really plan for an outing. I've got to head to the bridge soon, and take care of running the ship."

The girl responded exactly as the captain had hoped. "Oh, could I come with you? I loved seeing the bridge last time! I wouldn't get in the way. I promise!"

Taramay hesitated uncertainly. Eve looked up at her, eyes pleading, and said, "Please?"

Even if she hadn't already planned to take the girl along, the captain wasn't sure if she could have resisted that face. "Okay," she capitulated. She waved an admonishing finger at the youngster. "But you behave yourself up there, do you hear me? We've got lots to do and we can't be distracted."

"I'll be good," the girl insisted, and just like that, they were on their way to the bridge.

Exiting the elevator at the command floor, they walked together toward the forward section of the ship. The entrance to the bridge waited at the corridor's end, and they stepped through the doorway into the large circular chamber.

Even though she'd been there once before, Eve stopped just inside and gazed around at the hemispheric view of open space, entranced. Taramay smiled and continued alone to her command dais. Settling into her chair, she gazed around the room. Everyone was at their appointed places. The drama could now play out.

Taking a slow breath, Taramay spoke. "Ms. Stepanovich, have we received any further communications from Space Command?"

"No, Captain. All channels have been silent so far."

"Scanner readings, Mr. Cotton?"

"All clear, ma'am. No enemy presence detected."

"How far are we from home, Lef?" the captain asked, glancing surreptitiously toward Eve. The girl had shifted her attention from the overhead view and was now listening intently to the officers' exchange.

"We're approximately seven days out," the navigator replied.

"There's been a change of plan. I opened our sealed orders for the last portion of this mission. We've been instructed to report to Command Base before dropping off the refugees," Taramay said. "Plot a direct course for Clandesta at once."

"Plotting." Lt. Debartolo tapped instructions into his console, pulling up the star map and other images that Lt. Cotton had recently created. Only a portion of this was fabrication; the ship actually would alter course toward the asteroid to keep up the charade.

Taramay tried to appear relaxed as she kept her eye on Eve. The girl was slowly walking toward the navigator, her eyes fixed on his console. She almost seemed in a trance, so deep was her concentration. The captain wondered if the Crabs had somehow been able to prioritize specific objectives within the girl's programming. It certainly appeared that way. The captain couldn't remember seeing Eve so focused.

The girl approached Lt. Debartolo's chair from the back, her feet hardly making a whisper on the bridge floor. Now close behind him, she peered directly over his shoulder. The navigator's startled reaction when he realized she was there wasn't feigned. He said, "Eve! You nearly scared me to death, girl!"

She immediately looked chagrined, and he smiled to put her at ease, saying, "It's okay, silly. I didn't know you could be that quiet! You could be a stealth warrior with those skills."

Eve's face lit up, and she moved to stand next to the lieutenant's chair. "What is that?" she asked, pointing to the viewscreen. "It looks like a map."

Leofric quickly closed the screen, saying, "Oh, that's classified, sweetie. You shouldn't be looking at that. I don't want you to get in trouble."

"That's okay," the girl said, smiling. "There are a lot of other things to see up here. I'm just happy to be out of the cargo room."

The lieutenant chuckled. "I'll bet you are. That hold wasn't designed for comfort."

Taramay watched the exchange while pretending to work on her viewscreen. Eve chatted with the navigator for a bit longer, and then she moved around the room, visiting the tech officer, the gunnery officer, and the com officer.

At each stop she engaged the adults in conversation, as vivacious and chatty as ever. But the captain now observed the girl with knowing eyes. She saw that Eve fixed her gaze on each officer's viewscreen even while carrying on her dialogue. Gathering information, storing, collating, even without being conscious of it. *Good*, she thought to herself. *Keep working, Eve. Give them what they want. Then I'll give them what they deserve.*

16.

Later that evening Taramay walked Eve back to the cargo hold. "Thank you, Captain Taramay," the girl said cheerily as they reached her cot. "It was great seeing the bridge again. Everyone there is so nice to me. But most of all I love spending time with you. You're my best friend in the whole universe."

Taramay felt a stab of guilt as she hugged the girl and bid her good night. Part of her hated using Eve in this manner. Rationally she knew that she wasn't responsible for the child's situation. Nor could SpaceForce afford to let a critical opportunity pass due to ethical concerns, when the enemy had no such compunctions. Humanity was literally fighting for survival.

She walked alone from the cargo hold with the debate still raging inside. Try as she might, she couldn't shake the nagging voice that protested her betrayal of the youngster's trust. She fought it down, telling herself that this plan wouldn't harm the girl, and she could save many lives if it succeeded. The deception was necessary for now. Squaring her shoulders, she resolved to see this through to the end. She would make it up to Eve when it was all over.

Back in her quarters, Taramay readied herself for sleep. She felt restless and on edge, wondering if her plan would come to fruition. In her gut she felt that it would happen soon. They had given the girl enough vital information that it should trigger her programming. At least that was the hope. Lying on her back in the darkened room, she stared at the ceiling as the endless minutes ticked tediously away. Eventually she resorted to reciting poems in her head, trying to relax so she could get some badly needed rest.

It seemed only a few seconds later when she awoke to her wrist alarm's insistent beep. Looking fuzzily at the dial, she saw that the time was just past two hundred hours. Her finger tapped the answer icon. "Yes?"

"Captain, we have activity on the lower deck," a male voice

spoke. "It looks like a child is on the move."

"Be sure everything is recorded," Taramay commanded, already grabbing for her uniform. "I'm on my way."

She made the bridge within three minutes. Her arrival was just in time to catch Eve on the video screen, moving through shadowy gloom toward a glowing wall terminal.

Just as before, the child's body tilted forward stiffly, holding the unnatural position as her forehead touched the interface screen. There she stood for long minutes, while on the hushed bridge the officers watched spellbound.

Finally the indistinct figure broke away and slowly shambled off into the dark. Collective breaths were let out in unison, and the captain slumped back in her chair as the tension drained from her body. She remained silent for a moment, staring at the floor.

When she looked up her expression was one of steely resolve. She said, "Okay, people, it looks like we got what we hoped for. We need to confirm that she sent a transmission, and analyze its contents. Give this highest priority, and message me with your findings."

"Will do, Captain," the night tech officer answered, saluting.

"I'm off to my quarters," Taramay concluded. She turned and walked slowly toward the exit, her legs feeling as wooden as little Eve's had appeared on camera. For better or worse, events had been set in motion, and it was now out of her hands. Only time would tell whether it was the right choice.

* * * *

"Good morning, Captain," Lt. Debartolo greeted her as she reentered the bridge six hours later. "We've got some updates for you. I think you'll like them."

Lt. Cotton nodded enthusiastically. "The intel people worked overnight to decode the transmission that Eve sent. It definitely went out, and it definitely included the information we wanted the aliens to get."

Taramay smiled briefly. "Excellent. Now we have to hope that the Crabs decide to act on it."

"I think that they have already done so," the tech officer said.

The captain's eyebrows rose, and she asked, "Why?"

"Because the alien ship appears to have moved away. Scanners indicate that as of this morning, it is no longer pursuing us," Bruce replied.

"It seems they've gotten what they wanted," Taramay concluded.

"And they may also want to contact their fleet without us intercepting their signal," Leofric added. "A little distance between us would make that easier."

"Well then, let's set the next phase of the plan into action," the captain said. "From this point forward, all refugees are prohibited from accessing any computer terminals, day or night. I don't want anyone sending out a transmission that exposes our plan. Our little spies are officially shut down."

"I'll see to it," Leofric replied.

"Once we've verified that our shadowing vessel is gone, we can communicate more freely with Space Command," Alena spoke up from her com station. "Should I send a message updating them on current events?"

"Yes," the captain said. "Mr. Cotton, monitor your scanners closely for the next three hours. If they read clear, then Ms. Stepanovich can send a tight beam transmission bringing Command up to date. Advise them that the Knackers may be moving on Clandesta very soon. They'll need to get our fleet coordinated in time to respond. Hopefully the asteroid has already been brought out of hibernation and mined with explosives. We'll want any human presence long gone when the Crabs arrive."

"We're on it, Captain," Alena said, nodding. "I'll advise you of Command's response when it arrives."

"Fine. I'm going to do some housekeeping: stop by the medical wing, check on the refugees, etc. You can reach me on wrist com if you need me. Carry on." The captain glanced around the bridge and snapped off a quick salute before exiting.

Around midday Taramay met with Eve for lunch. They ate in the officers' mess, enjoying the simple pleasures of good food and companionship. Meals together had become their island of sanity in the midst of wartime. Taramay knew from hard experience that such interludes could be short-lived. She vowed to cherish the time they had.

Later, in the captain's quarters, they relaxed on the bed as had become their habit after meals. Eve searched for fun articles on her digi-pad, and they read them while sipping fruit juice from pouches. When they tired of that, they lay on the cushions just chatting. Taramay grabbed a brush from her bedside cabinet, and began to run it through Eve's long hair.

No longer worried about what the girl might report to the enemy, Taramay wanted to learn more about how Eve experienced her nighttime forays. She waited for a pause in their conversation, then said, "Last night I had a strange dream about visiting my aunt and uncle. It seemed so real. Have you have any good dreams lately?"

Eve giggled and said, "Yes, I visited grandma in my dream last night. I had a lot of things to tell her about my adventures on the *Goliath*. It was real hard getting through her door locks and everything, but it was worth it. She was very happy to hear about all the stuff I've seen and done." The youngster smiled at the memory. "She even gave me some cookies. It was a nice dream."

"It sounds like fun," Taramay agreed. "I always loved seeing my grandparents when they were alive."

"They're not alive now? Did they die when the Knackers came?" Eve asked in a muted voice.

"Oh, no, dear! Nothing bad happened to them," the captain said, smiling at the youngster's look of concern. "They died of old age."

"I guess that's okay, then," Eve said, looking thoughtful, "but I'm still sorry they're gone. It's sad when people in your family die."

"Yes, it is. Unfortunately, people all die, sooner or later. We have to make the most of the time we have, right?"

The girl nodded, and with the movement Taramay felt the hairbrush catch on something on the girl's scalp. It was down near the nape of her neck, just above the hairline. Frowning, she said, "Tip your head forward for a second, please."

When Eve complied, Taramay ran her fingers over the area. She detected a small raised knot, and parting the child's hair, observed what seemed to be a pale scar.

Looking up, she said, "You've got an old wound here, girl. It's all healed, but there's a nice lump left behind. How'd you get that?"

Eve looked puzzled and shrugged. "I don't know. I might have fallen when I was little, I think. It's too long ago for me to really remember."

"Well, it's nothing to worry about now," the captain reassured her. "And it's in a good spot, no one can see it."

The girl grinned and Taramay resumed brushing her hair. "I wish I had hair like yours," she told Eve. "It's so thick and shiny. You're a very pretty lady, you know."

"You think so?"

"Yes, I do." She put the brush aside and turned the girl to face her. Caressing her cheek gently, Taramay said, "You're a beautiful person, Eve, inside and out. I'm very happy that we got to know each other."

Tears welled in the child's eyes. "I'm happy too," she said. "I don't want to go away to live with strangers. That's what will happen when we get to Eden, right? Because I have no family left."

"I'm not sure exactly what will happen, my little one. I do know that Eden is a wonderful place, and whoever you live with will take good care of you. I'll make sure of that." She brushed away tears from the child's cheek. "Hey, don't cry. I can come visit you on Eden, did you know that? I get shore leave now and then, like a vacation. We'll still get to see each other."

"Not very often," the girl said unhappily. "Not like this."

"No, not like this," Taramay agreed. "Still, Eden is a lot better place for a girl to grow up than a metal spaceship."

She hugged the youngster tight, savoring the contact for a few long seconds. Then she kissed the top of Eve's head, saying, "Come on, I'd best get you back to the cargo hold before lights-out. It's late, and things always look better after a good night's sleep. Let me know if you have any good dreams," she added with a wink.

Eve managed a smile and obediently took Taramay's hand as they stood up from the bed. As they turned toward the door, the girl swayed unsteadily on her feet, and might have fallen except for the captain's hand gripping hers tightly.

Taramay stared at her through narrowed eyes, concerned. "Are you okay, Eve?" she asked.

"I'm fine," the girl assured her, nodding brightly. "I was just dizzy for a second. I'm pretty tired I guess."

"Okay…well, let's get you to bed then," the captain said, watching her for a moment longer. Satisfied, she led the way out of the room and down the corridor.

They approached and entered the lift, and Eve exclaimed, "Can I push the button for the lower deck? I know which one it is!"

"Sure, give it a try."

The youngster reached out and thumbed the control panel, glancing up questioningly at the captain. Taramay smiled and nodded. "Good work, corporal!" she said.

Eve beamed happily as the lift began to move. "Maybe I'll get another promotion before I leave the *Goliath*," she said. "I could—." She broke off, her eyes wide and puzzled. "That's weird. I feel…" Suddenly her gaze lost focus, and her pupils rolled up into her head. Then her legs buckled and she crumpled to the floor.

Taramay quickly dashed over to the prone figure and knelt by her side. By then the girl had begun to convulse violently. Eve's limbs tensed and thrashed, her back arching impossibly. Her head slammed into the wall of the lift violently enough to leave a deep dent in the hard material.

Taramay fought to control the girl's movements, trying to prevent serious injury. Eve's teeth were clenched, pale froth spewing from her mouth. Her breath came in harsh wheezes. The captain glanced at the girl's eyes and all she could see was the whites.

The seizure continued for what seemed like an eternity. Finally the lift door opened, and Taramay yelled, "Help! Help us! Medical emergency here! For Ares' sake, we need help *now*!"

A startled-looking corporal appeared in the doorway, freezing as he took in the scene inside the lift. The captain barked, "Don't just stand there, get a medic!" He nodded, and ran off again.

Soon several medical staff rushed in, and Taramay backed off to give them room. She hovered just beyond the cluster of bodies, watching and listening to the dialogue as they worked.

"She's got blood in her mouth."

"Looks like she bit her tongue; I got a soft gag in place."

"Get her arm restrained; I need to access a vein fast." And eventually, "Okay, we've got meds on board, she's relaxing."

With the convulsions abating, they were able to load Eve onto a floater-stretcher and carry her to the medical ward. There she was whisked into a treatment room and laid on an exam table. Dr. Lott hurried into the room a moment later and began to assess the girl's condition. "What's the history?" he asked, glancing at the captain. "Did anyone see what happened?"

"Yes, I was with her," Taramay replied. "She seemed fine, other than a brief dizzy spell, and then suddenly she passed out and convulsed."

"No signs prior to this?" the doctor asked.

"None that I'm aware of."

The medic looked Eve over, pulling up her eyelids and shining a light into her eyes. "Pupils are responsive," he muttered to himself. Turning to an assistant, he said, "Get a venous line into her and start her on fluid support. We need a complete blood profile stat, including screens for pathogens and toxins. Let me know as soon as you get results. In the meantime I'm going to perform a cranial scan."

After a few more minutes examining the girl, the doctor walked over to Taramay. "As far as you know, she's had no recent head trauma?"

"No," the captain said. "I saw evidence of an older trauma, but it's long since healed."

"What do you mean?" the doctor asked.

"There's a small scar just above the hairline on the back of her head. It doesn't bother her, and it's old, so I can't see how it would affect her currently."

"I see," Dr. Lott said, brows furrowed. "I'll check it out myself." He jotted down a note on his digi-pad as he spoke. "Just for curiosity's sake I may examine the other modified children, to see if they sport similar marks."

"Do you think the Knackers could have left that scar on her?" Taramay asked.

"Possibly. I don't know. Hopefully I'll have answers for you soon. For now, her condition seems stable."

"Good. Message me the moment you have any useful information." The captain turned to leave, and as she walked away she said over her shoulder, "If Eve's status changes, I want to know about it."

"Affirmative," the doc called after her.

* * * *

Atom stood under the shower atomizer and let the warm droplets of water caress his skin. The sealed stall featured spray nozzles on two separate walls as well as the ceiling. It was morning, he had this work shift off, and he'd just finished a very enjoyable breakfast with Adara. All in all, the day was starting out quite well.

Eyes closed, he turned his face into the water jets. A sense of total relaxation pervaded his being. Just then he heard the door click open behind him, and a moment later a soft hand slid around his stomach from behind. He gasped as even softer lips caressed the base of his neck.

Reaching back, he felt Adara's nude form standing close. His hand grabbed her supple waist and pulled her tight against him. She slid her wet body against his sensually, nibbling his ear. Breathing heavily, he turned, maintaining the bodily contact. Now face to face, their mouths met, tongues dancing and probing as their hands roamed over each other's naked skin.

Adara slid her mouth slowly down his body as her nails raked his back. He groaned with pleasure, his pulse rushing in his ears. His hands and tongue returned the favor, teasing and exploring. He slid a finger between her legs, reveling in the way she eagerly responded. When an involuntary moan escaped her lips, he felt an incredible thrill of excitement surge through him. He wrapped her tightly in his arms, wanting to experience every inch of her.

Finally she broke away, turning and planting her hands on the wall of the shower stall. Bent over at the waist, she looked back over her shoulder teasingly. That was all the invitation he needed.

He took her from behind, gripping her hips, matching her rhythm, slowly at first, then building to a hard, fast tempo as their passion swelled. They were both panting now, consumed by animal hunger. Grabbing her hair, he thrust harder. Suddenly he felt her body clench as she cried out and reached orgasm, and he met her there, holding on tight and riding the waves of pleasure until he was spent.

They passed most of that morning in bed, talking, sharing, cuddling. The ongoing war, and the uncertainty that accompanied it, had given both of them pause when it came to pursuing a relationship. In the end, the mutual attraction had proven too strong to resist. Ever since they had made the decision to become intimate a couple of days before, they had spent nearly every spare minute together.

Atom lay on his side gazing at Adara, drinking in the curves of her face and body, letting her voice caress him as she talked of her time on Nueva Terra. Her life before the Knackers, a normal life full of gloriously mundane pursuits, wherein the biggest worries were which boy to date, which relatives to see on the holidays, which lake to picnic at. A life that had been stolen from her, perhaps forever. Yet here she was, alive and real and willing to share her love with him unconditionally. Somehow she was still capable of that. An odd thought occurred to him, that her body perfectly reflected her persona: soft and beautiful on the outside, but with a steely strength hidden beneath.

His pleasant musing was interrupted as Adara giggled and poked him in the ribs. "Have you heard anything I've been saying?" she said mischievously.

"I was lost in good thoughts," he admitted with a sheepish grin.

"Aww, I can tell," she said, her expression softening. "Were they about me, by chance?"

"Do you really need to ask?" he replied, chuckling.

"Yes, I do. I like to hear it from your lips," she said tenderly, her fingertip gently brushing against his mouth.

"Well, if you like a man who says what's on his mind, you're going to love me," Atom said with a grin.

"Oh, I already do," she breathed as she leaned in to give him a lingering kiss. That effectively ended all conversation for a good while.

* * * *

Taramay was eating her evening meal in the cafeteria when a page came through her wrist com. She touched the screen and said, "Yes?"

"Sorry to bother you at dinner," Dr. Lott's voice emanated from the speaker. His image was tiny on the miniscule display, but the worried look on his countenance was still evident.

The captain convulsively swallowed the bite of food in her mouth, and asked, "What is it?"

"I've got test results on Eve," the medic replied. "I'd like to go over them when you have a moment, preferably in person."

"I'll be there in a few," Taramay replied. The doctor nodded and she killed the screen.

She gulped the rest of her now-tasteless meal at a pace that would have made the doctor shake his head in disapproval. A few minutes later she sat in the medic's office, listening numbly as he recited his findings.

"Serum chemistries were mostly normal," he began, "but analysis of her cerebrospinal fluid showed increased protein levels and leukocytes indicating inflammatory response. Brain scans did not find any visible pathology in the cortex, where seizures would originate."

He paused, gazing at the captain with a heavy expression. "However, the mass in Eve's midbrain has grown significantly since the first scan. Alarmingly so, for such a short time interval. There is also fluid accumulating in that region. I suspect this is causing pressure and inflammation in the brain, likely leading to the convulsion she experienced."

"Why is it growing?" Taramay asked. "Is it cancer?"

The doctor shook his head uncertainly. "I don't know. It's behaving like a neoplasm, in layperson's terms a tumor, yes. The other children show no progression in their masses, so I don't think this was a development that the Knackers foresaw or intended."

"The damned Crabs couldn't care less about the welfare of these kids," the captain growled. "People are just tools for them to use and discard."

"I agree that our enemy has little concern for a human child *per se*," the doctor said. "But they likely wanted these children to remain functional, and normal to outward appearances, for as long as possible. That is how they could remain useful. Eve's condition is making her ill, and it's drawing attention. This cannot be intentional. Something went awry with the tissue that they implanted. I think it was supposed to grow and develop, then remain stable from that point on."

"Implanted?" Taramay interrupted. "So the growths were put into the kids somehow? They didn't develop with the children, like genetically engineered?"

"No, I believe that our initial impressions were correct. These children started out as normal humans, and were abducted and modified. Their childhood memories appear too detailed and...too real, for lack of a better term. Dr. Roman agrees with me on this. The Knackers are advanced, but they don't have a great feel for human psychology. We don't think they could implant a false personality and memories into a person, not well enough to pass for a normal human child."

"Then how did the masses get into the center of their brains?" the captain asked.

"The scar you found on Eve was present on every modified child. No scars existed on the other children; I checked in case it was some odd vaccine protocol on Nueva Terra or something. The wound was too small to allow direct insertion of a full-sized mass like we detected. The children's skulls were intact as well, except for a tiny focus of reactive bone under the scar, such as might occur with a needle puncture through the skull."

"So they inserted something into the head," Taramay said.

"Yes, we think a small bit of tissue was implanted, and then grew into the functional structure we see in the children today. It makes sense really. A small intrusion is far less traumatic to the brain. It also is much more likely to escape detection than a more invasive surgery."

"So Eve and the other children are real people, victims like everyone else," the captain concluded.

The doctor nodded.

"That's a great relief." A brief smile flitted across the captain's features, but as quickly vanished. She folded her arms and locked her gaze on the doctor. "Now, what about Eve?"

Dr. Lott shifted uncomfortably. "Well, I've got her on medication to suppress seizure activity; it's made her a bit sleepy, but otherwise she acts fine. I also prescribed anti-inflammatory meds to reduce intracranial swelling and pressure. She's stable for now, but these are stopgap measures. Something is wrong with the tissue that the Knackers bio-engineered. It likely will keep growing. If that happens, Eve's survival time may be measured in weeks, not years."

"Can you help her, Gerold?" Taramay asked anxiously. "Can you fix this?"

The doctor shook his head. "Sadly, no. I don't have the facilities onboard this ship. There are procedures at planetary hospitals that might eliminate the mass, provided it doesn't spread."

"Such as what?"

The doctor rubbed his chin as he considered his answer. "For starters, Tuned Electromagnetic Wave Interference can selectively cauterize a controlled area inside the brain. Possibly immune-cell modulation aimed at the abnormal mass could also be effective. This would utilize the patient's immune system to attack the foreign tissue. It works anywhere in the body, and would clean up stray cells if the tumor is spreading. Wave therapy would probably be used first, as it can kill most or all of the mass instantly."

"Where would Eve have to go for this type of procedure?"

"Any developed world would have facilities which are capable," the doc said, "provided that enemy attacks haven't destroyed the infrastructure of that planet."

"Eden, perhaps," Taramay mused. "We're to take the refugees there anyway. How much time do we have?"

"To avoid irreparable damage to Eve's brain, we need to get this done within the next one to two weeks at the latest. I can't be sure how fast this lesion will grow."

"I'll send a message to Command, and let them know that we have a patient needing immediate attention when we arrive at Eden," Taramay said. "That's the best plan at this point." She managed to muster up a smile. "Thank you very much for your help, doctor. It's a relief to hear that she's stable."

"Glad to be of help. I just hope we can keep her from deteriorating until she can receive proper treatment."

Taramay's expression brightened as a thought occurred to her. "Say, can Eve have visitors now?"

"Oh, yes! She's been sleeping a lot, mostly due to her medications, but I'm sure she'd love to see you," Dr. Lott said, moving toward the door.

"Okay, hold on for a minute, please." Taramay tapped her wrist com, and when it lit up, she said, "Bridge."

"Yes, Captain," Lt. Stepanovich's voice answered after a brief pause.

"What are the deep space scans showing? Any sign of our pursuer shadowing us?"

The com officer could be heard consulting with Lt. Cotton, and then she said, "No, Captain. All clear so far."

"Good. Transfer me to Mr. Debartolo."

"Affirmative."

In a moment the navigator's voice came through. "Yes, Captain?"

"Lef, we're resuming our original flight plan, now that the

Crabs aren't watching over our shoulder. Abort our approach to Clandesta and set course for Eden."

"Yes, ma'am."

"Captain out." Turning back toward the doctor, Taramay said, "We'll get help for these children as fast as possible." She motioned with her arm. "Okay, lead the way."

They snaked through a couple of short hallways and past the main treatment room, eventually entering a spacious ward. A line of beds, identically clad in standard brown and white hospital linens, flanked the left wall. At the near end of the row a small figure lay sleeping. Though the person's face was turned away and partly covered by a blanket, Taramay recognized the black shock of hair spilling over the bedding. She stepped forward hesitantly, calling softly, "Eve?"

The slight form stirred restlessly but did not awaken.

The captain glanced at the doctor, who nodded encouragingly. She walked slowly to the bed and put a hand on Eve's shoulder. "Hey there, sweet girl. Guess who's here."

The youngster turned over and squinted sleepily up at the silhouette standing over her. Taramay bent down closer, watching anxiously as the fog cleared from the girl's eyes. When it finally came, the smile that lit Eve's face was as glorious as a dawn sun breaking over the horizon. In a tiny voice she said, "Captain T! You came to see me!"

"Yes, I did. You didn't think I'd forget my best crewmember, did you?"

The girl shook her head, grinning. They looked at each other for a moment, and then Eve reached up and wrapped her arms around Taramay's neck. She nestled her head into the captain's hair, and whispered, "I love you."

Taken by surprise, she wasn't sure how to respond. Reflexively she returned the embrace, and after a moment's hesitation, she said, "I love you back, little angel."

The small arms gripped even tighter, and Taramay patted the girl's back, glancing over at the doctor self-consciously. He appeared to be studiously examining his shoes while fighting to suppress a smile.

Eve finally released her grip and fell back to the bed, looking fatigued. Her cheerfulness remained, however, and she talked with the captain for nearly a half hour before the doctor stepped in.

"Okay, Eve. We'd best get you some food, and then rest," he said, tapping on his digi-pad. "I've ordered you dinner. Be sure you finish it this time. No sneaking it into the recycler," he warned with a stern look.

"Okay, I promise," the girl said contritely. "The last meal just didn't taste very good."

"That's hospital food for you," the captain quipped. "It's always that way, supposedly healthy but tastes like recycled hyperdrive coolant. Why is that, doc?"

The physician shrugged, straight-faced. Taramay returned his serious look for a moment, and then a smile broke through and she began to laugh. Eve joined in, and seeing that he was outnumbered, the doctor abandoned his serious façade and started to chuckle as well. The medic headed for the door, shaking his head and waving his digi-pad at them as he left. Taramay gave Eve a kiss on the forehead and turned to follow the doc out.

"Come see me again soon! Please." Eve called from her bed.

"Count on it, soldier," the captain answered. The image of the girl's smiling salute stayed with her all the way to her quarters.

17.

They were three days out from their destination when Lt. Stepanovich announced an incoming message from Space Command.

Taramay stood up from her command chair. "Play it on screen as soon as it's loaded," she commanded. She waited impatiently for the file to play. One of the biggest problems with interstellar distances was information sharing. Even with faster-than-light transmissions, it often took hours to days for a message to reach its recipient. This precluded direct two-way conversations except when both parties were within a half-lightyear of each other.

"Message playing," Alena announced, and the captain turned her attention to the port side of the domed viewscreen. There a familiar rectangular projection materialized. The seal of the Core Planets Alliance came into focus, an eight-pointed star with the member planets arrayed at the tips. The auburn-haired figure of General Naismith was once again seated at her desk. Her steel-blue eyes held an intensity that demanded attention.

"Greetings, *Goliath* and Captain Dent," the officer began. She glanced down at the digi-pad she held in her hand. "We've received your action plan and status updates. SpaceForce is currently on track for the Clandesta operation. Enemy ship movements indicate a high probability of impending attack on the asteroid base. Based on available intel and our calculations, the Knackers will mount a large offensive. This requires us to bring every available resource to bear.

"Consequently, your orders have been modified. The *Goliath* is to proceed at maximum safe speed to the fleet staging area at Stannos 3; details are provided in the attached documents. Unfortunately, you will have to delay delivery of your civilian refugees, plus the enemy data you procured, until after Clandesta."

The general set aside her digital tablet and rested her hands on the desk. "Captain Dent, this operation is of utmost importance.

Thanks to you, we have the opportunity to strike a significant blow in this conflict. I've recommended commendations for all of the *Goliath*'s senior officers. I hope to present them in person when this is over."

Her gaze softened, and when she continued, it was in a less formal tone. "I know you have people on the *Goliath* who need help. Each individual matters, but the welfare of millions may depend on our actions here. When this operation is concluded, I'll do what I can to facilitate medical aid for your refugees. Until then, fly safe, and watch your backside, soldier. Best regards, Naismith out."

The screen went blank. After a few seconds, Lt. Caine broke the silence. "It sounds like we're going to see more action soon. I should check with our department chiefs and be sure all repairs are complete before we're called upon."

Taramay didn't reply. Her heart had sunk with the general's words. There was no medical help coming Eve's way, not for a good while anyway.

"Captain?" the first officer prompted. "Do I proceed?"

She glanced at him and nodded wearily. "Do it, Mr. Caine. We need the *Goliath* as close to optimal as possible. This ship is more powerful than anything SpaceForce has, except for the Lampreys. We've got to be ready when the fighting begins." She clenched her fists and pounded them softly on the handrail in front of her. To herself she whispered, "Hang in there a little longer, Eve."

* * * *

Running at top speed, they reached their new destination within one standard day.

"We're on final approach to Stannos 3," Leofric announced from his station. "Cycling out of hyperspace now."

Taramay glanced up at the domed viewscreen just as the image shuddered. In a blink of an eye the shifting palette of pastels and colored orbs was gone, replaced by a motionless black vista dotted with white pinpoints. They were back in the familiar environment of normal space.

"Scanner report," the captain commanded.

"We're in wide orbit around Stannos 3," Lt. Cotton answered. "Scanners show that a large armada of federation ships is massed closer to the planet."

"Ms. Stepanovich, announce us to the fleet. Mr. Debartolo, approach and bring us into formation."

"Affirmative, Captain."

The bridge officers went about their tasks. Leofric brought the *Goliath* into close orbit around the third planet of the system. It was a gas giant, striped with bands of emerald and royal blue, and encircled by three rings, one at the equator and two at the northern and southern latitudes. The unusual ring arrangement derived from gravitational interactions with the planet's two oversized moons.

The human fleet swam into view around the curve of the planet, slowly growing in the viewscreen ahead of them. Lt. Jónsson, usually quiet and reserved outside of combat, couldn't help herself. "Look at that!" she enthused from her gunnery station. "I've never seen a more beautiful sight!"

Taramay suppressed a chuckle. Beauty was a subjective thing, and Greta probably needed to get out more, but the captain had to admit that the swarm of ships spread across the dark sky was impressive. Warcraft of all classes were on display. Their metallic bulks glowed as if lit from within, reflecting the intense light of the blue-white supergiant star that was this system's sun.

Altogether the fleet contained no fewer than fifteen destroyers, including the *Goliath*, plus three fighter carriers and six of the rare Lamprey super-dreadnaughts. The latter were so new to the theatre of war that Taramay had never seen more than two in any previous engagement. This was one of the largest armadas that SpaceForce had ever fielded. She felt humbled that her impromptu idea had grown into such a significant endeavor.

They slowly came up on the fleet and merged into it. As their sister ships slid past on the viewscreen, Taramay read off the familiar names. The sleek tapered shape of the destroyer *Xerxes* passed close on their port side. To starboard floated the lumbering mass of a fighter carrier displaying the moniker *Styx* on its flank. Then another destroyer, the *Sparticos*. Old acquaintances all…except for the Lampreys.

As they approached a super-dreadnaught, Taramay stared entranced at the huge ship. A half kilometer long, the cylindrical craft was so narrow as to appear almost tubular. The prow was a bulbous mass resembling the head of a serpent. The captain had heard that the Lamprey's name came from a legendary old Earth creature which the ship's odd shape vaguely resembled. Meter after endless meter, it slipped past the *Goliath* for what seemed like an eternity. Finally they passed the fore section, where the name of the ship was emblazoned in red: *Hunter*.

Lt. Debartolo moved the *Goliath* into a gap in the fleet formation, and matched velocities with the other ships. There they remained, awaiting instructions.

Within minutes an incoming message opened on the port-side viewscreen. The murky white field resolved into the image of a silver-haired officer clad in a dark blue uniform. In addition to the usual shoulder epaulettes indicating rank, his uniform was dotted with numerous medals and ribbons commemorating past accomplishments. He stood straight and tall on the bridge of his ship, his trim figure attesting to a lifelong commitment to fitness. Hands clasped behind his back, he nodded and smiled briefly.

"Greetings, *Goliath*," he spoke in a deep resonant timbre that belied his age. "This is Admiral Roswell on the flagship *Artemis*. I'll be commanding the fleet for the duration of this engagement. Captain Dent, I'm glad to see you. Your combat experience will be needed here, not to mention the firepower your ship brings."

"Happy to be of service, Admiral," the captain replied, saluting. "What is the situation?"

"Well, you arrived just in time. Current intelligence reports have the Crabs mobilizing. We expect the attack on Clandesta to begin shortly. I'm sending you the relevant intel now, along with the armada battle configuration. Obviously you've been unable to attend any strategy sessions; I need to get you up to speed quickly."

"Can you summarize the action plan?" the captain asked.

"Yes. Our destroyers will lead the attack, split into three groups that will surround the enemy fleet. The *Goliath* will spearhead group B. The Lampreys will form an outer perimeter, firing on enemy destroyers and pyramid ships from a safe distance."

"Intel received from the *Artemis*," Lt. Stepanovich piped up from her station.

"Why do we have carriers in the fleet?" Taramay asked the admiral. "There is no planet for fighters to invade."

"We've observed enemy carriers mobilizing along with their destroyers and pyramids. I suspect the Crabs will deploy fighters to attack the base, after Clandesta's main defenses are breached.

Smaller craft can penetrate blast doors and open up routes into a structure without killing the personnel within. Remember, the Crabs will want trophies, not just a military victory. That's why they're bringing pyramid ships."

"Don't remind me," Taramay said through clenched teeth. "Still, there are no humans inside Clandesta, and Knacker fighters won't pose much risk to our big ships, unless one loses its defensive screens. They're almost an afterthought."

The admiral replied, "Not entirely. The Crabs seem to have learned from our use of the Lampreys' solid projectiles. Energy screens don't effectively repel that sort of assault. The enemy doesn't possess an equivalent weapon, but they've turned to crashing their fighters into our big ships. With their hive mentality, they don't seem to mind sacrificing themselves for the greater good."

Taramay was taken aback. "I've not heard of that tactic before now," she said.

The admiral shrugged. "It's a recent development. So far it's been used sparingly, mostly by fighters that have incurred damage and are useless for anything other than ramming. Nonetheless this is a real danger. That much mass hitting a destroyer at high speed could incapacitate it. Simply put, we need to neutralize all enemy craft, large or small, so our fighters will likely be called upon."

"When do we mobilize?" Taramay asked the admiral.

The grizzled officer glanced behind him as one of his bridge officers spoke. He listened for a moment, nodding. When he turned back to face the captain, his expression was somber. "The time is close at hand. We've received word of multiple Knacker warships jumping into hyperspace. We have surveillance drones in the asteroid field around Clandesta. When we hear that the base is under attack, we will head toward our target."

The admiral paused, narrowing his eyes thoughtfully as he gazed at Taramay. "Captain Dent, you and your crew have gone up against the enemy, and survived, more times than most fleet officers. I also hear that you personally hatched this whole Clandesta plan. Do you have any input regarding the battle strategy?"

"It sounds viable," Taramay commented, choosing her words carefully. "You've mustered more ships than I could have hoped for. That said, I think that the timing will be the most critical aspect."

"Explain," the admiral said.

Taramay felt the weight of expectations on her as the admiral's eyes bored into hers. She gulped and tried to collect her thoughts. "First of all, we don't want to attack too early, before all the enemy forces have appeared. We'd have hostile ships coming in behind us, and potentially get caught in the crossfire. Ideally, we arrive after the entire Knacker fleet has taken position, but before they have overwhelmed the base. We want them preoccupied, and facing the asteroid."

"I agree," the admiral said. "To that end, we sent in technical crews ahead of time to activate Clandesta's defense systems. After many years of neglect, things weren't in great shape. The techs had their work cut out for them, and limited time in which to do it. To their credit, they got the basic hardware powered up."

"What defenses does Clandesta currently possess?" Taramay asked.

"Mostly automated shields and plasma weapons. Standard armament from ten years ago, nothing enhanced. The base will put up a good fight, but it will be no match for the Crabs. By the time we arrive there, the enemy should have recognized that Clandesta's firepower isn't a serious threat. Once they're confident in their superiority, they'll move in close to the asteroid for the kill."

Taramay nodded. "Massing their ships in juxtaposition to the base was a vital point to my plan. We took out an enemy destroyer with a proximity blast on our rescue mission. Drawing them in is the key. The base detonation must damage enough enemy ships to give us a clear advantage."

The admiral said, "We've got human life sign generators scattered throughout that rock. To the Crabs it will look like a bona fide feast. Once the defenses are buckling, they'll come in, all right."

"What are the tactics after we arrive?" the captain asked.

"We'll trigger the antimatter charges the moment we come out of hyperspace, while we're far enough away to avoid damage. With a little luck, the explosion will take out at least half of the Knacker fleet. After that, we'll need to close distance with the enemy quickly, while their ships are in disarray and still bunched together. Then we can surround them and hit them from all sides."

"With the super-dreadnaughts along, it seems like destroyers aren't really needed. We could just hang back and blast the enemy from a distance," Taramay suggested.

"Yes, the Lampreys could take out a number of enemy ships, I'm sure," the admiral agreed. "But if their fleet is damaged by the blast, and then winds up facing our super-dreadnaughts, the enemy may simply choose to flee. We don't just want a victory here; we want to eliminate every alien ship. Destroyers will be needed to hem them in and prevent the enemy from running."

"That makes sense. Thank you for the briefing, Admiral," the captain replied. "Today we'll take the fight to the Crabs!"

"That's the idea," the senior officer said with a grim smile. "Await the signal from my ship, and be ready for immediate action. *Artemis* out."

Taramay saluted as the admiral's image faded from view. Turning toward her crew, she said, "You heard him, people. Sound the battle alert. Mr. Caine, are all systems optimal?"

"Yes, Captain. All department heads report full capability."

The twin alarm claxon sounded, announcing combat status. Battle lighting flooded the bridge in amber hues.

"Now we wait." Taramay sat back in her chair and relaxed her breathing, staring at the viewscreen. Unbidden, a stanza from Eve's battle poem, *Darkling Dreams*, intruded on her thoughts:

> *"In quarters close, two warriors clash,*
> *and strain to gain the upper hand.*
> *In sweat and blood their story's etched,*
> *at glory's end one left to stand."*

Let's hope we're the ones standing at the end of this, Taramay mused grimly. In reality, there was rarely glory in war, only death and loss. Loss of loved ones, of freedom, of innocence.

The moments of actual combat weren't the worst part. Space warfare was fast and intense, demanding a focus that left little room for reflection and anguish. The aftermath—that was where the scars showed. And the waiting. The waiting was hardest of all.

It turned out that they didn't have to sit for long. Barely ten minutes after the admiral's sign-off, his flagship sent the signal to mobilize.

"Engage hyperdrive," the captain commanded, sitting up straight. "Set destination to coordinates received from the *Artemis*."

"Ay, Captain," the navigator barked. "Hyperdrive engaged."

"Estimated time to destination, Mr. Debartolo?" Taramay asked.

"Fifteen standard minutes."

"Defensive screens at full intensity," the captain ordered. "Power up the plasma cannons, and place all non-essential systems on standby. Lock down all blast doors. Have the deck hands secure the passengers in the cargo hold. We don't want people slamming off of bulkheads or floating in zero-g if we take a serious hit."

The refugees' bunks, like most things aboard ship, were fastened to the floor to prevent shifting. Taramay had ordered makeshift restraints installed on each bed when she learned that the *Goliath* was going into combat with passengers. The civilians could lie down and fasten straps across their torsos to keep them in place in the event that gravity was lost or the ship experienced any violent maneuvers.

The captain tapped her fingers distractedly as the time clicked slowly past. "Ten minutes to Clandesta," the navigator eventually announced.

"Mr. Cotton and Ms. Stepanovich, I want real-time intel reports from now until the battle is over."

"Ay, Captain," the tech officer said. "Scanners show heavy activity around the asteroid. Energy surges characteristic of large-scale plasma weapon discharges."

"Any estimation of enemy strength?" Taramay asked.

Bruce shook his head. "No, ma'am. I can't get exact numbers until we're out of hyperspace."

Alena interjected, "Reports from robotic probes indicate nearly twenty Knacker vessels, mostly destroyers, but a couple of Pyramids and fighter carriers as well."

The navigator whistled. "That's a formidable force. We'd better hope that the initial blast takes out a bunch of them. Even with the Lampreys, I don't like our odds if the Crab fleet is mostly intact when we engage."

"Agreed," Taramay said. "Each of their destroyers is worth two of ours. It's remarkable that they allocated that many ships for a non-planetary target. They must believe that Clandesta is a major asset."

Lt. Cotton smiled. "I played it up pretty heavily on the data screen that Eve saw. The base was designated as our central military command nexus, a key component of SpaceForce's defensive capability."

"Ah…good work, lieutenant," the captain said, grinning. "Big bait lures a big catch."

"Communication from the *Artemis*," Lt. Stepanovich called out. "The fleet is ordered to observe radio silence until the engagement commences."

"Acknowledge," the captain said. Alena nodded and spoke quietly into her com-set.

The human armada hurtled through hyperspace at fleet combat speed, dictated by the maximum safe velocity of the slowest class of vessels, in this case the fighter carriers. Taramay scanned the sky around them. Amidst the colorful sea of stars and dark matter, the ghostly shapes of Goliath's sister ships flickered in and out of visibility, cocooned by the halos of their hyperdrive fields. Up ahead, the beautifully blue-tinted horizon masked the deadly danger which awaited.

"Nearing our destination," Lt. Debartolo called out several minutes later. "Preparing for jump to normal space in approximately one minute."

"All hands ready for combat!" Taramay commanded. "Ms. Jónsson, you are clear to fire at will on enemy targets after the asteroid detonates. Mr. Debartolo, maneuver as you see fit, unless I command otherwise."

"I'm detecting heavy energy pulses and radiation from the region of Clandesta," Lt. Cotton announced. "It looks like the base is still fighting."

"Intel from the battle scene is sketchy," Lt. Stepanovich added. "Most of our spy drones have gone silent. However, the enemy forces appear to have converged on the asteroid, and no new ships have arrived for the past several minutes."

"Good. Let's hope their entire fleet is engaged and in proximity to Clandesta," Taramay said.

"Ready for jump," Lt. Debartolo barked. "Expecting the signal from *Artemis* in approximately fifteen seconds."

"Link the signal to the automatic jump controls."

"Already done, Captain," Leofric responded. "Cycling down in ten seconds….five seconds….jump signal received."

In a flash the multicolored universe twitched and went dark. Fleet ships were popping into view all around the *Goliath*, their vast shapes cleanly defined against the black of normal space. It was an inspiring sight, but Taramay only had eyes for the scene ahead of them.

In the near distance a swarm of asteroids blanketed the star field in a broad band which stretched away to infinity on either side. The dark grey rocks were starkly highlighted by the rays of the yellow dwarf sun which lay at the fleet's back.

Dead ahead of the human armada, a lightning storm of energy bolts flashed and flickered. The activity was centered on one of the more prominent rocks at the edge of the asteroid belt. A flotilla of alien ships hovered there, unleashing their combined firepower at their objective.

Even at this distance it was obvious that the Knacker vessels were dauntingly large. A fleet of blunt-nosed heavy destroyers spearheaded the assault. Taramay also picked out the sprawling angular shapes of fighter carriers, plus a couple of gigantic pyramids, lying in wait behind the attacking ships.

The asteroid was dealing out punishment in return. Its computerized battle system was firing powerful plasma weapons at inhuman speed, pummeling the numerous targets in front of it. Defensive screens flared on both sides of the conflict as energy hits struck home.

For a scant few seconds the *Goliath*'s bridge crew stared at the violent tableau, and then everything vanished in a brilliant ball of light. Fifty antimatter charges detonated at once, releasing an unthinkable amount of force that instantly fought to escape the confines of the relatively small planetoid. A miniature sun materialized where none had existed previously. The mass of glowing energy blew outward, obscuring the Knacker armada within milliseconds. Then the wave of destruction bore down on the human fleet.

"Shockwaves incoming!" Lt. Cotton called out, and an instant later, their ship was battered by a long rumbling impact. A cloud of incandescent plasma engulfed them, the entire viewscreen flashing brilliant white before the dimmers kicked in. Taramay held onto her chair as the deck lurched and heaved beneath her, hoping desperately that their ship wouldn't be crippled again.

Her wishes were answered. The Clandesta blast was vastly more powerful than the one they had triggered in the pyramid. However, this time the *Goliath* was much farther from the epicenter of the explosion. Incredibly destructive at close range, the intense energy dissipated rapidly as it expanded outward. By the time it slammed into the human ships, it held only a fraction of its original potency. The physical impact amounted to little more than a hard nudge, and the electromagnetic pulse was attenuated enough to be reflected and absorbed by the defensive screens. The *Goliath* rode the shockwave easily, with little more than a brief flicker of the interior lights to indicate the impact.

"Systems status!" Taramay barked as the viewscreen slowly cleared. "Scanner report!"

"Weapons and screens nominal," the gunner called out.

"Propulsion on line," the navigator added.

Lt. Cotton said, "Scanners functional." He tapped in commands on his screen, and added excitedly, "The enemy fleet appears to have taken heavy damage, with many of their vessels obliterated."

The captain stared at the viewscreen. The glowing haze gradually parted, revealing a scene drastically altered from mere moments before. The asteroid belt now sported a large gap where once had existed the Clandesta base. In the midst of an expanding cloud of debris floated the remaining Knacker fleet.

Taramay felt a thrill surge through her as she realized how diminished the alien armada was. The destroyers that had been nearest to the asteroid had simply vanished, pulverized by the antimatter detonation. Others had survived, due to being positioned further away or having been partially shielded by the forward ships. The blast had tossed their ranks into disarray, with vessels rolling and tilted at various inclinations.

The captain thrust a fist into the air. "*Yes!*" she exclaimed. "We've hurt them badly! Forward quickly and engage the Knacker fleet!"

"Ay, Captain!" Leofric replied. "Closing at full acceleration."

Taramay scanned the field as the *Goliath* leapt forward, using a few precious seconds to assess their adversary's strength. Out of the fifteen or sixteen original Crab destroyers, only eight remained, and many of those carried visible damage. Two large Hades class warships had collided and were locked together, the prow of one ship imbedded deep into the flank of the other. The pyramids and carriers had remained further out from the asteroid, and appeared to be mostly intact.

They bore down on the enemy fleet, their sister destroyers keeping pace on either side. Taramay gripped the arms of her command chair, eyes fixed on the viewscreen as she barked, "*Gunner, fire at will!*"

Greta Jónsson didn't have to be asked twice. Her hands scurried like spiders across her board as she tracked enemy targets. The hyper-focused energies of *Goliath*'s plasma guns stretched out toward the Knacker vessels, and where they touched, destruction ensued.

The enemy ships were turning sluggishly to meet their attackers, but many had their flanks and sterns exposed. Plasma rounds from fifteen human destroyers ripped into the alien fleet, raining damage upon their opponents.

This was what they had planned for, that golden short interval where surprise gave them the advantage. They had to pounce on the opportunity while it lasted. Once the Knacker destroyers were able to turn and face them, the aliens' superior firepower could make short work of the human ships.

"Signal incoming from the *Artemis*," Lt. Stepanovich announced. "The admiral commands that we take group B and flank the enemy fleet to the left, circling around and hitting them from behind. Group C will flank them on the right, and Group A will meet the Knackers head on."

"Acknowledge," Taramay said, "and hail the ships in Group B. We will take point on the approach; have the others fall in behind us."

They continued to rush forward, all weapons blasting. The alien ships began to return fire, but it was sporadic and lacked coordination. Only a few rounds struck the *Goliath*, and those appeared to be from the enemy's secondary cannons. They were being fired seemingly in a random saturation pattern, as if the Knackers had neglected more precise targeting. Taramay found this puzzling, but she welcomed the ineffective tactic if it gave her ship better odds of survival.

Her confusion was justified. The alien destroyers were normally superior to their human counterparts in both offensive and defensive capabilities. However, their proximity to the antimatter detonation had altered that dynamic. Although half of the enemy warships had survived, few had escaped unscathed. The shock wave and asteroid debris had torn through the Knacker fleet like shrapnel, ripping open hulls and damaging weapons emplacements on the ships facing the explosion. The accompanying electromagnetic surge had penetrated the destroyers' electronics, scrambling circuitry and causing partial or total failures in key onboard systems.

The net effect was that many of the enemy vessels were significantly compromised. Their defensive screens were unstable or even nonexistent, and the warships' plasma weaponry and targeting systems had taken a beating as well. The widespread damage had rebalanced the playing field in favor of the humans.

"Direct hit!" Lt. Jónsson exulted as the front of a Knacker ship exploded in a fountain of molten metal. "Their shields were only at fifty percent. That's no match for our new guns!"

"We're angling off the enemy's flank," Lt. Debartolo cut in. "Initiating a rounding slide maneuver."

The exercise he referred to was a common flanking move, designed to keep the ship's prow presented to the enemy as they circled. In this way the destroyer's main guns remained focused on the opponent. There were also advantages from a defensive standpoint: a ship facing head-on presented the smallest profile for enemy weapons to target, while allowing the stronger energy screens at the front of the vessel to provide maximum protection.

The navigator set a course to the left of the Knacker fleet, aiming the *Goliath* on a straight line past their adversary. He waited, fingers hovering above his controls, as they closed in at top speed. Just prior to flanking the enemy ships, he cut the main engines. While momentum carried them forward, he hit the lateral thrusters, slowly turning the huge ship to face the Knackers as they slid by. The other vessels in her group followed suit, synchronizing their movements in a delicate and dangerous ballet.

As one of the leading ships, the *Goliath* was a prime target. Her defensive screens began to flare with increasing plasma hits, still mostly from the Crabs' secondary cannons. The bridge crew strapped into their chairs as the deck pitched and rolled.

The weapons officer retaliated with gusto, firing primary and secondary plasma cannons with precise abandon. Using the situational advantage to the maximum, Greta made sure that the *Goliath* gave out more damage than she took. The human destroyer flung round after round of hyper-focused plasma at their adversaries. Although they were moving past the enemy at high speed, Lt. Jónsson's targeting was deadly accurate. Time and again, molten metal sprayed from deep wounds gouged into the vulnerable Knacker vessels.

After a minute of intense fire and counter-fire, the navigator spoke up. "We've passed by the enemy forces," he said. "We'll be taking up position on the far side momentarily."

As they completed the lateral flanking maneuver, their momentum carried them beyond the enemy fleet. Now they were flying backwards, their prow still aimed back at the Knackers. At precisely the right moment, Leofric fired the main engines, and the *Goliath* slowed, sliding around behind the aliens and matching velocities with them. The pilots of their four companion destroyers expertly slid in alongside, and as a group they continued their onslaught.

"Command reports all three destroyer groups are in position around the enemy," Lt. Stepanovich called out. "We've got them in a crossfire pattern now."

Hitting the Knackers from multiple directions gave the human fleet a significant advantage. It prevented the enemy from massing their firepower. More importantly, the alien warships couldn't protect their flanks from attack. No matter which way they turned, a human destroyer would be behind them or flanking them, firing at the more vulnerable sections of their hulls. The aliens were also hemmed in, minimizing the chances for escape.

Taramay watched as one, and then another, Knacker ship was sliced apart by plasma rounds. "That's it!" she barked, fist slamming onto the arm of her chair. "Keep at it; take them down!"

The *Goliath* fired both primary and secondary cannons at an enemy destroyer directly in front of her. Two of her sister ships discharged their own plasma beams almost simultaneously. The weak screens of the enemy ship flared and vanished under the onslaught, and the prow of the Knacker destroyer exploded outward in a deadly flower of red flames.

Instantly the alien vessel's weapons went silent, and its engines flared and died. The stricken destroyer began to list sideways, pushed out of striking position by the weapons impacts. The cauldron of flame and smoke at the front of the ship was testimony to the fact that it would not fly again.

"Alert, Captain!" Lt. Cotton called out. "Scanners show that the two conjoined Knacker ships are active!" He pointed to starboard, where the vessels in question were visible in the near distance.

Taramay followed his direction and spotted the warships. Left mostly untouched by the human attack, the stricken destroyers now showed signs of life. Along both ships' hulls, the violet flames of positional thrusters had blazed to life, as the Crab crews desperately tried to free their vessels.

For a moment it seemed that their efforts were for naught, and then the two giant hulls began to separate. Slowly, ponderously, the prow of the intact destroyer retracted from deep inside its companion. Flashes of energy discharges and small explosions lit the interior of the impaled sister ship as the two vessels tore apart. Metallic debris from the damaged hull sprayed outward, decorating the space around the vessels like silver glitter.

Then they were free, and both warships immediately turned toward *Goliath*'s destroyer group. It suddenly occurred to the transfixed human observers that the two enemy vessels might be battle-capable. *"Hard to starboard!"* Taramay shouted. "Face the enemy! Fire at will!"

The navigator rushed to comply. Main plasma cannons in both fleets had a rotational range of approximately twenty degrees to port or starboard; the ships needed to be aligned within those angle parameters to get off a shot. The panorama on the viewscreen shifted sideways as they veered to face the new threat, but the enemy beat them to the punch. The more intact Knacker destroyer reached attack alignment first, and it fired. Unfortunately for Taramay and her crew, the enemy ship had full use of its primary plasma cannon.

The beam impacted the starboard side of the *Goliath*. In a split second the energy overwhelmed the defensive screens and struck hull metal. From there it bit deep, punching completely through the ablative surface armor and depressurizing the forward lower compartments.

The weapon impact rang the ship's hull like a gigantic bell tolling. Deeply wounded, the *Goliath* lurched sickeningly, as the harsh reverberation hit the bridge crew's ears with painful intensity. Portions of the viewscreen went blank; those that remained lit showed a grey cloud of outgassing air spewing into space from the stricken portion of the ship.

"Starboard screen is down!" the gunner reported. "Weapons still on line."

"Pressure doors and bulkheads holding," the first officer called out. "Damage appears limited to storage and secondary weapon compartments."

"Still rotating to starboard," the navigator barked. "Aligned for attack...*now*!"

"*Firing main guns!*" Lt. Jónsson said.

Both adversaries unleashed rounds from their primary weapons simultaneously, the two energy beams passing each other en route to their targets. The *Goliath* had repositioned to starboard after the first energy hit, and the enemy destroyer's guns were not precisely aligned when its second strike came. The deadly plasma bolt glanced obliquely off of the port-side screen of the human ship, causing minimal damage.

The humans' return salvo did not miss. Lt. Jónsson had learned from their encounter at the pyramid, and she knew precisely where the Knackers' main gun emplacement was located. She had to rush her shot, but her aim was true.

The plasma round from *Goliath*'s enhanced weaponry struck home. At this range, it was lethal even against a fully capable Knacker destroyer. The concentrated beam punched an opening through the aliens' defensive screens, and another, much larger hole in the prow of the Crab destroyer. The enemy's main gun instantly ceased to exist. "*Dead hit!*" the gunner crowed, a hard grin splitting her face.

The Knackers' secondary plasma weapons were still operational, however, and they began spitting fury in rapid-fire progression.

"We've seen this before," the captain said. "Keep our starboard prow protected, Lef."

"On it, Captain," the navigator nodded, watching his readouts closely. The other four destroyers in *Goliath*'s group had now turned to join the fray, and they began to pummel both of the

Knacker destroyers. Giant lances of glowing energy spanned the empty space between the combatants, flaring against screens and gouging chunks of molten metal from their targets.

The disemboweled Knacker ship had also joined the fight. The vessel was surprisingly capable, her propulsion and main weapons systems still fully on line. Her midsection was vulnerable, however, with the open wound presenting a sizable gap in both hull armor and defensive energy screens.

That was a weakness that could be exploited. Taramay frowned in thought, arms folded, and then spun and issued commands. "With our starboard shield down, we're handicapped in a head-on fight. Alena, signal the *Tamaris* to follow us. Let's flank that injured ship."

While their companions continued to engage the enemy, the two destroyers pulled back and circled around. They angled parallel to the embattled ships, making it appear as if they were heading away to help other parts of the fleet. When they were almost past the enemy vessels, the two destroyers abruptly turned and targeted the Knacker ship from the side.

The *Goliath* and the *Tamaris* fired a coordinated burst, hitting the damaged section of the aliens' hull with their main guns. Internal explosions rocked the Crab destroyer, finally stilling its weapons. More detonations followed. Fire and debris belched from the vessel's interior, and in slow motion the vast hull split in two, each section twisting away in opposite directions with a debris trail extending behind.

"Excellent!" the captain exulted. "That's another Crab ship down. We're going to win this!"

"Captain," the gunnery officer interjected. "We've lost our front port-side shield as well; it must have incurred damage from that second plasma round we got hit with."

"Damn!" Taramay said. "That pretty much ends our day, unless we can hit someone from behind. We're wide open if we try a frontal assault. Well, at this stage it looks like the fleet can get it done without us. Stand down, everyone."

Across the battlefield, SpaceForce was indeed gaining the upper hand. The Knacker destroyers were outnumbered and handicapped by the damage sustained in the Clandesta blast. They steadily took weapons hits, losing capability until one by one they were destroyed. Currently only four were still fighting.

The human fleet did not go unscathed. Taramay saw several SpaceForce ships bleeding flames out of badly damaged hulls. One of *Goliath*'s sister craft, the *Nannis*, passed directly in front of a disabled Crab destroyer. The enemy ship was immobile, and its guns had ceased firing after its targeting array had been fused by a plasma round hit. Unfortunately the Knackers' main weapons still had power. As the human ship passed across its firing path, the enemy destroyer unleashed a round from its primary energy cannon. Then another, and a third, all within a span of a few seconds. The human ship didn't stand a chance.

The point-blank plasma beams shredded the *Nannis*'s screens as if they were nonexistent. As the human destroyer slid past the enemy vessel, the three impacts were spread along the length of the hull. The ship's flanks were not as well protected as its prow, and the Knacker weapons were superior to anything SpaceForce had been able to develop. At such a close range nearly a hundred percent of the plasma's energy made it to the hull. The rounds passed clear through the human destroyer, exiting on the other side in massive gouts of flame.

The *Nannis* went dead instantly. The blue-white exhaust jets from her engines shrank and vanished, her running lights winked out, her radio went silent. Horrified, Taramay stared at the viewscreen, unable to tear her gaze away. "Mr. Cotton, can you give me scanner readings on the *Nannis*?" she asked, afraid of what the answer would be.

"Minimal life signs registering," the lieutenant replied in a muted voice.

The captain's heart sank. Thank Ares that they were too far away to visualize bodies in the floating debris. "Hit that Crab ship with everything we've got," she gritted out. "I want nothing left but space dust."

Lt. Jónsson nodded and turned to her console. A few seconds later the captain gasped as the alien destroyer suddenly expanded and burst open at the seams, jetting white flame from multiple rents in its armor. The entire port side of the ship blew open, spilling the inner contents of the hull out into the raw vacuum of space. No portion of the vessel was left intact; it had been rendered into a burning cinder within seconds.

Stunned, Taramay turned to the gunner. "I know I said to destroy that ship, but…what the hell did you do, Greta?"

The lieutenant shrugged, her expression puzzled. "Nothing, Captain. I didn't even fire a shot. The ship just exploded."

"What the…" the captain began, and then her eyes widened as the realization hit her. "Ah-ha! The Lampreys have joined the party!"

"It's about time," Lt. Cotton growled. "Our destroyers have been doing all the dirty work. What took them so long?"

"I suspect they had to wait until things cleared a bit, so that they could minimize collateral damage," Taramay replied.

"It's not that hard to avoid our ships," the tech officer retorted. "Destroyers are really large vessels, and we have good targeting systems. Is it really that likely they'd hit us?"

Greta Jónsson spoke up. "It's not just a matter of aiming straight. You saw how that Knacker ship blew open on one side. The Lamprey round probably exited the hull there, and continued onward at high velocity. If one of our ships had been in the line of fire, positioned behind the target…"

"A Lamprey round can penetrate all the way through a destroyer?" Lt. Cotton asked incredulously.

"If it's a flank shot, then yes, it could pass through fairly easily," the gunner replied.

The tech officer just shook his head, at a loss for words. Then he glanced down at his console, and sat up straight in his chair. "Fighters incoming!" he said urgently. And sure enough, the viewscreen showed approaching swarms of small ships, appearing like tiny insects compared to the destroyers around them.

"Message coming in," the com officer announced. "One Knacker carrier has released its fighters; Admiral Roswell has ordered our carriers to respond in kind. The second enemy carrier was destroyed by our Lampreys before it could deploy its complement."

"Fighters aren't much of a risk to our big ships," Taramay commented. "Avoid targeting them. They're too mobile for our weapons to easily hit, and there will be friendlies out there as well. Let our fighters handle this."

The battle was over for the *Goliath*. The bridge crew sat and watched as fighters wove and spun in intricate maneuvers, jostling for positional advantage. Small streaks of plasma jetted between the tiny ships. Here and there a bright flash heralded the death throes of a fighter as its fusion reactor lost containment and detonated.

Off across the battlefield, much larger flashes and explosions signaled the impacts of Lamprey railgun rounds as they obliterated Knacker targets. The remaining alien destroyers became nothing more than mangled space junk, along with the carrier that had launched the fighters. Win or lose, the pilots of those small craft would have no base to return to.

When the battle's outcome had become evident, the pair of alien harvest pyramids had begun to edge away from the asteroid field. Large bodies of matter, such as planets or asteroid clusters, were able to warp space around them. This made hyperspace jumps extremely dangerous to attempt. The alien pyramids had to put distance between themselves and the mass of the asteroids, if they wanted to use their hyper-drives to escape. To this end they tried to sneak away, moving so slowly that they might appear to be simply drifting.

By the time the human fleet had eliminated the Knacker destroyers, the pyramids were nearly to the jump horizon. A few more klicks and they would be safely away.

That was as close as they would get. The human fleet had been tracking the giant craft, even while dealing with higher priority targets. The moment their weapons weren't needed elsewhere, several Lampreys turned their bulbous noses toward the distant pyramids.

The super-dreadnaughts were a modern incarnation of a very old weapon, the railgun. A solid metal projectile was accelerated by magnetic fields and expelled at extreme velocities to the target. Instead of gliding down a metal rail as in ancient versions of the weapon, the Lamprey rounds slid between force screens which acted as frictionless guides. This maximized muzzle velocity and minimized internal wear in the weapon. The railgun occupied nearly the entire half-kilometer length of the ship, allowing for generation of tremendous speed by the time the rounds were expelled.

The tungsten-coated slugs fired by the Lampreys were 100 kilogram cylinders of depleted uranium alloyed with titanium. This material was extremely dense, providing maximum mass in a relatively small volume. In addition, the outer layers pulverized on impact, producing a cloud of metallic dust that instantly ignited into an intense fireball.

Railgun rounds were admittedly 'low-tech' and depended on sheer velocity and kinetic energy to do their damage. Nonetheless, they packed a devastating punch, and the Knackers' defensive screens were powerless to stop them. This made the super-dreadnaughts the most important innovation that the human fleet had brought to bear against their adversary.

Four Lampreys unleashed their weapons at the pyramids. Flickers of blue energy briefly jetted from the ships' prows, as the exiting projectiles pulled the railguns' intense magnetic fields with them. The rounds themselves were invisible to the naked eye, leaving the ship with a muzzle velocity of over 800,000 kilometers per hour. By the time the Lampreys fired their volley, the pyramids had moved a full twenty kilometers away. It took less than 0.1 seconds for the rounds to reach their targets.

Each of the four super-dreadnaughts fired twice, with four rounds impacting each alien pyramid. The small projectiles effortlessly pierced the armor of the Knacker vessels, leaving entry wounds that were little more than specks on the huge surfaces. The pyramids absorbed the hits and for the briefest of moments, appeared unfazed. Then the smooth hull faces began to buckle and heave, almost like the surface of a boiling liquid.

Internally, incredible forces were warring with the pyramids' extraordinary mass. The rounds had delivered kinetic energy to each target equivalent to a two kiloton bomb blast. The extreme size of the vessels precluded the rounds exiting out the back as often happened with lesser ships. Instead, the entire energy content of the impact was transferred to the interiors of the pyramids.

There was simply no way to contain that much force. The hull surface instability grew and then both ships burst open, revealing a sea of glowing liquid metal and fire engulfing their innards. To the observers it was evident that not a single Knacker warrior on board could have survived that inferno.

With the destruction of the last large enemy vessels, all that remained was eliminating the pesky fighters swarming throughout the battlefield. Many were now harassing the human carriers, which were more vulnerable than the other warships. The tiny attackers carried surprisingly powerful plasma guns, and they made repeated strafing runs at the ungainly SpaceForce ships. Surface damage was visible on at least one carrier, and human fighters had rushed to defend their mother craft.

Taramay watched the swirl and flow of the battle from her vantage point on the *Goliath*'s bridge. With magnification, the combatants were easily distinguished, as the ovoid shapes of the Knacker fighters contrasted sharply with the sleek arrowhead profiles of the SpaceForce ships.

The human fleet had fielded the newest Avenger class of single-pilot fighter, which had recently proven to be the equal of their alien counterparts. No longer did they have to accept a four to one loss rate in dogfights with the enemy.

Even so, it was a close contest between the opposing forces. The factor tipping the scales for the humans was that they had fielded three fighter groups, while the Knackers only had one vessel successfully deploy. The alien carriers boasted a larger complement of ships than those of SpaceForce, but the humans still fielded over twice the number of fighters as the Knackers on this day.

Slowly the SpaceForce pilots shot the enemy out of the sky. Fewer and fewer ovoid craft remained flying, and the human fighters began to gang up on the stragglers. The day was won.

Taramay sighed and leaned back into the cushions of her command chair, closing her eyes, letting go of the tension. Her plan had worked, better than she had dared hope. It was finally over.

"*Captain*!" Lt. Cotton's panicked voice bolted Taramay upright. "Crab fighter incoming! It looks badly damaged, but it's heading right for us at top speed!"

"We've got no front shields," the gunner said. "It's on a suicide run."

"Taking evasive action," the navigator stated as his fingers danced across his board.

The star field shifted to the right as the Goliath veered sharply to port. "No good," the tech officer called out. "The Crab ship is compensating; still on collision course. Impact in less than ten seconds."

"I can't target something that small," the gunner said helplessly. She added in a resigned tone, "I'm not sure even shields would have helped much."

Now Taramay could see the incoming fighter straight ahead of them. The oval shape was blackened and spewing smoke but appeared to be under power. Its flight path was erratic, possibly deliberately so, to avoid being hit by the *Goliath*'s weapons should they attempt to manually fire at the small target.

In the Knacker ship came, rapidly swelling in size as it closed with them. Taramay gripped her chair helplessly. This was going to be very bad, and they could do nothing to stop it. Five seconds until impact, four, three…

Twin lances of energy hit the alien fighter from above, and it exploded into a dozen pieces which scattered in every direction. Two seconds later the debris hit the *Goliath*'s hull like high speed shrapnel, glancing off the armor plating with impacts that made the ship shudder. Even situated near the ship's center, the bridge crew could hear the deep thuds. Another section of viewscreen blanked out as an external scanner array was hit, and then it was over.

Taramay let out her breath, and then flinched as a SpaceForce fighter jetted close across their bow.

"Message coming in from that fighter," Alena said.

"Put it on speaker," the captain replied.

A male voice filled the bridge. "Calling *Goliath*, calling *Goliath*, please respond. Are you okay?"

"We're fine," Taramay answered. "Just a little banged up I think. It would have been much worse if not for your help."

"Sorry I couldn't hit that Crab sooner; I was at distance and coming in at a severe angle. Had to anticipate his trajectory and also avoid hitting you."

Taramay was impressed. "That's some fine marksmanship. What's your name?"

"Major Simon Roy, at your service."

"Well, Major Roy, I'll be sure to put in a good word for you with the admiral."

"Thank you, Captain. I've got to return to my carrier now; our fighter group has been recalled."

"Fly safe, soldier."

"And you as well. Roy out."

18.

With the fighting over, the human fleet began the task of securing the battlefield. This included scavenging ruined ships, both human and alien, and retrieving the bodies of the SpaceForce combatants who had lost their lives in the campaign. Some intrepid survivors were found aboard the *Nannis* and were rescued.

Services were held for the deceased, and space burials were performed. The wrapped bodies were cast into the deep, on trajectories that would send them into the system's sun. The cremation would ensure that Knackers could not harvest any of the human dead for food.

Once their work at Clandesta was finished, the fleet ships began to return to their bases. The *Goliath* resumed her journey to Eden, where the civilian refugees would find a new home awaiting. After dropping them off, the destroyer would head for Iliana IV, where her damaged hull could be repaired at a fully-equipped space dock.

As soon as the situation was secure, Taramay had made a tour of her vessel, wanting to assess the damage firsthand. On the lower deck, she found blast doors blocking her access to the aft sections. The engineers confirmed that the area beyond the barrier was depressurized and uninhabitable. Per standard combat protocol, all outer hull compartments had been evacuated prior to entering combat, so no lives had been lost.

Touring the stern cargo bay, she found the refugees shaken but unharmed. Following instructions, they had remained tethered to their cots until the battle had passed. None had suffered so much as a scratch, although fear was still plainly written on many of the faces that turned her way.

She shook hands and smiled, offering reassurance to anyone who looked like they needed it. Eventually she made her way to Adara's cot.

The young woman was sleeping when Taramay approached. The captain contemplated the peaceful scene for a moment, smiling. Then she leaned over and gently put a hand on Adara's shoulder.

The woman's eyelids fluttered and she started awake, sitting up groggily with a frown of concern. "What…what's happening?" she mumbled, still half asleep as she gazed around her through squinted eyes.

"You're fine, nothing is wrong," Taramay reassured her with a grin. "What's happening is simply a visit by your captain."

Adara focused on her visitor's face as the fog cleared from her eyes. She flashed an embarrassed smile, brushing her hair back with one hand. "Hello, Captain. Wow, I'm sorry about that. I was sound asleep and I didn't recognize you for a moment."

"You must have been tired," Taramay said sympathetically. "I probably should have let you rest."

"No, it's all right, I'm glad to see you!" the young woman replied, waving off the captain's concern. "But yes, I was exhausted. We were all on edge knowing a battle was coming, so no one slept much…and then when it actually happened, people were scared to death."

"It was quite a ride down here, I imagine," the captain said with a wry smile.

"Oh, yes!" Adara exclaimed animatedly. "We got thrown around quite a bit, and I swear a couple of times it sounded like the ship was exploding! People were screaming, and I wanted to help them, but I was too scared to do anything but hang on and hope."

"You couldn't have done much strapped into your cot, anyway," Taramay replied. "It turned out okay; no one was hurt." She paused, and then shook her head as she reflected on the battle. "You know, I was so busy running the show on the bridge, I didn't have time to think about what it was like down here. You probably had it worse than I did, not being able to see what was happening." She cocked her head, and grinned as she added, "I suspect that weapons hit was probably louder on the lower deck than where I was."

Adara's eyes widened as she said, "It was plenty loud, I can assure you! My ears were ringing for quite some time after."

"Are you okay now?" the captain asked.

"Yes. The doctor checked me out earlier and said everything's fine. My hearing is back to normal."

"Well then, your ears will be happy to hear that we're heading for Eden. We should be there in a few days."

Adara's face lit up with excitement. "That's great! I can't wait to get off this ship." Her expression fell and she stammered, "I'm sorry! I didn't mean to say that I don't like the *Goliath*. You've been so nice, coming out to rescue us and taking us aboard and all—"

Taramay broke out laughing at the dismay on the young woman's face. She held up her hand, cutting short the apology. "It's perfectly all right, Adara. I know exactly how you feel. The *Goliath* is my command, in fact most of the time she's my life, but right now I can't wait for some shore leave! You can only walk these decks for so long before you simply need to…get away."

Adara nodded, looking relieved that her *faux pas* had not caused any hard feelings.

"Has Atom been down to see you?" the captain asked.

"Oh, yes! He was actually here during the battle, with some of his security guards, maintaining order and making sure people stayed strapped into their bunks. They brought water and snacks around when the worst part was over."

"I suspected he'd find a way to check on you," Taramay said with a knowing smirk.

"Hey, do you know how Eve is doing?" Adara asked. "I've been worried about her; she's not been in her bunk and Atom said she was pretty ill."

The question stopped Taramay in her tracks. Eve was isolated up in the sick bay, and was probably feeling forgotten. She should have checked on the girl first thing! "She's fine," she managed to say. "She's been stable and seems like her normal self. We'll be able to get better treatment for her illness when we reach Eden."

"Oh, good," Adara said with a look of relief. "I was hoping she was okay. I've become quite attached to her."

"You're not the only one," the captain said. "Speaking of which, I'm overdue for a visit with our little waif. Hold down the fort for me here, and I'll come see you again before we arrive at Eden."

"I'll do my best," the young woman said, smiling. She gave

Taramay a casual salute, reminiscent of the absent girl they were both thinking of. Taramay chuckled and returned the gesture before she strode away.

The captain hurried to the medical wing to see her young friend. Days had passed since her last visit, and she hoped that the child's condition hadn't deteriorated.

She was relieved to find Eve sitting up in her bed, eating a chocolate dessert. "That looks good!" she said from the doorway.

"Captain Taramay!" the girl exclaimed excitedly. Sweet treat forgotten, she threw her dish down on the bed tray and reached out her arms. The captain quickly stepped over to the bed and returned the child's hug warmly.

"Where have you been?" Eve murmured into the captain's shoulder. "I've been all alone here."

"I was busy protecting the ship," Taramay told her. "I didn't forget you, silly." She pulled back and looked at the girl with one eyebrow raised. "All alone? I think you're exaggerating a bit, hmm?"

Eve dropped her gaze and fiddled with the bed cover. "Well, there's doctors and nurses, but they don't spend time with me, like talking or playing games. They just want to poke me or feed me medicine." She looked back up at Taramay, adding, "And the food is bad."

The captain giggled, cocking her head and meeting the child's gaze. In a moment Eve gave up pouting and started to grin. They both broke into laughter then, and the girl said, "I can't keep a serious face when you do that."

"I know," Taramay replied. "Haven't you heard that laughter is good medicine?"

"Who says that?" Eve asked, looking skeptical.

"Well, I just did!" the captain retorted, hands on her hips. Seeing the child's frown, she relented and said more seriously, "Actually, I don't know where that saying started. It's been around as long as I can remember; my mother said it to me when I was a child."

"Really?" the girl said with a smile. "That's a long time. I like hearing about things from when you were little."

"Then maybe I'll tell you more stories, when we have time."

"That would be great!" Eve said, bouncing on the bed.

"Hey, you'd better finish your dessert," the captain said. "It's starting to melt."

"Okay, I guess you're right. I've waited all day for something tasty to eat." She grabbed the bowl and began to shovel in a scoop of chocolate.

"I'll let you finish, then I'll check on you a little later, okay?

Eve nodded, her spoon buried in her mouth.

The captain cornered Dr. Lott on her way out of the sick ward. "Any news on Eve?" she asked.

The doctor dropped his gaze a moment, looking unhappy. He finally met Taramay's eyes, and said, "She's had another seizure. The reduction in swelling we achieved with medication has been offset by further growth of the mass. Intracranial pressure has increased, and we're back to where we started. I increased the drug doses, but there's only so far I can go with that."

"Have we found someplace on Eden for her treatment? General Naismith said she would try to facilitate the process after we finished with Clandesta."

The doctor sighed, shaking his head. "I've been in contact with SpaceForce. A problem has come up that may delay her getting treatment."

"What sort of problem?" the captain asked, grabbing his arm. "Doesn't Eden have the facilities?"

"No, it's not that. The issue is a legal one," the medic said.

"*What*?! How?"

"The procedure isn't routine, because the lesion isn't," the doctor explained. "There are significant risks. This tissue mass is unique in our experience. We can't say with certainty that it will keep growing, or that treatment will cure it. The mass is interlinked with areas of Eve's brain; destroying it could have unforeseen side effects. It's not a given that she'll even survive the procedure."

"But treatment is the best option, right?"

"I think so, yes. Other experts I've talked to agree. But Eve is a child. Space Command is concerned that there are no adult relatives available to give consent for the procedure. That could have legal implications, if things go badly and then family shows up later to ask why."

"Their home planet was overrun!" Taramay exclaimed. "There may not be any relatives left."

"I know that. Nonetheless, Command wants a responsible adult to speak for Eve, and take the legal brunt if family shows up later and wants to cast blame."

"I don't believe this," the captain said, exasperated. "Can't they create a document stating that to the best of our knowledge, no family survives? Make Eve a ward of SpaceForce?"

"Well, you're on the right track, but Command wants nothing to do with Eve. They'll allow for her be declared an orphan, but a private citizen would have to get involved at that point."

"So there is a way?" Taramay pressed.

"Yes…but it would require sacrifice on your part," the doctor said, eyeing her evenly.

"Tell me what I have to do."

* * * *

Later that day, Taramay walked slowly down the corridor toward her quarters, head bowed in thought. She had to make a decision soon; Eve's life likely depended on it. So little time for such an important thing.

Over the course of her career, she had learned not to make snap judgments. Careful consideration was her usual approach, and it had served her well. But time was an asset she lacked; she had to act now or let fate play out as it would.

Taramay sighed, a deep exhale of frustration. If nothing else, she could sleep on it, and see how things felt in the morning. Reaching her cabin, she thumbed the fingerprint lock and entered. It was going to be a long, restless night.

* * * *

The next day, the captain awoke and had breakfast. Sometime during the night, she had made her choice, and by the light of day, she was at peace with it. Finishing her meal, she walked deliberately to the medical wing. Eve was there waiting for her.

"Hey there, little angel," the captain said warmly, sitting down on the bed beside her. She used a forefinger to brush back the girl's hair, and said casually, "Has the doctor talked to you about your illness?"

The girl nodded. "He said that I have to get treatment, or I'll probably get sicker."

Taramay smiled. "That's right, but the treatment isn't easy either. It could make you sick, too."

"But it could cure me, right?" Eve asked, her eyes searching Taramay's face.

"Yes, there's a good chance the doctors can fix the problem," the captain replied, hoping she sounded confident.

"Could I die from the treatment?" the girl asked bluntly.

Now was not the time to avoid the truth. "Yes, but it's not likely."

"Will this illness kill me if I don't have anything done?"

"Probably, yes."

"Then I want the doctors to treat it," the girl said, her face set in a determined expression. "They can do that on Eden, right?"

"Yes, but there's a problem," Taramay said. "You're not an adult, and so you can't be the one to say 'yes' to the procedure. An adult has to give permission, usually one of your family."

"But I have no one," Eve said, her voice quavering. "Only you."

"That's what I want to talk to you about," the captain replied. She reached out and held the girl's hands. "I can give permission for the treatment, but only if I do something first. It's something very personal, and I won't do it unless you agree."

"What?" the child asked, wide-eyed.

"I'll need to adopt you," Taramay said softly.

"Adopt?"

"Yes. I'll be like…a new mother to you." She paused and took a deep breath. There. She had said it. Eve wasn't running away screaming, so maybe there was a chance. In truth the child looked overcome by surprise, and hadn't uttered a word yet.

To fill the uncomfortable silence, Taramay began to speak again, and the words tumbled out in a rush. "I know I'm not your biological mother; I know that no one can replace her. You need to understand, if we do this, we won't be together all the time. I'll still be a SpaceForce captain, and you'll have to stay on Eden while I'm on missions in space. I've got a lot of shore leave built up, and I can come home to be with you whenever I get time off. When I'm away I'll have good people look after you."

She released the girl's hands, and crouched down so that they were face to face. Eve's eyes were swimming with tears, and Taramay caressed her cheek gently. She said, "This war will end eventually, and then I'll be home for good. I'll take care of you until you're grown up. We'll be a family, you and I. But only if you want it. Do you want this, little angel?"

Moisture was streaming down the girl's face, and she sobbed once. Taramay anxiously waited for an answer. She had opened her heart, which left her painfully vulnerable. What if her offer was refused? She held her breath…and then Eve nodded, and she smiled through the tears, and she reached out to hug Taramay with desperate strength. And it was all right, it was all going to be all right.

* * * *

The *Goliath*'s shuttles made several trips down to the surface of Eden, as they preferred not to pack the refugees in as tightly as they had the first time around.

Taramay took Eve on the very first trip down. Among the other passengers were two faces they recognized, Atom Granger and Adara Knightsbridge. They sat together, holding hands, talking quietly as they endured the bumpy ride through the atmosphere. Out of the corner of her eye the captain observed the couple; they seemed very happy together. She smiled to herself. Atom was a good man, and she was glad he had found the young lady from Nueva Terra.

Atom and Adara eventually noticed the captain and came over to say hello. Adara was excited to see Eve before they landed, as they had no way of knowing when they would be able to get together planetside. Eve made the young woman promise to look her up when she was settled.

When they disembarked, Taramay and Eve found an official SpaceForce vehicle waiting for them just beyond the shuttle. The driver opened the door, and ushered them both inside. They settled into the plush seats, grinning at the royal treatment. The door slid shut, and they were whisked away toward a nearby hospital where a top medical team awaited them.

Atom helped Adara off the shuttle, holding a combat bag full of personal effects and steadying her as she traversed the steep ramp to the ground. They walked a short distance across the pavement of the spaceport, trying to find a small island of privacy away from the crowd of disembarking passengers.

When they had gone far enough, they slowed and turned to face each other. Setting the luggage items down, they stepped close and embraced one last time. For the occasion, Atom had worn his best dress uniform, even though the refugees had only standard-issue fleet coveralls when they landed. He didn't care; Adara still made the outfit look beautiful.

He held her tightly, relishing the feel of her eager body pressed against his, the way his arms wrapped her waist so perfectly, the smell of her hair as it brushed his cheek. He wanted to absorb every sensation, hold it in his memory, as it would be all he had of her while he travelled far away from this place.

A warm, sweet breeze blew across them as they shared a lingering kiss. It was early summer in this hemisphere, and the planet was beautiful. Adara ground her body seductively into his, and giggled when he groaned softly. "I wish I could stay," he began, and she shushed him with a finger to his lips.

"We've talked about this," she said. "You have your duty, and nothing is more important now. If we don't win this war, no place will be safe for us. Do what you have to do, and I'll wait for you. Just promise to come see me as often as you can. Don't forget me."

"That's the easiest vow I've ever had to make," he grinned. He leaned in to kiss her one more time, and the shuttle's claxon sounded behind them. Reluctantly he pulled his lips from hers. "They're getting ready to take off again. I've got to get on board."

"Go. I can get the luggage from here, and if not, I'll just find someone to lend a hand."

"You be safe while I'm gone," he said in a mock-fatherly tone.

"Always. And you be careful, soldier. Come back to me."

"I will. Nothing could keep me away."

He released her from his embrace and stepped back, and she reached for his hand, wanting to extend the contact for just a moment longer. For a few seconds they stood like that, fingers touching, and at last he saw her brave face waver a bit, and her eyes turn wet.

"I'm afraid it's time to say goodbye," Atom said.

"I'm going to miss you so much," she replied with a sad smile.

"Keep me in your thoughts, and I'll always be close," he said gently. "I love you, Adara."

She silently mouthed the words back at him, and reluctantly let go of his hand. Turning quickly so he wouldn't see her tears, she bent and grabbed her bags. She had promised herself to be strong, to not make him feel sorry for her when it was time to go. Staring straight ahead, she hurried toward the spaceport terminal.

Halfway there, she thought better of it, and looked back to see her man one last time. He was still standing where she'd left him, watching her. She smiled and waved. He waved back, and apparently was satisfied, as he finally turned and strode toward the shuttle. Her eyes followed him up the boarding ramp, until he disappeared from sight in the bowels of the ship.

Blinking to see through a blur of moisture, she gripped her bags tightly and turned back toward the terminal entrance. She began to walk, hesitantly at first, and then step by step her stride became stronger and more confident. Her back straightened and her face took on a look of calm determination.

Things weren't all bad. Despite the war and the damage it had wrought, it was good to be alive and in love. Fate had given her a second chance, and she was determined to make the most of it. She would create a new life here, and from Eden she would do everything in her power to help her home world.

When it was time, she would eventually return to Nueva Terra and find any relatives and friends who survived. Meanwhile she would do what she could to make them proud. She focused her gaze ahead of her; the concrete and glass front of the terminal loomed close now. Beyond those doors her new world awaited. She marched through them with her head held high and a smile on her lips.

* * * *

Taramay sat in the hospital's waiting room, anxiously watching the clock. It had been nearly three hours since Eve had gone in for her procedure, and no word had come as to its outcome. She was nearly beside herself with worry. Was this what it was like to be a mother? She now understood why her own mom had been such an annoying hand-wringer when she was growing up.

Finally the doors to the surgery ward swung open, and the doctor in charge walked through them. He looked tired, but he was smiling as he approached. Taramay hoped that was a good sign.

"Hello again, Captain Dent. We've finished the primary procedure on your daughter."

Taramay felt a strange thrill course through her at his words; it was going to take some time to get accustomed to Eve being her child.

"How is she, doctor?" she asked nervously. "Did things go well?"

"Yes, very well," the surgeon said. "It looks like we were able to ablate the entire mass with minimal damage to surrounding tissues. The post-operative swelling appears minimal; we can manage that with medications for a few days until it resolves. She appears to be stable and functional at this time."

"Any sign of the mass spreading?" Taramay inquired.

He smiled and shook his head. "The scans all appear clean. Of course, that doesn't rule out microscopic tissue invasion, but targeted immune therapy should wipe out any stray cells. We obtained a needle biopsy of the mass before cauterizing it, which will let us tailor a therapy against the abnormal tissue."

"So the prognosis is good?"

"I'd say very good at this point," the doctor said, beaming. "If she recovers as expected, we'll be performing similar procedures on the other children who are affected."

"That's great news!" Taramay felt a giddy rush of relief wash over her, as the burden of worry that she'd carried began to finally lift. "When can I see her?"

"Not quite yet. She's heavily sedated right now, and she's hooked up to a lot of monitors in the intensive care unit. If she does well, she'll be awake and stable by later tomorrow."

"It's all right, I can wait until she's ready," Taramay said, as she rubbed her forehead wearily.

The doctor gave her an appraising glance, and smiled sympathetically. "I'd recommend that you go home and rest; you look worn out. Come back tomorrow afternoon and hopefully you can visit."

"I'll do that. Thank you very much for all you've done." Taramay shook the doctor's hand gratefully, and gave him a quick hug before heading for the exit. She suddenly realized that she was starving, and a good meal at a quality restaurant sounded like the perfect cap to the day.

Later that evening, with her stomach pleasantly full, she finally crawled into bed. She expected the day's events to keep her awake, but she was unconscious within minutes, and she slept more soundly that night than she had in a long time.

Early the next morning Taramay called the hospital for an update on Eve's condition. The nurse on call informed her that the girl was recovering well, and that she could come by to visit around fifteen hundred hours.

She was at the hospital thirty minutes early, and was so nervous that she could hardly keep herself seated. Fidgeting with her clothes, she waited for what seemed an eternity before a nurse in a red smock came to escort her to Eve's room.

She walked the sterile hallway alongside her guide, trying to ignore the smell of disinfectant that seemed to pervade all such places. They passed several patient rooms with curtains masking the entries. Eventually they halted at a doorway on the right. The nurse smiled as he gestured toward the door. "This is Eve's room," he said. "Please go right in. If you need anything, press the yellow button on the touch-screen by the bed."

Taramay thanked him, and he turned and walked back down the hall. Gathering her resolve, she reached out and pulled aside the door curtain, stepping hesitantly into the small room. She wasn't sure what she had expected; perhaps Eve's head shaved and swathed in blood-stained bandages, with wires and tubes running from every part of her.

Instead she saw a cute girl alertly sitting up in bed, eating what looked like fruit pudding out of a plastic cup. There was only one fluid line attached to her left arm, and most of her hair appeared untouched. She actually looked…normal.

Eve glanced up and saw Taramay standing there. "Captain T! Look at me! I'm okay!"

Taramay smiled broadly and moved quickly to her bedside. She leaned down to give the girl a careful hug. "Yes, you're going to be fine," she said. "How do you feel?"

A little sore, back here," she pointed at the back of her head. "They shaved off some hair there. Does it look funny?"

Taramay glanced at the small bald patch, and shook her head with a deadpan expression. "It looks really stylish; I hear it's the latest fashion on Eden."

Eve looked at her askance for a moment, trying to decide if she was serious, and then she giggled. "That's not really true. You're fooling with me!"

"Maybe I am," Taramay admitted, grinning. "Anyway, it doesn't look bad. You can comb some hair over it if you like, until it grows in."

"Nah. I can't see it, so I don't care."

"That's a great attitude to have," Taramay laughed. She watched the girl eat for a moment, and commented, "It looks like you're hungry! They must have better food in this hospital."

Eve nodded enthusiastically. "Definitely!"

"You're scraping the bottom of the cup there. Would you like something else to eat?"

"Yes, please," the girl said.

"How do you go about ordering food?" the captain asked her.

The girl pointed to a small touch-screen at the side of the bed. "Pull that up where we can reach the screen."

Taramay did so, and then said, "Okay, I see a menu button on the display."

"Yes, push that," the girl mumbled through a mouthful of food.

"Okay, let's see what they have to offer," the captain said, looking the screen over.

"I looked at the menu this morning. They've got quite a few things for breakfast, and even more for dinner. I can't remember all of them; did they have boroberry pancakes?"

"Yes, they do, smart girl." Taramay grinned, and then stopped short. "I thought you said that you'd already looked at this menu."

"That's right, at breakfast. Why?"

"But you don't remember everything on it?"

"Well, I remember some things, probably a lot of them if I think real hard…but no, I can't recall all of it. There's a lot of stuff on there!"

"Yes, there is," Taramay agreed, patting the girl's hand. She felt a small twinge of regret; it seemed that Eve's extraordinary memory was fading along with her implanted tissue. Such an ability would certainly have made the girl's life easier. On the other hand, she'd trade that away in a heartbeat to keep from losing her.

She smiled and said, "I'm putting in an order for pancakes with boroberries. That sounds yummy!"

"Thank you, Captain Taramay."

"You're welcome." Taramay looked at Eve thoughtfully for a moment, and then added playfully, "You can't call me Captain forever, you know."

"What should I call you, then?" Eve asked her, looking confused.

"Well, I guess you could just call me by my first name, Taramay."

Eve's brow furrowed. "I guess I could. I never called my mom or dad by their first names though. It sounds kind of odd, like you're just a friend, rather than my parent."

"What name would you like to use, then?"

The girl hesitated. She looked up timidly, and said in a small voice, "Can I just call you mom?"

Taramay fought to keep her own voice from cracking as she said, "Yes, sweet girl, if that's what you want."

"Is that okay?" Eve asked uncertainly.

Taramay leaned forward and planted a kiss on the child's forehead. "It's very okay. I'd love it," she said with a smile. "And I love you, my angel."

As she wrapped the smiling girl in her arms, the captain reflected on how one small person could have such a big impact on her universe. Standing alone, she had fought the Knackers for most of her adult life, but she had struggled to find any personal sense of hope and meaning in it all.

Now, with someone besides herself to care for, all that had changed. She had discovered motivation in Eve's plight, and had turned that to their advantage at Clandesta. And she had found inspiration in a little girl's love, which had given her a reason to live when the fighting was done. In all the cosmos, could anyone ask for more?

ABOUT THE AUTHOR

Dr. Mark Burgess is a practicing veterinarian in the Portland, Oregon area. Currently 95% of his practice is exotic pets, including ferrets, rabbits, rodents, reptiles, and a plethora of other small critters. His previous works of fiction include *Dog Daze and Cat Naps*, a humorous account of four years in veterinary school, *The Battle for Eden*, another tale of the Human-Knacker War, and "Outside Looking In," a short story featured in the anthology *Yondering—To the Stars and Beyond*. He enjoys his family, exotic plant gardening, science fiction, hiking, and the universe in all its complexity. He is graced with his loving wife Denise, wonderful children, and the ever-snuggly kitty, Scout.